The Sarrington Estate

All the best,
Jennifer Murdoch

Copyright © 2013 Jennifer Mardoll
All Rights Reserved.
First Edition
ASIN-B00D1G4ROK
ISBN-13:978-0615825847 (Northmen Press)
ISBN-10:0615825842

The Sarrington Estate is a work of fiction. Names, characters, places and incidents are products of the author's imagination or are used fictitiously. Any resemblance to persons or events, living or dead is merely coincidental.

Cover Design: Dawn Rajamaki
Cover Image: © User: Tischenko Irina; Shutterstock.com

For my husband, Josh.

1

Each life is made up of a thousand stories, this, is one of mine. I was taught to strive for a simple life. To know one's place and to be content with the hand dealt to you was held up by those around me to be the highest of virtues. I have to admit there seemed to be a restfulness to it, even, a pride in it. Such a person is a stark contrast to those who are never content, something inside of them frustrating them, whispering like the snake in Eden's garden, telling them they were born for something more, something greater, or maybe just something different. Pushing them, like a ruthless taskmaster up into the sky in hope and plunging them down to the pits of darkness in despair.

To such torture I never wanted to subject myself. I knew the life I was born to, and never sought to rise above my station. Fate has her golden sons, and her bastards. Those born with a silver spoon and those born to wash it. I was born the latter. Coming into the world on the cold February morning of the 17th, in 1912, in the neighborhood of Greenpoint in Brooklyn, New York -back when the Irish and Germans still outnumbered the Poles- in a small second floor apartment. The kind with newspaper and posters for wallpaper. The kind that has never seen a day that didn't include laundry strung up on a clothesline from one end of the kitchen to the other. I was christened Constance Mary Agnes Moore, lone daughter and youngest of 5 children. My parents, Molly and Ennis were Irish immigrants, both having come to America as children, in 1884 and 1881, respectively.

Their parents had been those who were never content. Like countless others from across the Earth they came. Abandoning the farms of their fathers and fathers' fathers they came to the cities, looking for something more. America was the great land of opportunity they had been told. You could be anybody. You could dream any dream. Dream, dream and stay there weary one. The reality of waking is cold and hard. They replaced the good earth, a mistress loving and harsh by turns, with the roads and buildings who were indifferent. The city doesn't need a farmer. The city doesn't need your love and devotion. It doesn't want your partnership. It doesn't even want you.

By boat they came, with dreams of riches and grandeur, of being like the men they had admired and reviled. Cramped, subjected to filth and sickness, the pain, the humiliation, the fear, difficult to bear, vanished with the first glimpse of the great lady, her hand jetting up into the sky, beckoning, "This way, I am waiting and will shine my blessings upon you." There she stood, the great mistress of hope, like a benevolent goddess of old, or, was it a siren?

They didn't know, as they looked up at her in awe, as they swelled with pride and relief, laughing, crying. They had made it! How could they know what was to come? The taunts, the hatred, the city's inhabitants eyeing them in disgust, another poor, dirty, stupid Irish immigrant here to take a piece of a pie that had long since run out, if it had ever existed at all. There were no open arms, only hard stares. No wide gates to the promise land, only doors slammed shut in disdain. "No Irish need apply." They fought and they pushed, any job, any place would suffice. In the dilapidated tenements they huddled and prayed for the day when they would finally escape. Again.

Their children watched as they tried to meek out a meager existence and hold on to the promise. They watched as the hope of their parents and grandparents, aunts and uncles, turned to bitterness, as their dreams fell around them like shattered glass and just as dangerous. They listened to the endless jeers from those on the streets and to the muffled sobs that came soft across the room in the dead of night. They watched and they listened and they learned. Dreams were for fools. Dreams left you hollow. Dreams killed. And they grew to adults and taught their own children the lessons that had been so hard won. Work when you can. Love when you can. Laugh when you can. But don't dream. Dreams may come true, but not for you. Not for us.

I learned this lesson well and I pitied those who did not yet know it. I grew up along the streets of New York, concrete underfoot just as naturally as my grandparents had had the grass and soil in their own youth. It was a carefree time for me as childhood often is and it was a carefree time for the nation. The Jazz Era, the Roaring Twenties, a grand, high, decadent time. The politians and the newspapers, the experts and the bankers cried from the rooftops to the people, "Come and get it! Buy on margin! It's easy. Don't be left behind." And the people listened, hungry for the dream to finally come true even if in reality it had only changed form, from dream to illusion. And they laughed without a care in the world, even if somewhere in the back of their heads a still, small voice nagged at them saying "This can't be right." All that mattered was that the ugly twin beasts of burden and want had finally been slain.

We watched with a mixture of pity and strange fascination those caught up in the frenzy of it all. The middle class suddenly being offered the prize they had always coveted. "So easy." sang the sirens "You can have it all. All we require is your freedom, your piece of mind. But don't worry; we'll come for that later." My parents declared them fools. The common man never got something for nothing they would say, something for nothing was the domain of those who didn't need it.

So we carried on as we always did. "The Lord lifteth up the meek and casteth the wicked down to the ground." my mother would say when she saw me look with longing on one of the pretty girls in their satin ribbons and fine coats. I would repeat it like a good girl, though little it did to abate the feeling in my gut as I would tug at my own plain cotton dress.

Every day that I wasn't in school I would go to work with her at the Clare Regency Hotel across the river. Early in the morning we would leave, often while it was still dark and late at night we would return to cook and clean. My father worked at the Greenpoint Ferry and my 3 brothers who were not yet married stalked the water's edge each day taking in what odd jobs they could find.

It was not necessarily a hard life, though to another it might have seemed so. For me it was all I had ever known, the constant work, the hard ground, the dirty air, the noise. It was all just another part of life, not to be begrudged, just to be lived. We laughed and sang and played. We had each other and we knew our place.

The Twenties waxed on and I grew towards womanhood. Teased by my older brothers, increasingly avoided by my father and a source of constant worry for my mother. A good Irish girl, chestnut hair, hazel eyes, full limbs. I was coming into form and I was enjoying it. I liked the look of my growing breasts under my dress and the feel of my hips swaying as I walked. I liked the way the neighborhood boys looked at me. I liked the sense of satisfaction, the feeling of pride. It was fun to play the game, to walk by them, to look them right in the eye with just the slightest smile. A smile that hinted of things I didn't really know and had no intention of finding out. Their lust fed me even if I didn't fully understand it. It was powerful and it would course through me like a drug, leaving me hungry for more, for just another pair of eyes on me, always another, confirming that I existed. That I wasn't just another face fading into the background, not then, not for that moment.

Despite it all I didn't succumb to the temptations and the slick words, a kiss here or there, but nothing too risky. I was a proper Catholic after all, though perhaps it could be said the blessed Virgin would not have approved of my vain indulgences. My mother had made it clear to me many times that the most important aspiration of my life, of any woman's, was to be married and simply put there were the kind of girls men married and the kind they didn't and it was my first duty above all else to make sure I was of the former variety rather than the latter.

And so life ticked on, until October 29th 1929 when the clock finally struck midnight and the golden coach showed itself for what it really was, a pumpkin. Black Tuesday as it would come to be known. The news came pouring in, 30 billion dollars lost, but for me this meant nothing. It was more than my experience would allow me comprehend. The city swirled around us, a whirlwind of panic, but in our own little world the consequences were not immediately evident. We were poor whether the stocks were up or the stocks were down. The worries of some fat cat didn't mean much to us, what did we care if he got skinned? He probably had it coming to him anyway. Everyone knew they were either new money crooks or inbred old money simpletons, more than likely crooks and simpletons both. The marks, well if they had been fool enough, then let them pay the piper. They should have known better and the fact that they didn't shouldn't matter to us.

We learned our part in it all soon enough. The already scarce jobs dried up. The shipping slowed and soon my brothers couldn't beg work. The months dragged on and next came mother and I. The hotel had fewer patrons and had to cut costs in these difficult times we were told, "We're sorry to have to see you go, but you'll be just fine. Two great ladies such as yourselves, you'll have no trouble finding good work, no trouble at all." The manager didn't even bother trying to look us in the eyes by the end of his little speech; he knew the score just as well as we did. My father's hours were cut, then his wage. But still we scrapped by, day in, day out.

It was the same all over the country. People scrapped by until they couldn't anymore. Then came the bread lines, the soup kitchens. Thousands of men throughout the city wandering aimlessly, lost souls looking for redemption. The local boys changed. Gone were their lighthearted calls. Gone were their winks and whistles. Gone too was my desire for it. It seemed so silly now.

No one was the same. It changes a man to have to beg for his sustenance. To bring home to your wife, to your children, bread you didn't earn, that you have no God given right to. It stripes away at them, and robs them of their most valued possession, their pride. What kind of man can't take care of his own? What is a man who has to go around on bended knee, pleading for scraps? The questions gnaw at him and the women watch as the light goes out of them, the fire that burns deep inside and says "I am", and left in its place, is dead, cold, hard resentment and it either paralyzes him to life and love and he becomes hollow, a thin vaporous ghost of a man, or it consumes him and fills him with hate. A hate he can't shake, a hate that grows until he no longer wants to shake it, he only wants an outlet for it, and it's you. He is Mr. Hyde, there is no other, Dr. Jekyll has long since gone.

The women watch on with no power to stop it, all-encompassing fear in their eyes that dart back and forth wildly, searching like an animal caught in a trap, but there is no answer, there is no escape, there is only that fear. They know nothing else now. The entire order of the universe is gone and they can't will it back, they can't pray it back, and they scream at the sky and cry to the ground, and they wait. A city, a country, full of women clinging white knuckled to hope and offering to their men the only thing they can, the only thing that sustains him even now, her belief in him, in the two of them together, that somehow, some way, they will carry on and this too shall pass.

I watched as it played out in our little apartment. My father once so lighthearted became sullen and distant. He didn't know the future and he didn't want to look upon our faces that called out to him for answers anymore. He didn't want to look my mother in the eye, the shame of it all. My mother always the strong one, began to falter. She would rally us onward, tell us not to give in, but we could hear her stifled screams into her pillow. We could see the desperation in her eyes as she would look at my father, silently pleading "Don't let your light go out. Don't give up. I need you."

The thickness of it all smothered us. My brothers became restless and destructive; prowling the streets until late at night, doing God only knows what, we didn't want to. I sat quiet, my stomach aching and my mind searching, and I watched them all, these people I loved, spiral downward, not knowing what to do. It was beyond the wisdom of my few years. On February 12th 1933, the worst blow of all came to our little house of cards when the final passenger ferry left Greenpoint and my father's job and our only steady source of income went with it. Day in and day out we walked the streets, each of us going our separate ways, trying to find work; a day's, an hour's, anything. A dollar, a half, a piece of meat; name your price. I longed to escape as one does when you're young and blessed with the freedom to run away, and the ignorance of not realizing, there's no such thing.

Salvation came to us on the first Friday of March in 1933 when a telegram arrived from Emma Shultz. Emma was 61 and had emigrated to the United States from Germany in 1892 with her husband and extended family when she was 20, and had worked at the Clare Regency since it had opened in 1904 before leaving a few years prior to the crash to work as a maid for a wealthy New York family at their estate along the Hudson River.

She was like a member of the family to us and we had taken her in after the death of her husband Gottlieb, until her relocation to the Sarrington Estate. She and her husband had had no children much to their sorrow and she had not wanted to move to Philadelphia where the majority of her relations resided. She doted on us as if she was our great aunt and we thought of her as such. Her presence alone was comforting and I wished for her to sit in the kitchen and tell me some parable that would make everything suddenly clear.

She wrote often to my mother of life in upstate New York. The beauty of the Adirondacks, the grandness of the house and furnishings, the news of the staff and her employers as if it were her own. But this telegram was different. One of the housemaids had succumb to a complete mental breakdown upon receiving the news that her only brother had taken his life by throwing himself in front of an oncoming train, the burdens of the times having been too much for him to bear "God bless her and may the good Lord rest his soul", and consequently Emma had convinced the housekeeper, Mrs. Casserly, to give me a trial at the position of between maid to take the place of the girl who would be moving up to fill the unfortunate's place. To us the letter was like a lifeboat, we had been treading water for so long. All had seemed hopeless when along came this message, a miracle from God Almighty.

My mother wept openly in relief and my father paced, his happiness showing itself after months of hiding, though visibly tinged with humiliation at the thought of his daughter of all people playing the part of his savior. Mrs. Casserly would be in the city the next day. I should meet her at ten o'clock in the front lobby of the Clare Regency. If I met with her approval I would accompany her through her errands and ride back to the estate with her that afternoon. If I didn't, she would go to an agency in the city and have a new girl within half an hour. It all rested on me and my ability to garner the good opinion of a woman I had never met and knew nothing about.

When morning came I sat fully clothed on my parent's bed, pulling absentmindedly at the blue yarn tied in knots over the threadbare patchwork quilt. My mother mostly, and father, had been so concerned that I present myself in the best possible light that they had given up their room to me for the night. My father had taken to the boys' room, relegating Pat, only 18 months my senior, to the floor. My mother had taken the folding cot in the kitchen that I usually slept on.

I had tried desperately to sleep, not wanting their generosity to be in vain, but finally gave up, figuring that it would be better to give myself over to chosen wakefulness rather than the resentment of unbidden sleeplessness. I sat perfectly still, looking out the window as the darkness slowly gave way to light. I looked at it with anticipation, and trepidation. I rose and went to the small mirror, staring at the face within. It seemed to say "What now?" and I shrugged my shoulders in response. With extreme delicacy I applied what little make up I possessed and smoothed over my dress for what seemed like the hundredth time. A light tap came and I turned to see my mother standing within the doorless frame. She walked over to me to appraise the results of my work.

"Are you excited my girl?" My mother asked as she lightly fluffed my hair though she wasn't really looking at it.

"I don't know." I answered. "I'm happy, but I'm nervous too."

"That is to be expected I think." My mother replied. "There is so much up in the air right now. I don't have any answers for you. But I think it'll all work out. God wouldn't get our hopes up only to let us down, not now, would he? We just have to have faith in him."

I nodded timidly in reply but I wasn't so sure. My mind filled with doubts and questions but what was there to say? She knew it all already. My stomach cramped like one big knot and I turned to face my mother. "But do you have faith in *me* Mama?"

I searched her eyes, waiting. She sighed and smiled, giving me a weak nod before leaving to prepare breakfast. I stayed behind at her request, though I would have welcomed the busy work of cooking, anything for me to focus on besides the hours that lay ahead, but she didn't want me to run the risk of messing up my dress or smelling of cooked eggs. Watching as she left the room, I fought the tears that were forming in my eyes. Her silence in answer to my question had been like a knife that cut clear and deep into my heart and yet I longed to run after her, to be near her like when I was small and frightened clinging to her leg and hiding my face behind her apron. I felt small and frightened now.

Breakfast was over quickly. My brothers said very little, being too enthralled with the spread our mother had laid out before us and the unusual as of late generosity of the helpings. The meal consisted of eggs, biscuits, gravy, fried potatoes and bacon. To this day I still do not know how she had managed the meat, though it didn't surprise me; that was mama. My father tried to be his jovial old self again, but it was contrived and hard to watch. I had hoped that my job prospect would help to breathe new life into him somehow, perhaps releasing some of the burden off of him. I wondered if that was even possible anymore.

When all was finished my father and brothers prepared to head out to look for work as usual. The boys were gone with a few quick well wishes, only Pat, with whom I had always been closest, took the time to give me a parting hug. My father stood in the center of the room, turning his hat in his hands.

"Connie Girl," he paused.

"Yes Da?" I asked when he didn't continue.

He fidgeted some more with his hat then after a moment he finally said "Y'll do fine."

He paused again, as if not sure what to do, then he put his hat on his head and nodding towards my mother, walked out the front door. It would be the last time I would ever see him. He left that morning to look for work as always, but he never returned. My mother and brothers, family and neighbors, scoured the streets to no avail. Death or desertion we would never know.

My mother washed the dishes as I sat watching. She began to hum 'The Nightingale', one of her favorite songs. I had heard her hum or sing it numerous times throughout the years, never giving it any thought but this time the sound seemed as necessary to my life as the blood in my veins. We had decided that she would accompany me to the hotel and stand watching from across the street so that she could know the outcome of my meeting with Mrs. Casserly. I don't know if she thought I would run rather than face them all if I failed or if like me she just wanted to spend as much time together as we could, but whatever the reason, I was glad of it.

Standing across from the hotel my mother and I stopped to make our farewells, should they turn out to be necessary. "Constance," my mother never used my full name, "I know that you're scared, but I also know that you can do it. You gotta do it. The time comes when the easiness of youth has to give way and we gotta grow up. For some folks it comes slowly, a little at a time, bit by bit, and for other people it's thrust on 'em all of a sudden. This isn't the way I wanted it to be for you. I had wanted that you would fall in love and grow a bit, and marry, and grow a bit, and get with child, and grow a bit, but that was not the good Lord's plan. Instead ya stand here in front of me barely a grown woman and I gotta ask ya to take on your shoulders the weight of the family and carry it. And it's more than you oughta have to bear, but I know that you can and I know that you will because you're strong Constance. You come from women who stood in the face of famines and crossed oceans and did what had to be done, because that's what women do. Do you understand?"

"I understand. I won't fail you Mama."

I had been into the lobby of the Clare Regency many times over the years, but never entering through the front door and while it had always been impressive to me, this time it seemed to magnify my insignificance. I quickly scanned the seating areas and noticed a tall thin woman with graying strawberry blond hair looking at me with lips pursed. Though she made no gesture or sound it was evident that this was Mrs. Casserly. I swiftly crossed over to her making a conscious effort to be as graceful as one unaccustomed to worrying about such things can be expected to manage. I put down my small suitcase and stood before her.

"You are Miss Moore I presume?" She made no pretense to hide as she looked me over.

I nodded meekly.

"You know why you are here?" Her manner was as curt as her appearance gave the impression of being.

"Yes Ma'am" I replied.

"I already have all the knowledge of you from Mrs. Shultz and from the hotel management here that I need. I have been assured that you are a good worker and now that I have looked you over and have seen that you do not appear slovenly nor do you seem to be sickly, I believe you will do."

Standing up quickly she walked past me and I scrambled to grab my suitcase and follow her out the door. My mother was watching as we exited the front of the hotel. I gave her a quick nod as Mrs. Casserly and I descended the steps and walked towards the waiting car. She waved and blew a kiss, neither of which I could return, and into the car I disappeared.

2

I will remember every detail of the ride to the home of John and Lily Sarrington for as long I live. The smooth tan leather of the seats, the various shades of brown in the wood paneling along the doors, the silver handles, the hum of the engine. I had seen such cars as the Packard in which I found myself sitting in Manhattan, but never had I dared to even look into the windows. To ride in one seemed too good to be true, and I was in awe at the splendor of it all.

What I was most taken by though was the beauty of the land as we drove. I had lived in the city my entire life and the closest I had ever come to wide open spaces had been Prospect Park in Brooklyn and also Central Park, which I had dearly loved, even though it had become merely a shadow of what it had once been, but this was something else. This was not a park, planned and controlled by man, but the land as it was meant to be, free and vibrant. The sunlight danced among the leaves casting rapidly changing shadows on the road in front of us. The trees jetted out here and there where they willed and others lay where they had fallen in peaceful sleep for all eternity. Here nature did not intrude upon man and therefore require his control as he liked to believe in the city. Here it was man who intruded upon nature, and you knew without doubt, that it was her superiority that was the true order of things, and always would be.

 Mrs. Casserly let me sit in my revelry. She did not say a word, not that she had said more to me than what was absolutely necessary since our first moments, but now she said nothing whatsoever and I couldn't tell if silence was just her natural way or if she did not deem me worth condescending to, but either way it didn't matter. I was happy and relieved to be left to my own thoughts and private worship of this new world.

The woods gave way to more ordered trees, and soon we turned onto a long driveway, trees lining the road in neatly spaced rows, the ground underneath them clear and trimmed. Up ahead I could see a large iron gate with bars that came to points on the tops like natives' spears and what looked to be a little house. As we approached a guard stepped out and we slowed to meet him. He was tall and thin though not lanky, rather his height suited him, making him fit and trim looking, with dark brown hair and eyes to match. Throwing a hand out in greeting to our driver Ken, he approached the window.
"Yes Frank?" Mrs. Casserly asked. She gave the impression of being annoyed that he had chosen to delay us rather than open the gate, but there was a falseness to it.
"Nothing Myrna. Just wanted to see our new house girl that's all." Frank replied, though he didn't look at Mrs. Casserly as he spoke, rather, he was looking at me, grinning.
"How do you do?" He touched the tip of his hat and gave a slight nod. "I'm Frank, one of the guards. You must be Connie. I've heard a lot about you."
"Constance." I smiled, correcting him. I didn't want to seem rude, especially to the first person I was meeting, and everyone did call me Connie and probably always would, but it felt odd to be addressed with such familiarity by someone I didn't know in a place I'd never been. "It's nice to meet you Frank."
"Constance. Yes, that is better." Frank said with obvious amusement. "Well Constance, welcome to the estate. I'm sure you'll like it here. If you need anything, just give me a holler." He turned to Mrs. Casserly. "Myrna." Touching his hat and nodding again he walked back towards the gate.
"Frank Golden." Mrs. Casserly said as she rolled the window back up. "He likes to think he's something special." She laughed at the idea and for a moment seemed to soften before quickly returning to her former indifference.
"That naturally was the guard house and main gate." She began as the car moved forward. "We will soon arrive at the main house. It consists of 21 bedrooms, including guest

bedrooms, 14 bathrooms, various secondary rooms; including a vast library, 3 offices, 7 sitting rooms, a ballroom and the like. You will come to know most of the rooms on the first floor. You will never be permitted on the 2nd and 3rd floors. The kitchen……."

I gasped and she stopped abruptly at the interruption. The house had come into view, although to call it a house seems like a lie. It was framed by an immense manicured lawn with tall square trimmed hedges and numerous topiaries. In front a large ornate fountain consisting of three circular tiers graced the center of a circular driveway. The top two tiers each held 4 spouts in the shape of lions' heads. On the uppermost tier, the heads were rather small, the second a bit larger and the bottom fitted with four full bodied lions each shooting water from their mouths. Behind the house at a respectable distance, though not too far, stood forest covered mountains, the Adirondacks I had heard so much about. The focus of this entire scene, the main house of the Sarrington Estate, stood 3 stories tall with uniform windows lining the front of the structure and graduating in size on each level from top to bottom. At the center of this imposing residence was a semi-circle of steps lined with columns, leading to two large ornate wooden doors, which made up the front entrance.

In truth I had seen many great buildings in the city, the Clare Regency after all was quite grand and large, but this with its magnificent white marble structure and its backdrop of large wooded peaks, was beyond anything I had ever seen or imagined. As we neared the house, the road split and we veered off to the right and continued around the house coming to the back. Here a large walking garden could be seen and a swimming pool. Closer to the house was a garage and our final destination, the servants' entrance.

Mrs. Casserly allowed me to take it all in as we exited the car and other servants rush out to unload it. None of them paused to speak with me though a few did look in my direction. Mrs. Casserly while observing this showed no sign that she intended to introduce me, rather, beckoning me to follow her, she began again as we walked through the door. "The kitchen and laundry will be where you spend most of your time, though you may be called upon to work in some of the house's common areas." She said pointing to the door of the laundry room as we passed.

I looked around unsuccessfully for Emma as we made our way past the bustling kitchen and into a narrow hall. "Down this hall are the rooms for most of the female servants. On the other side of the house is a similar hall for most the male servants, the upper servants have rooms upstairs close to the family and the other male employees, such as the guards and grounds men live in separate quarters over the garage. There is one bathroom at the end of the hall." Stopping in front a small door, 3rd from the bathroom and on the left, Mrs. Casserly paused and opened the door. "This is your room. It is the smallest of the rooms, but you will at least have it to yourself, many of the others don't. You've probably never had your own room have you?" I looked at the floor in embarrassment and shook my head. It was true. She began again "It's getting rather late and I don't have time right now to explain anything to you, so just try to get situated here and stay out of the way. We're getting ready for Mr. and Mrs. Sarrington's dinner. You will eat after they are finished and have retired. Someone will call for you then." With that she turned and retreated down the hall. I stood watching until turning the corner, she was gone.

I walked into my room in a sort of daze. It was small to be sure. Not much more than a glorified storage closet, it had a small single bed, which was about the size of my cot back home, but with a headboard. Next to the bed was a nightstand with a lamp and on the opposite wall stood a thin three drawer bureau with an oval mirror over it. There was a hook jetting out from the wall which held two crisp uniforms. On the bed was a pillow sleeved in a white pillow case and a grey blanket with a white sheet folded over the top. I put my suitcase on the bed and opening it, placed what few items of clothing I had in the dresser drawers and my toiletries on top of it. I hung my coat on a hook attached to the back of the door and placing my empty suitcase under the bed and sitting down, I surveyed the room in wonder. What an odd thing to think that while the country writhed in utter turmoil, I was experiencing one of the greatest luxuries of my life up to that point, my own bedroom, one with a door even.

I sat for what seemed like an eternity and I was starving. I had no idea what time it was but I knew it had to be getting late. Finally a knock came on the door and without waiting for a reply the doorknob turned. It was Emma Shultz. Sizable arms opened wide she crossed the small space and enveloped me, squeezing tight and rocking from side to side. "Oh Connie!" She let go and smiled wide, eyes dancing. "It is so good to have you here! I was so happy when Mrs. Casserly passed by me on the stairs and told me that you made it." She hugged me again.

"Emma!" Every feeling I had been trying to damn up flooded into me at that moment, leaving me in danger of crying, a fact that did not escape Emma's notice.

"There now, don't start crying." She said, standing back to survey me. "It's all done now. You're here. It's a good thing."

"I know." I tried to get myself under control. "I know it is. I'm just so happy to be here Emma."

"I know you are and you should be." she said taking control. "And we'll talk about it. But right now you need dinner! And so do I!" She laughed and we headed out of the room towards the kitchen.

I was not accustomed to having to wait for someone else to eat before I did and I cannot say that the idea sat very well with me, but that's just the way things are when you work for only one family. You bend and bow to their every whim and that's that. Since it was just Mr. and Mrs. Sarrington dining they had a "light" dinner of braised pork, boiled new potatoes, Waldorf salad, dinner rolls and a simple pudding for dessert. Since, as always, it was just the staff dining in the kitchen, we had bread, and a stew that was made up of mostly root vegetables and meat left over from the family's lunch. I'm not complaining of course. Not then, and not now. It was a meal after all in a time when those were hard to come by and I was glad to have it.

In addition to eating dinner it was also time for me to meet some of the staff. I say some because the entire estate staff consisted of forty-two employees, but for now I was only meeting most of those who worked in the house. The upper servants and Mrs. Casserly ate in the kitchen at the same time the family ate so they could help the "lord and lady" and their progeny -when they were home- prepare for dinner and then again with their needs after they had finished. The Upper Crust it turns out need those of the lower class to help them with pretty much everything and needed them constantly at the ready. God forbid if one of them had to tend to a zipper or figure out how to work cuff links on their own. The men who worked outside of the house, the guards and drivers and grounds men, ate before dinner preparations began for the family. It was the only way to get everyone fed.

It was fine with me that I was not going to meet everyone right then, truth be told it was the people I was with that I had interest in. The various maids, the footmen, the kitchen staff, the no names of the house. My kind of people.

There were twenty-one of us eating in the large, but not large enough, kitchen. By the open back door, trying to get some fresh, cold air into the stifling room, stood the men, all except Chef Henri –the only one of note among us- bowls in hand. Many of the women stood at different spots around the kitchen as well. There were only a hand full of chairs, which were usually reserved for the elders of the group like Emma, but they let me have one of them. Courtesy and good manners are not after all only the domain of the wealthy, we have our ways too.

Emma introduced me to everyone and I tried desperately to remember all of their names. There was Alan; he was a footman, around thirty. Tall, with brown hair and a large nose. Then there was Stephen, he was also a footman but his age was harder to place, his hair graying, but with the smile of youth. There was another footman and 2 male kitchen staff beside Chef Henri and the undercook Paul. There was Helen, a soft spoken woman of about 40 with mousy brown hair who worked as a parlor maid. There was also Ann, who was the eldest daughter of a Holiness preacher from rural Vermont. She was younger than the others, barely seventeen, with flaming red hair, green eyes and freckles covering her round face. She was the one who had moved up on the totem pole which I was to replace at the bottom. I think she was almost as happy to see me as Emma had been. I tried hard to remember as Emma went on. "Joan, Doyle, Nellie, Susan, Eloise............" but it was no use.

Everyone seemed friendly enough. They talked about their day. Nellie had caught a large gilded mirror just in time when it fell off the wall as she was cleaning it in the 3rd floor hallway. They talked about bits of news they had from relatives. Paul's granddaughter Garnet was teething, a letter he had just received that morning had informed him. And they even let me in on some of the house gossip, which of course is the quickest way known to mankind for employees of any stripe to bond.

"Two of the valets is fruits." Darla, the heavy set laundry maid said as she leaned in towards me pretending she didn't want anyone else to hear.

"Darla!" Emma cried out from across the table "Don't you be telling her that!"

"Well it's true." Darla responded. "And you know it!"

"I do not know it and you don't either."

"Do too! Saw em myself. Warren," she turned her gaze from Emma to me to explain, "he's old man Sarrington's valet. I seen him and Peter, that's Thomas, the younger son's valet. I seen em both round the back of the garage. I was comin' round the corner and they was real close to each other and holding hands. They saw me and backed up away from each other real quick like, then walked right past me. Didn't say a word. Hell, they wouldn't even look at me. They knowed they'd been caught."

"And knew you'd tell it too!" said Joan, a maid in her late twenties, with a full head of dark brown curls.

"Well," Darla looked a little embarrassed and began to pick at the underside of her splotchy red arm. "Folks gotta right to know that kinda thing don't they?"

"Do they now?" Joan replied "Do they gotta right to know why you was round back of the garage when you was supposed to be in the laundry ya old hen?"

"I ain't got no shame in that. I was goin' round to get me a smoke off my pipe. Myrna don't like me smokin, you know'd that. She says it ain't right for a woman to be smokin no pipe, 'specially one that works for people like the Sarringtons. But I ain't givin' up my pipe. And I was wantin' a few puffs, laundry or not." Darla said, chin up in the air defying us all.

Everyone laughed except Doyle. "Well it ain't right is it?" He seemed almost defensive.

"No it ain't!" interjected Darla.

Doyle nodded at her and began again "Two men, I mean, I'd rather know. I don't wanna take the chance of em rubbin' up against me."

"Woot!" Joan called out as she bent over and slapped her leg. "What makes you think they'd wanna rub up against you for? You couldn't get a hungry dog to rub against you."

"Is that right? I seem to remember at least one bitch that wanted to." Doyle winked at Joan and they both laughed, breaking the tension and freeing everyone else to join in. Ann leaned in to loudly whisper the obvious in my ear, "They had a thing going on a while back."

"Yes we did!" Joan said shaking her head and smiling. "Yes we did." She looked at Doyle and he smiled back her. "Anyhow," She continued "I don't see why it matters. They ain't hurtin' you or me or anybody else. As long as they're doing their job who cares." Helen nodded in agreement though it was obvious some of the others in the room weren't so sure.

"I don't want to hear about it." Alan said as he pulled out a cigarette and stepping just outside the open door lit up. "It's not my business" he blew out a puff of smoke, "and if it's not my business, I don't want to know."

"Well I still thought Connie might, bein' new here and all." Darla said. She glared at the stovetop, annoyed at Joan and Alan for not playing along the way she had obviously hoped.

The night and the talking went on. I sat through all of it, mostly silent, nodding my head here and there. It's funny how people don't really want to know about you went they meet you. They want to talk about everything else except you. They have to bring you up to speed on their lives and everyone else's to see how you react so they can know if you're worth asking questions about. That's what was going on then. They were putting out their little tests and sizing me up. Was I worthy? I tried to be.

I was tired, having not slept in almost 48 hours. More than anything I just wanted to go to sleep. I had attempted to stifle more than a couple of yawns unsuccessfully, when finally Mrs. Casserly came into the kitchen.

"Party tonight is it?" She said as she looked around the room, everyone avoiding her as best as they could. "Well it's over now. Go to bed." With that she turned and left the room as everyone reluctantly stirred.

Emma and I walked towards our rooms together. Stopping in front of mine she said "My room is on the other side at the very end if you need anything. We'll talk tomorrow, but for now you just get some sleep. Our days start early." She gave me another hug and turned towards her room.

"Good night Emma." I called out after her. "Thanks, you know, for this."

She smiled and nodded before disappearing into her own room. I could hear clanking coming from the remaining kitchen staff getting on with the night's clean up as I opened my door. I felt a bit guilty knowing I was to blame for what would be their long night.

Grabbing my things I went down to the bathroom which was surprisingly vacant and washed up for bed. I really was very tired which was nothing new. What was new was that I felt like I could finally sleep now, it was allowed. I hurried back to my room, put on my nightgown and climbed into bed. The bed squeaked just a little and continued doing so as I got comfortable. Finally settled, I lay on my back looking at the ceiling in the dim light that shone through under the door. I started to think of my family back home and whether or not they were sleeping easily, but it didn't last. My eyes grew heavy and soon all else was gone.

I awoke to the sound of light tapping on the door. As I looked around I could not deduce the time, being on the interior side of the hallway left the room windowless and the same darkness with a sliver of light shining in under the door enveloped the room as when I had first laid down. From down the hall I could hear clanking in the kitchen. Ten minutes could have passed or ten hours. The tapping came again, but this time it was followed by a voice. "Connie, wake up girl!" It was Emma. "You need to be getting ready and getting something to eat before there's no more getting to be done."
"Yes Emma." I answered. "I'm up. I'll be there in just a little bit."

Leaning up on my elbow I reached over and pulled the cord on the lamp, filling the room with a yellow glow. I looked briefly around the room and sat up fully. It was the first time I had slept so easily and so soundly in months and rather than feel better I felt heavy. My body had grown accustomed to the restlessness and didn't know what to do with hours of uninterrupted sleep. I slipped into my bathrobe and made my way to the bathroom to wash up. It was occupied, but only for a moment, by Ann who wished me a good morning. I was in and out as quickly as possible and back in my room surveying my new uniform. Black with white trim, except for the colors it was almost identical to the ones we had worn at the hotel. I lifted it off the hook. It looked about right in size. I realized with a small amount of panic that I should have tried it on while I was waiting to be called to dinner. Now I would just have to hope that Emma's estimate had been right or at least close. It had.

"Morning!" Paul said as I entered the kitchen. "Are you hungry?"

"Yes, please." I replied.

"Good. Take this and sit down." He said as he handed me a plate with eggs, ham and potatoes on it and a mug full of coffee.

"Thank you." I said.

I sat down and began to eat. It seemed almost too good to be true. I was eating breakfast again for the second day in a row and I had had dinner and also lunch thanks to Mrs. Casserly's generosity. Four meals in twenty four hours.

A few of the other servants milled around the kitchen. Emma stuck her head in the door briefly. "Just looking to see that you made it."

My mouth full of eggs I could only nod in return.

"Alright. Myrna will be here soon to take you around." With that she was gone again as the door swayed gently back and forth.

I had just finished eating when Mrs. Casserly came through the door. "You're up and dressed I see." She said as I stood to greet her. "Follow me and I will give you a rundown of your duties and a quick tour of the 1st floor." She turned abruptly and I followed obediently. The door led from the kitchen into the service room and from there into the breakfast room. It was very light and airy, bathed in yellow everywhere, from the sunlight shining in through the windows to the upholstery on the chairs that surrounded the large round table. It even seemed cozy, which was no small feat considering the room alone was as big as our entire apartment back in Brooklyn. From there we passed through another set of doors and into the dining room. It was large with tall ceilings and dark cherry wood panel walls. "This is the dining room naturally." She barely paused as we left it and entered into a hallway with doors lining the opposite side from which we had emerged. Pointing to the door closest to us, she continued on "That is the billiard room, on the other side of which is the smoking room and beside that, the gun room." We then proceed down the hall passing the salon and onward until coming into the entrance foyer.

It was as grand as anything at the Clare Regency. White marble floors that shone like glass, two staircases that arched around the oval room and a chandelier that looked like it was made from a thousand diamonds. I could not believe that it was all just for one family and a small family too! Two sons and a daughter, that was all they had, but here they were in this house as grand as any hotel and it wasn't their only one I had learned. They had a townhouse in the city and were building an estate in California, amazing. From there we went on through the other rooms. The gallery, library, music room, office and male servants' rooms made up the remainder of the 1st floor. As we entered the hallway once again Mrs. Casserly stopped and turned to face me. "When you are asked to help somewhere besides the laundry, kitchen and servants' areas it will be on this level. You will not enter the gun room nor will you enter the rooms of the male servants. You will also not ascend the stairs to the upper floors. Do you understand?" I nodded that I did and she began again.

"You will mostly be in the laundry, service room and kitchen and will help as the servants there instruct you. You will also clean the servant's hallways and bathrooms on both the men's and women's sides here in the house, not those above the garage. You should never have to go above the garage. As I told you yesterday over lunch you will receive your wage monthly. This isn't the city and this isn't a hotel. You do not clock out at five and you do not get every weekend off. You get every other Sunday off and if you need off another time for any reason you let me know well ahead, otherwise you are here at my disposal, twenty four hours a day. Do you understand?" I nodded again. "Good. Now go to the laundry room and help Darla. You follow her lead. She will let you know what to do, when you can eat and when you can stop. When she's finished with you go help in the kitchen. There is always something to do there and I should never see you just standing around. I have no tolerance for laziness."

"Yes Ma'am." I replied meekly. Something inside warning me not to even attempt Myrna. I wondered if any of the others besides Frank dared to say it to her face. I highly doubted it.

"Alright, go!" she waved her hand in a shooing motion and then turned making her way towards the foyer once again.

Susan, who was leaning over a mound of dough, looked up as I entered the kitchen. "Law!" Susan laughed "Your face is whiter than your collar! It's alright, she won't bite you. Myrna's nice enough once you get to know her, but she's in charge and she's gotta let you know she's in charge, know what I'm saying?" I nodded in reply and Susan asked "So where you working at today? In here with us?"

"No, at least not right now, but maybe later. Mrs. Casserly told me to help Darla in the laundry." I replied.

Susan shook her head and laughed. "Good luck!"

3

A week passed, then another. I got to know the rest of the staff. Peter and Warren, Darla's "fruits", who were aloof but nice, much nicer anyway than Ernest, who was valet to Robert. There was also Matilda, Mrs. Sarrington's lady maid and Emily, the lady maid of daughter Jane. The children did not need their attendants at present, all of them being off at school and it was obvious that the servants whose world had grown accustomed to revolving around one person did not feel comfortable without them. I also met Will and Greg, the other guards besides Frank, who really did believe himself to be something special with the ladies and who was obviously quite sure he would make his way with me. There were the chauffeurs Stanley, Ken and Charles and various grounds men, but the one who intrigued me most was the head groundskeeper, Eli.

Eli was tall, 6 feet at least and muscular, with skin tan from a life spent out of doors. His hair was blonde and shined in the sun as if gold was thread through it. He had bright blue eyes like the autumn sky and a wide smile that was self-assured and yet entirely unpretentious.

I liked to watch him. It didn't matter what he was doing. His movements were strong and certain. He lacked the self-doubt that hovered just under the surface of most men, and it showed in everything he did. Each day I hoped I would be in the kitchen working when it was time for him to come in and eat. I would look at him quickly and then look away. Often I could feel my face flush. It had to have been obvious to him that I was infatuated, but he didn't let on if he did know. He treated me the same as everyone else though sometimes I could see the slightest hint of amusement when he would smile at me.

I found myself thinking about him constantly, it didn't matter what I was doing. Eventually he worked his way into my dreams. They were simple, innocent dreams. Dreams of us sitting and talking or of the two of us walking in the gardens. In one we stopped and skipped rocks across the Hudson which made up part of the estate's border, just simple, he and I laughing and looking at each other out of the corner of our eyes. Soon I became jealous of his attention to the others in the house, but especially the other women. I was sure they all wanted him. How could they not? I hated to hear them speak his name and to hear him speak one of theirs was like a hammer to my chest.

I tried to carry on, to focus on the work in front of me, to try to redirect my thoughts when they would once again wander his way. I didn't know what to do. This was new to me. He was not one of the neighborhood boys. I didn't want his attention just for the sake of having it. Let the others have that. Let them be satisfied with a look or a nod or a greeting. I wanted him to want me, not lust after me, though I wanted that too. I wanted him to want to know me, to see me as someone worthy of his time, to be his equal. I wanted to know that he thought about me as I did him, and that his thoughts and his dreams, just as mine, were never left in peace. The desire for it burned inside me. Nothing mattered to me more than that. I had to show him that I wasn't like Ann or Eloise. I wasn't going to giggle and bat my eyes at him. I wasn't going to fawn over him, placing myself in the same category as the others, just one more infatuated girl. And yet I could feel my body betraying me every time we were near each other. My face would flush, my pulse would quicken. I felt as if my entire body, my entire being, gave off a heat that said "Please notice me." It frustrated me endlessly.

Finally I knew the answer, the only thing I could do. I began to stay away from him. I began to hope our paths would not cross. Perhaps what I needed was distance. Maybe my blood would cool and my obsession would wane. I prayed that it would, but even more than those dutiful prayers, I prayed that he would notice. That he would feel my absence and it would gnaw at him and then the desperation and the obsession would be his.

A week passed, then a second. Some days I would think I was on top of it all, that I had been right, that distance was all I needed. Eli held no power over me. He meant no more to me than I did to him. But I knew it wasn't true. It was just something I told myself. It would be no time before my mind would go off again into one of its many daydreams. It was all hopeless. There was nothing to be done. I was nothing. And besides it was forbidden for employees to form romantic partnerships. Mrs. Casserly would not tolerate it. She didn't think it was prudent and after she had had enough of being strung along like a wide eyed puppy after Frank, the victim of his careless bravado, she had decided with finality that it would be a danger no longer. That was why Joan and Doyle fought with each other as much as they laughed. It was the only thing they could do, the only defense they had against love and desire forcibly held captive by circumstance. Should I leave myself to the same fate? Better to never know, to wallow in a never ending in between than to taste it and have it taken away from me and yet never out of sight, to live each day in silent torment. No, this had to be better. I would resign myself to it and wait for it to fade.

I began to walk the grounds where I could be alone. The estate consisted of over 500 acres, most of it wooded and I roamed these areas whenever I could. I felt at peace there among the trees. It was the exact opposite of the city. In the city there was so much noise and activity that it all faded into the background and you didn't even notice it, but here, the stillness and the silence were over powering. You couldn't escape it. You couldn't ignore it. In the city, you built up a shield against the assault of an artificial environment consisting of unending noise and light and people, but here no shield would stand against the ancient call of nature to soul. It drew me in, this untouched, wild place. It was what man was meant for. I drank it in and it nourished me. And it frightened me, the realness of it. There was no place surer in the world than this, than nature in all its glory, untainted by man. In time I knew I wished never to live in a city again. The roots of generations past had awakened within me, healing something within my blood. Every fiber of my being called out, and the trees and the ground and the wind answered in sweet communion.

I had left the house early in the morning with a bag of food and a thermos of hot coffee. It was my day off and I planned to climb the mountain ridge behind the house. Up until this point I had stayed on the flat lands that bordered the river but now I wanted to see the skyline, one made up of trees and rolling hills. I reached the top a little after nine. At first it seemed the same as every other place I had walked; I could see nothing but trees. I continued walking along the top until I came to a clearing made of large smooth boulders emerging from the mountain top. They looked like the shoulders of ancient trolls that had slept so long the earth had grown them a blanket. I climbed on top of one and looked around. The view was wondrous. Down below was the house and other estate buildings nestled in vast expanses of lawn bespeckled with frost; from there the woods fanned out in all directions as the river glistened through it like a silver vein among green skin, a dragon in the land. I had heard people use the expression "picturesque" but had never really seen anything that fit such a description, even this did not, because this was more. This was something no picture could ever hold.

I sat down and pulled the thermos out of the bag when I got the feeling I wasn't alone. Truthfully, I have never felt alone in the woods because there is no alone in the woods and you know there isn't. Sometimes there is a welcoming and sometimes not, sometimes there is the sense of otherworldliness, but there is never an alone and I had grown accustomed to that, but this was a different not alone. This was the feeling not of things more ancient than you, but rather the familiar feeling of human eyes, and I found that much more unsettling.

I turned and searched the trees behind me. There leaning against a pine was Eli.

"Good Morning." He said as he began to walk towards me, smiling. "I hope I didn't frighten you. I heard you approach and thought perhaps you were an animal, a deer or a bear or something and I wanted to see what so I stayed quiet. Then when you came up I saw the look on your face as you surveyed the land and I couldn't bring myself to interrupt."

I turned my head to the side and looked at him doubtfully. I felt self-conscious and annoyed. I had come there in part to get away from him and yet there he was, and watching me no less.

Eli continued. "And then so much time had lapsed I didn't know how to call out to you. I didn't want it to seem weird. But I guess it does." He laughed.

"It does seem weird." I said. "You should have said something when you first realized I wasn't a deer or a bear or whatever else. What am I supposed to think now?"

'Well, I don't know. Why don't you just not think about it at all. I shoulda, and I coulda, but I didn't. No reason to make it more'n it was and ruin the morning for both of us." He answered.

"So, what do you think of the place?" He said, trying to change the subject as he sat down beside me. "I know you haven't been here before. I could see it in your reaction, and besides, I come here every Sunday, and you're not here."

"I think it's beautiful. I've never seen anything like it."

"Really? That's a shame." He turned his face from me to the land. "Yes, it is beautiful. It reminds me of home."

"Where are you from then?" I asked even though I already knew the answer.

'Tennessee. I grew up in the foothills of the Smokies."

"How did you end up here?" I looked at him, the feelings I had tried to fight bubbling to a rolling boil inside of me as my anger faded.

"Ah, well, it was just one of those things I guess. When I was eighteen I went to Nashville looking for a job and got hired on doing grounds work for the city, then after a couple years I left with a buddy who got us on working for a rich family in Atlanta. They bought a place up here and brought the head groundskeeper with them; he in turn brought me and made me his sorta second. He eventually came to work for the Sarringtons and I followed again, but then he passed away three years ago and I moved up the ladder." Eli paused and looked at me. He seemed to be waiting for a reply, but when I didn't offer one he began again. "It's alright though. I like it here and I like working the grounds. I always liked working with the land back home but I didn't wanna farm. This lets me have it both ways, and I'm good at it too. I'm headed out to California for a bit soon." He waved his hand towards the house. "They're building another place out there and want me to look at it. They hired a landscape architect, but old man Sarrington says he wants me to see it too and give him my opinion on it. Says there's college know how and there's real world know how and that I've got the second and often times that's what's more important. It'll be nice. Maybe I'll work my way up out there, become a landscape architect myself. Have both kinds of know how. Be damn near unstoppable then won't I?!" He laughed and I smiled back at him. It was a wonderful laugh.

'So," he said, "what about you? You like it here?"

"Yes very much. " I replied, which was true. I did. I liked all of it. The work, the people, the land. It seemed to me to be pretty much perfect, with the exception of my silent agony caused by the man sitting beside me. Though truth be told, I liked that too.

Eli laughed. "You don't talk very much do you?"

"No." I could feel myself blushing. "I've always been quiet."

"A woman of few words, hmmm, what a thought!" Eli smiled wide and brought a pack to his lap from which he pulled his own thermos. "Mind if I sit here with you for a while?"

"No." I answered looking directly into his eyes for a moment before turning back to the horizon. "Not at all."

We sat there on the mountaintop for hours. He told me about Tennessee. What it was like, how he grew up. I told him about Brooklyn and my family. We talked about the Depression and Roosevelt and the hope that came with him. We talked about the Sarringtons and the staff. Eventually we decided that it was time that we head back down. The sun was sinking lower in the sky and though he wasn't worried about himself, we both knew that if I did not return to the house before dusk Emma would have the entire house out and searching.

We walked down the mountain in silence, but it was a comfortable silence. Occasionally Eli would turn to look at me. He wouldn't speak, only look and smile. It made me laugh, not out of nervousness but just out of the impossibility of it. I had been both avoiding and obsessing over this man and yet there we were spending the day together as if it was the most natural thing in the world, and it was. It seemed as if I had willed one of my dreams into reality.

Over the next few weeks we spent an ever increasing amount of time together. As before, Eli would come and sit in the kitchen sometimes and talk while I and the others worked. But he would also show up just to see if I wanted to walk the grounds with him. Depending on the time, sometimes we would just stay in the gardens. Other times, if it was early enough, we would go down to the river together and sit, watching and listening to the rushing water as it spilled over the rocks, laughing as it went. Each Sunday that I had off we would climb the mountain to sit in what I was being to think of as "our spot".

Emma watched us, a mixture of happiness and wariness. Mrs. Casserly was gladly, rarely around the two of us together but she eyed us suspiciously when she was. There was nothing she could say however. We were friends. That was all. As far as I knew I was nothing more to Eli than a person who shared his love of being out in nature and I could only hope that as long as I was unsure of his feelings, that that is what he assumed I thought of him as well. If only it were true.

My time with Eli was a sweet sort of agony. It was like the feeling you would get watching a bubble as a child. A thing you can't help but find magical and beautiful yet it must remain elusive. You can't try to get too close. You can't try to touch it lest it pop and be gone forever, but there is nothing you want more than to try. So frustrated you will yourself to hold back and savor it for what it is, a moment of fleeting perfection.

That was how I felt about our time together. That each moment was beautiful and perfect and fragile, and I worried that the slightest misstep could cause them to disappear forever.

I loved to look at him when I didn't think he would notice. His forehead was high and his thick golden hair swept over it carelessly. He had a prominent nose, straight and perfectly proportioned like a Greek statue. His chin was strong and well defined, neither pointy nor indistinct. He had high cheek bones and his clear blue eyes shined whether he was laughing or deep in thought. All of this sat on a rugged, masculine body, hard and capable. The kind of body that makes you think of cowboys in the open West. The kind of body that calls out to a woman silently but powerfully on a primal level far older than words. It calls not to her mind, not to her heart, not even to her womb, but to the hungry, wanting part of her loins.

Watching him I would grow hot and flush, lost in feeling. Catching me he would smirk, and ask some inane question that should have been easy to answer but that my mind struggled and rushed to make sense of. Even now thinking about those days is almost overpowering.

    I had been sending home the bulk of my pay to my mother, leaving only enough for myself for a few things in town, such as toiletries, and I had splurged once to buy a book, *Walden,* which Eli had suggested to me. My mother and I had been writing each other often and though her letters were nothing if not cheery it always seemed as though something was not quite right, as if she was trying too hard to convey happiness. On the 1st Sunday in May I found out why. Mrs. Casserly came into the kitchen holding a letter for me that had arrived at some point during the week and had somehow fallen behind her desk while she was sorting through the mail.
    I had written my mother telling her that I had Mother's Day off and was hoping to find a ride into the city to spend it with her and the rest of the family. She wrote me in return asking that I not come and informing me that my father had never returned home the Saturday that I left. She wrote of how they did not know if he was alive or dead, not a single clue to point them in one direction or the other though they searched and continued to do so, taking time away from searching for jobs and that because of this I was the only thing that kept them from complete destitution. She said that it would be more helpful to her if I could pick up extra work on Mother's Day rather than come to the city to partake in what would only be another day of searching and probable disappointment.
    I tried to focus on the tear stained paper through my own tear filled eyes, my hands shaking and head swimming. I couldn't believe it. Not my Da. He wouldn't do this. He wouldn't just abandon his wife of nearly 30 years. Not the man I knew, the man I idolized. Never. He must have been hurt, maybe roaming the streets with amnesia or as much as I hated the thought, maybe he fell into the river and drowned, but not abandonment. No matter how the Depression had

changed him. No matter that countless men across the country may have been doing it. He wouldn't, would he?

I was sitting at the table eating my lunch when Mrs. Casserly had given me the letter and being ignorant of its contents had not bothered to retire to my room to read it. The others in the kitchen including Emma had been watching me, at first waiting for my news from home to share in my joy, but as I read their interest changed to concern.

"What is it Connie? What's the matter?" Emma asked. "Is everything okay?"

I couldn't speak. I just shook my head as tears began to roll down my face. It was all too much. I couldn't bear the news and I couldn't bear eyes on me while I received it even if they were only the eyes of those that wished me well. I had to get out. I pushed the letter to Emma, she was as good as family and had a right to the news, and I knew that her love for us would keep her from turning the letter's contents into fodder for gossips.

Then I ran. I ran past the garage and through the gardens. I could hear Eli calling my name as he saw me rush by, but it didn't matter. I had to get to the river.

The sun shined on the top of the water, a testament to the consistency of nature. Our lives and problems come and go but it goes on as always, oblivious. I fell to my knees burying my face into the soft green grass along the river's edge and I let it flow out of me. All of it. The wandering the streets of Brooklyn begging work and food. The hunger pains and sleepless nights. The terror of the unknown. The uprooting of my life. Eli. The disappearance of my father. Everything I had pushed down for days and months and years. I didn't want it anymore. I was tired of holding it inside of me and I could do it no longer. I let it all fall out of me in cascades of tears and sobs and screams into the ground. I let the earth have it all, my hurt, my disappointment, my anger. I let it flood into her, and she took it willingly.

I don't know how long I stayed by the river, but I could tell it was late in the afternoon as the sky had taken on the comforting orange and gold hue of approaching sunset. I wasn't hungry but I was tired. My eyes ached and my ribs hurt, but I felt relieved somehow. The weight of all that I had been carrying like a tumor had lifted from off of me and I felt lighter because of it.

Pressing my hands against the ground to push myself up I noticed a small white flower shaped like a six pointed star growing in the grass. I reached over and picked it. Standing, I brought the flower to my lips and said a silent prayer for my father and kissed the tiny blossom. I threw it into the current with the wish that the Hudson would send it, along with my prayers and my love, back to Brooklyn and my Da.

As I approached the lawns I grew fearful. My mother had just told me how important my job was and yet I had immediately jeopardized it in my panic. As I topped the hill where the garden began I saw Eli sitting on one of the benches. It was far enough from the water to have allowed me my privacy but still situated where neither I nor he could be missed on my journey back to the house. He rose and walked towards me.
"I don't know what's going on Connie, but Emma told me if I saw you to tell you she talked to Myrna and you can take whatever time you need today; that it's okay and that Ann took your place and you can take hers next Sunday."
He stood very close to me, our chests almost touching. I didn't want to look up at him.
"Connie, you don't have to tell me what this is all about but please, just let me be with you. Wherever you're going, just let me come along alright."
I nodded in consent and we turned back away from the lawn and towards the river from which I had just come. We walked along in silence following the water. Every so often one of us would bend down to pick up a stick or rock to throw, but otherwise we kept a steady space. The golden sky slowly turned soft periwinkle before giving way to darkness.

The stars appeared one by one and the moon full and round rose above us, its twin dancing in the water below.

Finally I stopped and sat down and Eli did the same.

"Do you want to talk about it?" Eli said after a while.

"No." I replied.

"I want to be here for you Connie. I care about whatever hurts you or whatever makes you happy. I hope that you know that. I hope that you can see that I care. That I'm here." Eli paused "If you want me."

I could feel his entire body facing me and I turned towards him. His face was illuminated in the moonlight and I could see the concern in his expression and in his eyes. He looked as if he hurt at the thought of me in pain and my heart was lost to him completely in that moment. I reached up, my hand unsteady and slow, and caressed the side of his face. In reply he lifted his hand to cup my cheek in his palm and leaned in towards me. I closed my eyes as I felt his lips press against mine. My chest filled and my throat burned. I had forgotten how to breathe. He pulled away and I opened my eyes. He rose up onto his hands and knees and leaned in to kiss me again, slowly moving his body forward as our mouths took each other in.

I leaned backwards until I could feel the cool ground underneath my back, my body flat. Eli hovered over me moving slowly, catlike, his hands and lips moving tenderly but with a hint of desperation. I could feel his body hard and warm against my own, our legs intertwined, his stomach pressing against my side. Feeling the hardness of him against my hip, my own womanhood responded with the aches of longing.

He unbuttoned my uniform from top to bottom and pushed it down along my sides. Then gently helping me out of my underthings, and exposing me to the night sky, he leaned back and smiled at my smooth white skin almost luminous in the moon light. Bending down again his mouth found my breasts and I moaned at the exquisiteness of the feeling of his lips on my tender skin. I could feel him as he tugged anxiously at his belt and worked his pants. As he lowered himself onto me, I buried my face into his neck, taking in the smell of him. Gently he went into me and I gasped at the pain as my maidenhead was claimed. Tears welled up in my eyes once more and I closed them in reply. This was what I wanted after all, wasn't it?

Afterwards he lay beside me slowly caressing my arm. He seemed in no rush to go back to the house and I was unsure I would be able to move even if he was. I stared up at the stars and thought about all that had happened.

Eli rose up on his elbow and looked at me. "I love you Connie." He said. "I have loved you almost from the beginning. As I watched you work and the way you would blush when I would look at you. You were so beautiful. Then you avoided me." Eli laughed. "It was torture and it only made me want you more. But when I saw you up on top of the mountain and I saw how you looked out over the horizon. I knew then that I wanted you to be with me always."

I couldn't say anything. It couldn't be real. There had to be some other explanation.

"Do you love me?"

"You know I do." I replied and he leaned down to kiss my shoulder.

After a while we dressed and sat up but we didn't stir to leave; not yet. I leaned into his chest and told him everything. He didn't reply in words, just the occasional kiss on the forehead or a tightening of his embrace. When I was finished we sat quietly and listened instead to the owls and the frogs until we knew we couldn't risk staying any longer.

As we approached the house it had to be nearing midnight and I was hungry and tired. Eli stopped and took my hands in his.

"I leave tomorrow and I don't know how long I'll be gone." He said looking from me down to the ground and back again. "I have to go to California. I wish I didn't, not now when you're going through all of this, but I have no choice."

I had known this of course but I had forgotten. Now the blow was fresh and hard as if I had never heard it before. After all of this I had felt like I could stand again with Eli to support me and yet here he was about to take away my new found crutch.

"Connie, what I said was true. I do love you and I do want to be with you. This is horrible timing, I know, but I have to go. It's not forever. I plan on making my own way in the world and this is my chance." Eli's words came faster as he grew excited. "If I can do this, I can make something of myself. What I was talking about on the mountain that first day wasn't just a joke even though I pretended it was because I wasn't sure if I could reveal myself to you. I will become a landscape architect, it's what I want. I won't just be a groundskeeper for ever, see Connie, so think of that when I'm gone. It's not just the job that's taking me away from you, it's the future, our future."

My eyes grew wide. His words were like a hot poker and I shrank away from them. I wanted him as I always had and I knew that I loved him but I knew what dream chasers were and I couldn't reconcile that to my idea of him.

He dropped my hands and we continued on, parting ways at the garage. Entering the house Paul and Joan looked at me, they were the only ones still working and I nodded at them as I walked on to the hallway grateful that they had remained silent.

I was too tired to wash or even to change. I simply slid off my shoes and laid down. It had been a day of highs and lows. I had been crushed by the unthinkable and overwhelmed by the attainment of all that I had dared to wish for. I didn't want to think of what any of it meant, I just wanted the escape that sleep alone could offer.

4

I opened my eyes to the sound of rapid taps on my door. The door opened and a faint light flowed into the room, followed by Mrs. Casserly.

"It's early." She said. "None of the other girls are up yet. Yesterday Emma gave me some details of what has happened. Don't be upset with her. She only told me what was necessary. I am sorry for your bad news."

"Thank you." I said, reaching over and turning on the lamp.

"Paul said you got in late. I won't ask you about that. I am sure you did what you had to do, but when I asked, he also said he heard you come in here and never go to the bathroom. That's why I decided to wake you up early so you could have some time to collect yourself and more importantly, wash yourself, before you start work."

"Thank you." I said again.

Nodding, Mrs. Casserly walked the short distance to the door. Reaching it she turned around and looked at me again. "I am sorry Connie." She said before exiting the room and closing the door behind her.

I found out some time later that Myrna had been abandoned by her husband Mike Casserly about two years after they were married. She was 19 and 5 months with child when he disappeared along with her cousin Sandra. They had left no note and there had been no warning of their love affair. No one had voiced any possible connection at the curiousness that they both should go missing at the same time, though it was undoubtedly in everyone's minds. Finally a week later when a visiting friend mentioned seeing the two of them together in the neighboring town the morning of their disappearance it could no longer be denied. Myrna, shamed and pregnant moved back in with her family. In the spring she gave birth to a baby girl which she named Rebecca, who succumbed to influenza nine months later. With no husband, no daughter, and not even a divorce releasing her to find someone new, she fled Ohio for New York City seeking solace wandering anonymously among the masses. In time she picked up the broken pieces of her life and eventually found her way into working for the Sarringtons. She threw herself into her job completely, giving to the estate the devotion she had nowhere else to lay.

She had never had any other serious romantic prospects. In her early days in New York she wasted herself with various men as she tried misguidedly to regain a sense of pride in her ability as a woman, but when it dawned on her that the desires of these men had more to do with booze and convenience then her, she gave up.
That is until Frank Golden appeared. Frank stirred in her feelings long since dormant and his attention filled her with hope, but his attention wasn't hers alone. Between longing and humiliation she continued to maneuver when I had arrived.

I slowly gathered my things, still sore from the previous night and made my way to the bathroom. It was not my day to shower, as we had a schedule, but I decided to disregard this. I was sure that Mrs. Casserly must have had that in mind when she thought to wake me as early as she did. I wondered anxiously if she somehow knew of the previous night's deeds. Laying my things aside and starting the water I looked into the mirror as I waited for the water to warm. I wasn't sure what to think of the girl standing in front of me. Was she even a girl anymore? So much had changed since the last time I had looked at my own reflection even though it had only been less than twenty-four hours. Girl or woman she looked back at me with eyes still swollen, red and sore, and a mouth turned down. She looked lost.

The mirror began to fog from the bottom up and I turned away and stepped into the shower. It still hurt me to move, the area between my legs sore and swollen, much like my eyes, but for different reasons. I touched the area gently, cleaning the residue from my riverside activities. I felt odd. I didn't know what to think of myself. With all that my family was going through to have succumbed to such a thing was surely shameful. And besides that there was the fact that I was not married as I should have been. I hadn't done it right. I had gotten caught up in a moment and was weak and sinful. I wondered what would happen now that the morning light had come? Would Eli even dare to look at such a lowly creature, a woman who would give in so easily to his will? Women were supposed to be on the moral high ground were we not, the ones with the willpower to say no and keep us and our men on the straight and narrow. But I had failed.

Still another part of me didn't care. And that part of me jutted its chin forward in pride and defiance. Why should it matter? It was mine to give was it not? If I chose to surrender it then why should there be any shame in it. Eli loved me and I loved him and it was beautiful and pure. What dictate should have the right to rob me of it, to have the right to taint it? It was a struggle that raged inside of me as I am sure it has inside countless other women from time immemorial and one that would take far longer to reconcile than the length of a shower.

I heard the door open and expected to hear the voice of one of the other maids or Mrs. Casserly, but no sound came, not even the sounds of movement. I peeked out of the shower and saw Eli. Gasping I pulled the shower curtain around my body clutching it tightly which made him laugh.

"I think, my darling, that it's a little late for modesty don't you?" He asked raising one of his eyebrows in mock questioning.

"It's never too late." I replied. "And why are you in here? Are you crazy? You could be discovered at any moment. You have to leave."

"Is that anyway to treat the man you love? Besides, I've already been seen."

"By who?!" My heart jumped in fear.

"By Paul, but he won't say anything. I went to your room to speak with you but you weren't there so I came down here. I'm glad it was you in here and not someone else." Eli laughed again.

"I think that if I wasn't in my room at this hour, here was a pretty good bet Eli." I shook my head.

"I thought so too, obviously." He winked at me before coming over and kissing me.

I closed my eyes and moaned as he drew away again. "So why did you risk both of our jobs and my reputation?" I asked.

"I wanted to say good bye. I knew that once everyone was up there would be no chance. Also I wanted to see what you looked like as you slept, but I must admit, this is better."

I turned away blushing and he reached into the shower and cupped my breast before letting his hand slide down my side to my hip. I turned towards him again and looked into his eyes. Words felt inadequate for what I was feeling. I could only hope that he could somehow see it in the way I looked at him.

He kissed me again, slower and longer this time before pulling away and heading for the door. Putting his hand on the knob he smiled large. "Bye."

"Bye Eli."

With that he slowly and quietly opened the door and slid out as I stood there thinking that it was worth any risk to have shared such a moment.

By the time I was finished getting ready the rest of the house was beginning to stir. I sat on my bed reading *Walden* and thinking to myself how nice it was to have such free time before starting the day and how much nicer still it was to have such visits.

After a while I headed out to the kitchen where others were beginning to sit down to their breakfast. Paul looked at me and smiled as he handed me my plate and I felt my face go red. He shook his head and his shoulders moved up and down in silent laughter as he turned away. I quickly scanned the room to see if anyone had noticed but thankfully everyone seemed too tired or too busy with other concerns to have seen it. I sat down wondering what Paul must think, but after a while I decided that it didn't matter. What was done was done and I could only hope his own convictions were either high enough to show me mercy and overlook it or low enough to see nothing of it.

I sat eating my breakfast, lost in thought, when Mrs. Casserly came in. Emma startled me by asking her if I might help with the valances in the dining room as she felt she was getting too old and unsteady to be standing on a ladder trying to clean them. Mrs. Casserly pursed her lips for a moment looking as if she was just going to suggest someone else take the job from Emma completely before coming to the conclusion that it was an acceptable request and allowing it, perhaps thinking that in light of my recent news I needed to be near my friend.

The dining room windows faced the front of the house and on them were some of the heaviest and most cumbersome window treatments you could ever hope to see, a heavy silk taffeta of a rich burgundy color with muslin backing which in turn was covered in a pale, shell white linen. The valances were especially tiresome since they hung in a soft curve made of numerous thick folds of fabric and they had to be dusted just as anything else, but it was a very delicate matter because for one you can't just dust them with a duster or dry rag, nor could you just wet a rag because silk taffeta will show the spot where water has saturated it forever thereafter. Secondly and more importantly, to me anyway, it is difficult because you have to clean them while standing on a ladder and with your arms working uncomfortably above your head. Why Emma would wish this job on me was a mystery but I still followed behind her ready to obey.

When we reached the dining room Emma gestured with her head towards the window. Sitting in the circular driveway was a beautiful Rolls-Royce Phantom II. I had ridden in my first high end car, a Packard, on my way to the Sarrington Estate with Mrs. Casserly and it had been more luxury than I had enjoyed at any time in my life, but the Phantom II was beyond even that. The Packard had been black on the outside, all black with the exception of the silver hardware. But the body of the Phantom was the color of coffee mixed with too much cream and the roof of coffee mixed with too little. I could almost imagine the silver here and there as little spoons sticking out of the surface. That was not however what held my attention. What did that was Eli.

He was standing in front of the Phantom talking to Stanley as they waited for Alan and Stephen to load the Sarrington's luggage. Within moments it was done and a handful of upper servants appeared as did Mr. and Mrs. Sarrington. I had spent all my time thus far at the estate in areas not frequented by the Mr. and Mrs. and as a result had not had a chance to see them in person. Well not up close anyway, though I had seen them from afar as they walked the grounds, particularly Mrs. Sarrington, and I had also seen them in paintings within the house, always staring over my head calm and benign. But this was the first time I had seen them both fairly close and in the flesh.

John Sarrington was an average looking man in his late 50s, though how late was a matter of debate amongst the older staff. He had black hair that was balding on the very top of his head and he wore glasses, whether he always had or whether they, like his hair, were just another accessory of age I could not tell. He seemed to be rather rigged in his movement and looked impatient to be headed along. Mrs. Sarrington's age was an even greater topic of debate, but the consensus was that she had to be in her forties at least considering the ages of her children were 18, 22 and 23. If Lily Sarrington was forty she was not the forty I was accustomed to seeing. She radiated a youthful vitality and always wore a smile which may have been the cause. Her blonde hair was pulled into a low sleek bun that rested almost on the nape of her neck, a hint of her age that her face did not confess. Although I could not see her eyes from where I stood, I knew that they were pale blue unlike her husband's which were brown.

Stanley rushed over to open the door to the car. Once Mr. and Mrs. Sarrington were inside and the door was closed Eli gave a small quick wave to the gathered staff and climbed into the front passenger's seat. Within moments they were off, headed to the city and the train station and California. The entire scene lasted perhaps three minutes at most, but I was grateful to have had them.

Once the car was out of sight I looked down at Emma.
"Thank you Emma." I said.
"You're welcome." She replied. "But now we better get to work. You know Myrna wouldn't be happy to turn the corner and find us talking, but talk I want to, so come lunch time lets you and me take ours and go sit in the garden, okay."
"Alright. Can we do that?"
"Sure we can. Myrna will lighten up a little bit, not much mind you, but some since none of the Sarringtons are here. She always does. And we might as well enjoy it while we can. By the end of the month the kids will be back here from school and she'll be right back like she always is."
"Kids?" I asked.
"The Sarrington children; Jane, Thomas and Robert. Well, they're not really kids anymore, but they're still 'the kids'."
"Oh yes, of course, those kids. Are they nice?" It really didn't make any sense that I should want to know or care if they were nice or not. In the two months I had been at the estate I had never once had an encounter with Mr. or Mrs. Sarrington and I couldn't imagine that it would be any different with their progeny, but I suppose that I was curious in the same way any young person is curious about other young people or women are curious about each other. It's just natural I guess.
"Eh, I've never talked to them much really. They're young like you but it's different. You are used to deferring to your

elders and working and being seen and not heard. They're not. They're use to telling people what to do and using people as they see fit and they certainly aren't used to working, not like we do anyway. Probably they work real hard at their schooling or maybe they don't. Maybe school's just like everything else in their life." Emma sighed. "Ah well it doesn't matter. More than likely you won't see them at all anyway."

Cleaning the drapery took up the entire morning and was very tiring work, still in addition to getting to see Eli off it was nice to be out of the laundry room and away from Darla, though I knew I would find myself right back in that very spot after lunch. It wasn't that Darla was cruel, because she wasn't, it was that she was petty. Although I had no doubt that she would surely help anyone who needed it, it was a simple fact that for some reason she had a need to tear people down. It was never truly mean or spiteful nor did she try to set people up, it was just little things. Small judgments and criticisms, and a true love for gossip, even if she had to dig for it. I knew what she said to me about the others and with the amount of time I was spending with her, despite my goal of silence when possible, I could only imagine what she was saying to the others about me.

Emma and I put away our cleaning supplies and went to the kitchen for plates full of beans and cornbread which we carried along with glasses of tea to a bench in the garden. The garden was beautiful with low lying trimmed hedges, fountains and pools, and flowers everywhere. When I arrived to the estate it was barren, the winter snow just beginning to melt, but then came daffodils, crocus, hyacinth and snowdrops, followed shortly thereafter by the tulips, that were in turn followed by the lilac bushes, which although small of bud and really to be honest scraggily of limb, rival the hyacinth and the rose in scent and being the flower of the wee folk, had my vote for the best of the three. The redbuds were just finishing their display as were the dogwoods and in summer the roses would begin to appear as beautiful and majestic as little queens at court.

I was very hungry, still not having recovered from the two missed meals of the previous day. Though it had only been a couple of months since I had went full days without much more than a bite or two of bread and broth, the body gets spoiled quickly.

"I'm sorry about your father Connie." Emma hung her head shaking it. "I just can't believe Ennis would do something like that to Molly and you kids. I really thought I knew him after all these years. I guess you never know what someone will do."

"You do and he didn't." I replied. "Something has happened. I'm sure of it. He's hurt or he fell into the river."

"Maybe, I suppose that is possible." She replied, though obviously more for my benefit. "I surely hope it's true and that wherever he is he's safe and they find him real soon."

We sat quietly for a while watching two gray squirrels chase each other around the garden. I assumed that the one in front was trying to get away, but just when I thought it might it would double back and the chase would continue on. It finally dawned on me that the one in the front was playing hard to get, just not too hard.

"So now Constance." Emma said my full name, putting me instantly on guard. "You and Eli. Would you like to tell me anything about that?"

"I like him Emma. But you already know that, so what else could I have to tell you?" I answered hoping that by some miracle I sounded impassive, though I knew I didn't.

"You don't have anything you would like to tell me about last night?" She looked at me, eyes large and probing.

I hated this game. I had played it many times with my mother and always wished that if something was known she would just be out with it, but that was never the way it worked. Because the object of this game was to try to trick me into revealing just a bit more than what she was actually privy to.

"What about last night Emma?" I finally said.

"Connie," she sighed. "I'm just going to say it because as much as I'd like to, we can't just sit here all day. I know Eli had you last night."
I could feel my eyes widen and my face flush.
"I know you let him. You don't have to tell me you did. I've been around long enough that I can tell. It's not in the way you look or anything so obvious. You have to be someone who pays attention and I'm someone who does."
Emma's eyes seemed to be boring into me.
"I can tell it by the way you ate your breakfast like you had a secret you didn't want anyone to know and sure it could have been what happened with your father but it wasn't. Because you didn't look sad, you looked like you felt exposed. And you kept one hand in your lap like you were trying to cover yourself. And I could tell in the way you looked at Eli when he was leaving. It wasn't the same as how you've been looking at him ever since you got here, like a schoolgirl watching a crush. You were looking at him like a lover, because that's what he is to you now. "

I looked down at my lap, not wanting to meet Emma's eyes as I admitted to my sin. "I won't try to deny it."
"Good. Thank you for not insulting me with a lie." Emma reached over and patted me on the leg. "It's alright." she said. "Well, it's not completely alright. You shoulda been married. Your poor mother would be heartbroken. But you know that already and what's done can't be undone, but now he's gone and that's good I think. You won't be running off doing it again anytime soon. Maybe it'll give you and him some time to think about it, though I can't imagine time would change his opinion on it much. But I hope it'll change yours. You need a husband in this world Connie. You can make it without one, I've been doing it and Molly is gonna have to do it, but it isn't easy. It isn't something you want. Every woman knows it and always has. You've got to get the best husband you can. Somebody that's gonna take care of you. We ain't men Connie. We only got so many options and Eli's a good

one for you, but you can't expect him to marry you if you make things so easy for him."

I could tell she was getting upset now. It was important to her that I understood what she was saying.

"Think about it. What if you went and got pregnant? What are you gonna do then? You think Eli will marry you? Maybe he will, he seems honorable enough but you can't tell for sure. He's free and you've got no hold on him. If he just wants to walk away, he could do it and you with no ring and no prize to dangle in his face."

I could feel my face growing hot again, though this time it was from anger rather than shame.

"You say I don't have any hold on him Emma, and maybe I don't, but maybe I do. Maybe he does love me. And if he doesn't a ring isn't gonna change that. If he wants me, he'll marry me and if he doesn't he won't and if he does is that a guarantee? It wasn't for Mama. It wasn't for Loraine O'Hare that lived in the building beside ours. He could marry me and leave me anyway. Maybe it wasn't the best way to do it, but it was pure and it was honest. I wasn't trying to trap him and I can only hope that he wasn't just trying to take advantage of me. And no Mama wouldn't like it and neither would God and neither would Mrs. Casserly but don't none of that matter. All that matters is me and Eli and what we felt. I'll deal with the rest of it as it comes."

Emma looked down shaking her head again. "Fine Connie. I won't say any more about that, but you remember this, Myrna doesn't like this kind of thing and you need this job, not just for you either. Your mother is depending on you and I stuck my neck out for you. I can't believe the way you're talking to me right now. I know sometimes young girls get caught up in their feelings and the moment. I can understand that, you wouldn't be the first and Lord knows you won't be the last. But I never thought I'd see the day when you'd act so disrespectful. Maybe it's just that you've been through too much in such a short time and I'll just believe it and leave it at that."

Emma got up and started back towards the house. I knew I needed to as well but I couldn't bring myself to get up and walk beside her. I wished I could take it back. I knew what I felt but just because I did didn't mean I had to say it and definitely not like that. I waited until what I thought would be enough time for her to get back to the house then I stood up and started that way myself.

When I entered the house Henri, Paul and the rest of the kitchen staff greeted me with odd looks. It was probably just that Emma had come in from our lunch upset, which is out of character for her, but with so much I was trying to hide it made me paranoid, especially considering Paul was privy to my morning rendezvous in the shower. Mrs. Casserly was in the kitchen as well and she directed me to the laundry. That wasn't a surprise, she was usually directing me to the laundry, but of all the people I did not want to see at that moment, Darla was at the top of the list.

Darla looked at me as I entered the laundry room. The excitement obvious on her face, she'd been waiting for this all day. She almost pinched her finger in the rollers as she fed in a sheet, she was so distracted. Wouldn't be the first time.
"Oh Connie," Darla said putting down the sheet and crossing over to me. Within seconds she wrapped her large arms around me and squeezed tight for emphasis. She held me for a minute then pulling away she began again "I ain't gonna ask'd ya what happen. I knowed it mus' be some'in bad, what with ya runnin' off liken you did, but no, I ain't gonna ask. I knowed some people jus' don't wanna talk about them kinda things" Darla raised her hands and waved them back and forth in front of her "but if you're wantin' an ear I'm here for ya girl. I am. I like ya. I liked ya from the first and ya know me, I'm there for folks when they need me. And you and me we's more'n friends ain't we, why, I could be your auntie, so you jus' thinka that if you get ta feelin' like ya need to talk to somebody."

"Thank you Darla." I replied. "I'll keep that in mind. But I don't think I'm ready to talk about it just yet."
"That's alright, that's alright. Jus' remember what I said."
"I will. Thanks again."
Darla settled back to the washer as I plugged in the iron and began to set up the board. I knew that silence would be too much to ask and I was right; though Darla did pause for at least ten minutes between the time I declined her offer and her starting in with something new which could have been counted as a small miracle.
"Emma looked to be upset when she came in from lunch." Darla finally said, almost panting, she had been holding it in so long.
"Did she?" I replied.
"Yes, she sure enough did. I was wondering if everythin' was alright seein' as the two of ya were out there eatin' lunch together." Darla answered.
"As far as I know she's fine." I said.
"Well, alright." Darla sighed "If 'n ya say so."
Darla looked as if she was trying to decide if she should say something or not. I hoped she would settle on not, and apparently she did, because the way in which she uttered her next words gave the hint that they were not really what she wanted to say at all.
"Won't be long for the Sarrington kids come home." She said.
I looked up at her and smiled, glad for a safe topic.
"Yes that's what I heard this morning. Are they nice?" I asked the ridiculous question for the second time. It would be better to keep her focused along these lines rather than others.
"Eh, I reckon. I don't spend no time with em. They're alright when their parents is home, but they can get a little wild when theys not. That's kids though. Guess it don't matter none whether they're rich or poor. When the cats away and all that."

"Yes, I suppose you're right." I agreed. "So what do you mean wild?"

"Nothin' too much really. They like to have their friends over and get liquored up. That kinda thing."

"Oh I see. That's normal for college kids I guess huh." I said.

"Eh, all kids that can I reckon. What about you, you ever get all liquored up? I bet you ain't." Darla laughed and I laughed a little in return.

"No you'd be right there. I've never had anything to drink." I answered.

"Not even when you was out with Eli?" Darla asked, looking at me with one eyebrow cocked and a smirk on her round red face. That was it. Eli was what she had wanted to bring up. I should have known that it would not escape the notice of *some* that while I was gone for most of the night, so was Eli.

"No, just coffee and water. You can't do much hiking if you're drunk I'd imagine." I replied.

"Hikin' huh. That's all you two did in all that time?"

"Well," I said forcing a laugh "What else would we have been doing?"

"Well, I don't know if you don't. If you says you was hikin' I guess you was hikin'." Darla huffed. After which she was quiet and instead began to sulk as she always did when things didn't go the way she had planned.

Luckily for me there was not a lot of laundry to do and I was out and in the kitchen in less than two hours. Those within the kitchen had the good grace to not ask me about the letter or Emma or Eli and for that I was grateful. I was happy to just be able to listen to their stories and conversations as I went along with my work. Doing so was calming and just what I needed, to be able to get lost in ordinary, everyday cares that had nothing to do with anything of importance and especially not anything to do with me and my many predicaments.

I spent the next few days in a state of depression. I don't know if that's normal or bad or maybe it's good, maybe it's a short amount of time considering the rapid ups and downs I had endured. I like to think that it is. I have always considered myself not only an optimist but a 'pull yourself up by the bootstraps' sort of person. Even so, I did need some time to be sad and hurt and shocked. Time to wallow in self-pity, and I took it.

I didn't join in much late night conversation during those days. I wanted more than anything to be outside. Since arriving at the estate nature had become my refuge and my sanctuary and it was where I wanted to be in my times of joy and times of distress, but instead, this time, nature held me at bay.

All had been bright and sunny without a cloud in the sky when Eli and the Sarringtons left. It was the kind of weather that fills you with hope and happiness and makes people want to be out and about at lakes and parks. There wasn't the slightest warning that things wouldn't continue to warm and brighten with nothing but carefree summer days ahead. You could say that the weather of that day was the perfect metaphor for what had been my life the past month. A rumble in the distance came ever so faint. So faint in fact that you couldn't be quite sure that that was what it was at all. Then the winds picked up. What had just minutes before been nothing but a light breeze that caused the flower heads to wave lazily in greeting, became stronger with each passing minute. Soon the trees began to bow sharply with each increasingly strong gust before springing back to attention. Next the thunder grew louder and the horizon flickered with distant lightening and the sky darkened though it was only around five thirty in the afternoon.

I looked around the kitchen to gauge the reaction of everyone else. I always hated storms, not rain, that I didn't mind. Rain is calming and uniform. But thunderstorms I despised. I like routine. I like to know what I'm in for, but thunderstorms are unpredictable. Crashes and booms and bursts of light and wind without warning. I don't like surprises and I was liking them even less as of late. The approaching storm almost offended me at the rudeness of its appearance then of all times. I felt betrayed by the very nature I loved. When it rains it pours they say and that was truer in that moment for me than at any other time I can think of.

I looked around worried and trying hard to conceal it, but everyone else just went on about their business. Then it was as if the heavens suddenly shattered and rain and hail and lightening descended all around us. The thunder was loud and hard, instantaneous with the lightening, making the ground shake underfoot. They all paid attention now.

Darla came out of the laundry and the others came in from the rest of the house. No one wanted to admit fear, but no one wanted to be alone either. Even the upper servants found their way into the kitchen. I suppose the ingrained idea of safety in numbers applies even when the danger is something that isn't swayed by a crowd any more than it is by a lone wolf.

We all stood around in silence. Every once in a while one of the men would try to make a joke, but the uneasiness in their voices was evident and only added to the tension in the room rather than doing anything to abate it. Mrs. Casserly made a few attempts to preoccupy herself with busy work, such as trying to straighten a stack of plates, or doing other tasks that made no sense like folding the wet wash cloths. But her efforts were always interrupted by a close flash of lightening and simultaneous thunder causing her to forget whatever it was she was doing.

The hail passed quickly but the rain continued on seemingly forever and the lightning and thunder came at an almost continuous rate. It appeared for a moment that the rain had lightened and the wind was dying down a bit when a deafening crack came and the sky and kitchen filled with a brilliant white flash followed by darkness as the ground shook beneath us.

The power was out. Ann was frantic. She cried and let out a little scream with every lightning strike. Emma and Helen busied themselves trying to calm her. Mrs. Casserly ran for the storage and Stephen began to rummage through a drawer until he found a flashlight and he and Alan took off for the fuse box on the other side of the house. When Mrs. Casserly appeared again she was holding a box full of half used candles and looking more like her usual self, happy to have some way to take control of the situation. Mrs. Sarrington didn't like the look of old candles in her candelabras and as a result quite a collection of 3, 4 and 5 inch burnt pillars had been amassed.

Mrs. Casserly lit one, then lighting others off it passed them around as she instructed Joan, Nellie, Emily and Ernest to gather all the holders they could find throughout the house as long as they weren't crystal or porcelain and bring them to the kitchen being careful to take the nearly new candles and lay them gently aside before doing so. Better to use discarded candles she said, then waste oil and dirty the lamps; especially with only us in the house.

Stephen and Alan returned to the kitchen shaking their heads. As far as they could tell the fuses were fine. A discussion began about what should be done next and soon the kitchen was filled with the glow of dozens of flames dancing to the beat of the rain that drummed its song softly outside. The worst of the storm had passed, for now.

5

Storms continued off and on over the next few days forcing me to spend the time I wasn't working in my bedroom with a book and a candle. A power line pole had snapped south of the main gate and we spent the week without electricity. It probably would have been longer had Mrs. Casserly made the electric company aware of the fact that Mr. and Mrs. Sarrington were out of town, but she did not. What the company didn't know wouldn't hurt them and seeing that there is no way they would leave those as important as the Sarringtons without power for a second longer than absolutely necessary, what they didn't know could only help us.

Actually the storms weren't forcing me to my bedroom, just keeping me indoors. I could have spent the nights as the others did, sharing stories and laughter in the kitchen. It was my desire for seclusion that had me take to hiding in my room night after night. I had a lot to think about with what was going on with my father and also with everything that had happened with Eli, but the truth is that while I did think about those things quite a bit, I was simply being a coward.

I didn't want to face the others. I had been doing a good job so far keeping everyone at bay while working, but after work socialization was a different matter. I didn't want to have to endure the questions that would surely come, the sympathetic glances in my direction from those who perhaps knew a bit more than I would have liked or the smirks from those who assumed other things that I equally had no desire for them to know. I also didn't want to face Emma. I knew that I needed to and that she deserved an apology and wanted to make amends, but I was still too raw. I had a good suspicion that talking about any of it with anyone, even her, would only produce the same results as it had in the garden.

So I sat in my room being cowardly and if we are really going to be honest, lazy and selfish too. Because while I was avoiding everyone for my own comfort, and while I was denying Emma the apology she deserved, I was also not responding to my mother's letter. I kept telling myself that she wouldn't be expecting a letter yet and that was true enough, but she would expect one sooner rather than later. I was sure she would have tried to calculate when her letter would arrive and how long a letter would take to get back to her assuming I replied immediately. But I didn't know what to say and really, I didn't want to talk to her. A good daughter would have responded at once and set her mind at ease, but maybe I wasn't a good daughter after all, maybe, all I was anymore was just an angry one. She had lied to me. She denied me as a daughter, as a member of the family, the right to be concerned and worry and pray, just as she was denying me the right to come down to Brooklyn to help in the search. And what gave her that right? Yes she was my mother, but that couldn't be enough justification. And in denying me, she had lessened my place in the family to that of a distant cousin or far-flung aunt who you only catch up with from time to time. It hurt and I didn't know how to go on with everything from there and I was too tired to try to figure it out.

So I didn't try. For the first time in my life I immersed myself in books. I had always enjoyed reading when I could but we didn't own many books at home and though I never regretted it growing up, I had never spent much time in a library either. Now my mouth nearly salivated at the thought of the books that the libraries of New York City must hold.

Eli had suggested that I read *Walden* and seeing as I wanted to make him happy and touch anything that had touched him I sought it out in town a few weeks prior. My life at the estate up until this point had left me with little time to spend in reading it, but now I devoured the book, working my way through it as I could. I cannot say that I am well educated or that I have any claim on natural intelligence, which at times made it difficult for me to understand everything that Thoreau was trying to say, but it didn't stop me from soaking it all in like the rays of the sun and being warmed and enlivened by it. As I approached the end his words reverberated within me like a bell that has been struck and continues on filling the room and the listener with its vibrations even as the sound fades. There was so much to it, more than I could grasp at the moment but what I did started a ripple within me that echoed in my mind and soul. "The universe is wider than our views of it." and again "Explore thyself." I loved it. I may not have fully understood it, but I loved it still.

When *Walden* concluded I snuck into the Sarrington's library and explored, finding the writings of Emerson and also Whitman's *Leaves of Grass*. The waters of wisdom and beauty ran deep and I drank until I was refreshed and ready to face the world once more, renewed.

I spent the weekend setting things to right. I began with an apology to Emma and tried to be pleasant and sociable as much as I had always been without seeming worried that anyone had anything they could say that would upset me or put me on the spot, and they couldn't really. I did feel strengthened and sure of myself and now that I was on my own, I was beginning to feel some sense of personal authority, which was something that had always eluded me. Because of this I was able to find that I enjoyed the company of the others even more than I had before, knowing that I didn't have to answer their questions if I didn't want to or even remain in their presence if I felt uncomfortable. I began to realize that I had a choice and didn't necessarily always have to bend to the will of someone else.

I also wrote a letter to my mother which I enclosed in a box containing the gift I had planned on giving her in person, which I would have to be content to give to her by other means. It was a set of three handkerchiefs, not an expensive gift by most people's standards I realize but I had been sending most of my earnings to the family already and had only kept a very small portion for myself, though after the news I felt guilty about having done even that. Just another reason she should have told me earlier, so I could have sent every bit and made due, but there was no sense in dwelling on it and at least the handkerchiefs were needful besides beautiful. The few she owned had been worn for quite some time and were also rather plain. These were not the handkerchiefs someone like Lily Sarrington would use, but I was proud to be sending them and I knew my mother would be proud to receive them. They were white with a border of embroidered flowers, not stamped like cheaper versions. These were the type that you prized and handed down to daughters and granddaughters. Each one had a different type of flower. One had blue daisies, another, pink roses, and the other, purple violets. All the flowers were laced together by sage green embroidery floss. I was so proud when I bought them and showed them around to some of the ladies. While I thought later that they may have found me silly, for me it was the most expensive gift I had ever bought and who better to deserve it?

My letter was short and decidedly sweet considering. Thankfully pen allows you the time to work through your emotions and choose your words wisely in a way that face to face interaction never can. It offered her my hopes for my father's return, my request to do anything I could and my vow to pray without ceasing. Placing the letter in the handkerchief box and wrapping that in brown packaging paper I sent it along with Stanley, Joan, Doyle and Nellie who were headed into the city for Mother's Day. Stanley promised to drop it off on his way to visit his own family in the nearby neighborhood of Williamsburg in Brooklyn.

The house was fairly empty. Stanley's was not the only carful of employees headed out, both Ken and Charles had car loads as well, everyone who could was taking the opportunity to spend the holiday with their loved ones since the Sarringtons were out of town and work was minimal. The sun was shining in a cloudless blue sky and though I felt bad at the thought of leaving Emma, Mother's Day was hard on her, I longed to be on top of the mountain again and she wouldn't be alone after all, she had Mrs. Casserly, Darla, and Henri among others. I did my work as quickly as possible, finishing by noon, and after sneaking into Emma's room to lay a small box of chocolates I had bought for the occasion on her nightstand I headed out the door.

I set out with vigor and reached the boulders in record time. Looking out over the estate and beyond at the beauty and majesty of it all I felt whole and truly pacified for the first time in a week. As I sat down I thought of Emerson's words *"There is nothing that can befall me in life —no disgrace, no calamity (leaving me my eyes), which nature cannot repair."* Pulling out my thermos of water I offered up a silent toast to nature, and her admirers.

The sun was warm on my face and arms but a cool breeze blew steadily on my back keeping my body in a constant state of flux, like Goldie Locks between hot, cold and just right. The calm was disrupted by the sound of leaves rustling behind me and I turned half expecting to see Eli. Instead I was greeted by the sight of a deer. It was a Whitetail doe probably about 4 years old, more than likely foraging while her young lay in a den nearby, but I didn't know any of that at the time. This was my first experience of ever seeing a deer in person. I was lucky to have it. The breeze that had served to both cool and annoy me had also served to hide my scent.

When I turned she caught sight of me and stood perfectly still and my own body froze in solidarity. She was beautiful. Her long legs and face, her big dark eyes and long eyelashes. Everything about her seemed to radiate gracefulness and purity. She stared at me for only a moment before she darted away and was out of sight within mere seconds. My body remembered itself and my heart beat fast as I panted hard. I had not realized I was holding my breath. I had seen a few small animals since I had begun walking, squirrels, chipmunks, even beaver down by the river. I had also seen many birds from woodpeckers to hawks, but this experience changed everything. Nature took on a whole other dimension. Though I knew from Eli that other large creatures lived in these woods, I hadn't given them much thought. Now, I wanted nothing more than to see them all.

I returned to the house a little before six. Paul, who usually made the employee meals, was gone and whether it was the occasion, pride or kindness, Henri pulled out all the stops for our dinner. The guards and grounds men had eaten before us as always and he had made a nicer meal than usual for them as well, a roast with red potatoes, green beans, mushrooms, carrots, dinner rolls and gravy. We had rolls and red potatoes as well, but rather than roast for us he served asparagus cooked with lemon and butter and lamb chops cooked in a rosemary and balsamic vinaigrette reduction. I had never eaten lamb in my life and it was and remains even now, one of my favorite meals. The lamb chops were small, much smaller than the pork chops I had grown up with, but they were delicious. I sat relishing it all and thinking how nice it must be to be able to eat like this every day. And while I wouldn't say that the worries that began the previous Sunday didn't still way heavy on my mind, things were definitely looking up.

The next couple weeks seemed to fly by. I was reading and walking when I could, foolishly hoping to run into a bear or wolf and I had received a letter from my mother, thanking me for the handkerchiefs, though there was still no new leads on my father. Emma and I were back to the way things were, better in fact since I was spending more time talking to her and everyone else now that Eli was not around.

I had not heard from Eli, though I tried not to worry about that. I could come up with plenty of reasons why I had not. He was surely busy and of course there was the matter of not wanting to arouse suspicion, but in the back of my head a small part of me couldn't help but replay Emma's words. What if it had all been nothing more than a hunt for gratification, and I had never been anything more to him than a naïve, love struck girl, easily taken advantage of.

As the end of the month approached the house really began to come alive. The Sarrington children would be making their way home within days and though there was not much extra to be done to prepare, everyone was looking forward to it. It's one thing to work day after day, dusting furniture and cleaning mirrors simply for the fact that it's your job, it's another when it's both your job and someone is witnessing and benefiting from the results, even if in reality they're not paying attention to it. It still gives your actions weight and purpose. The upper servants were naturally more excited than us lower ones, but no one was more excited than Ann.

I had witnessed Ann with Eli and knew as any woman does, but especially one eyeing the competition, that she had been infatuated, as I myself was, and vying for his attention. I had seen the blush in her cheeks and the wide eyes when he was around, but none of that compared to the effect that the very name of the younger Sarrington son, Thomas, had on her. She would become flustered and giddy and it was both amusing and irritating to be near her.

I really couldn't see the draw. I had seen pictures of the younger Sarringtons. Jane the youngest and only daughter looked like a younger version of her mother, light blonde hair, blue eyes, and delicate features. Robert the elder son had brown hair and eyes like his father and appeared to always wear the same irritated expression. It could be said that just as Jane so favored the mother, so too Robert favored the father. Thomas however was a perfect combination of the two. Brown haired with his father's straight nose and blue eyed with his mother's high cheekbones and perfect lips. He was attractive no doubt about it, like a movie star, but to me he was too perfect, too beautiful, making him almost take on a hint of feminity.

Once they arrived my life didn't really change. It was much like it was when the elder Sarringtons were home. I didn't see the young Sarringtons except for an occasional glimpse of one or more of them through a window, usually as they headed to the pool to swim. I did however hear them quite often, at least the sons. They spent a good deal of time on the lower level, kitchen side of the house as that was where the billiard room was and as most men at their leisure and in their twenties, they could be loud.

Ann, who I had always been friendly enough with, but never been close to, had suddenly begun to take me into her confidence with the arrival of Thomas Sarrington. I can't say why this was exactly. Perhaps it was that she felt as a girl close to her age I would understand her feelings. Perhaps she thought that because I seemed to have gotten Eli's attention I might be able to give her some advice. Perhaps, she simply wanted to make me jealous if she could. I imagine that it was probably a combination of all three.

For the week that Thomas had been home she had managed to place herself in his line of sight on an almost constant basis. I really didn't know how this would help her situation. It had always been my experience that the rich don't pay much attention to the help no matter how often you're around them. Really it seemed to me that as far as they were concerned you might as well have been a lamp or a curtain or some other inconsequential object, just one that moved. While it is true that most of my experience came from working as hotel staff, my time at the estate so far hadn't given me any reason to think that it would be any different in the private sphere.

Apparently I was wrong. As I stood in the laundry guiding shirts through the roller, I saw Ann peek her head in. She was in luck, Darla had stepped around to the back of the garage for a smoke. Seeing that I was alone, Ann came running into the room and grabbed me by both arms.
"He smiled at me!" Ann blurted out.
"Okay."

"No, you don't understand, he *smiled* at me." She repeated. She was breathing fast and shallow. "It wasn't just a regular smile either. Not one that he would just give to anybody."
"How do you figure?" I asked.
"I don't know. It just wasn't. Ugh. I can't explain it. It was like, it was like." Ann moved her head side to side trying to collect her thoughts. "It was like, *the look*; you know what I'm talking about?"
"No. I can't say that I do."
"It's a smile but not a normal one. Not a have a nice day smile. What am I wanting to say?" Her eyes suddenly widened and her mouth drew up at the corners. "It was an impolite smile."
"What?" I laughed.
"An impolite smile." She repeated. "A cocky smile. A smile that implies things." She nodded her head in satisfaction.
I wanted to ask what it had implied, though I knew exactly what she was talking about, but at that moment Darla returned. Before Darla could even get a word out Ann was speeding out the door, calling behind her "Thanks! Talk to you later!"
"What was that about?" Darla asked.
"I really am just not sure." I said hoping Darla would either believe it or take the hint to let it go. She did. As it turned out she had other things she was more interested in talking about.
"Well now, you're never gonna guess what I jus' heard." Darla began.
'Probably not." I sighed.
"I heard the younger boy, Thomas, done flunked outta school."
"What? Where did you hear that?" I asked.
"Jus' now. I was round back taking a smoke when Frank came up ta me. Said that he heard it from Charles, who'd heard it from Ken. Ken, done been the one that drove the boys home and he'd heard the younger 'en talkin' to the older

'en about it and how he had ta make sure he gotta holda the letter before old man Sarrington did."

"I don't know Darla. That's a lot of people to go through."

"I don't see why that matters none." Darla replied, annoyed. "Theys grown men, they knows what was said and what wa'nt.

6

Another week passed, then another. I continued my reading. I had long since finished with *Walden* and Emerson's essays and was going through *Leaves of Grass* when I could tolerate it. Whitman may be a genius, I won't argue it; but poetry I was deciding, was not really my thing. I had also found a book on Queen Elizabeth while sneaking around in the library and was reading that when I could, drawn to the idea of a woman unto herself, and I continued hiking, still on my quest for the wildlife that wisely eluded me.

One Sunday I passed by the pool on my way to the river. The Sarrington children were swimming with some of their friends making enough noise that they could be heard from within the house. They had had many gatherings since they had returned, taking advantage of the fact that their parents were out of town and they had the place to themselves. They would host parties during the day, which were usually loud but mild, and parties at night which were not as loud but from what I could gather, not nearly so mild either.

As I walked by the pool the talking died down considerably and the feeling of being watched came over me as I went along. I didn't look over and within a few moments I heard someone laugh and say "Hey Tom!" followed by more laughs and the sounds of splashing. I didn't know what to think about it so I tried not to, but it made me self-conscious and I wished that Emma or Eli or even Mrs. Casserly were with me.

By the time I made it to the river my mind had one thing on it and that was Eli. I still hadn't heard from him even though it had been well over a month. My heart sank as I thought about the night we had shared before he left, of all the nights and days really, but especially that one. I had given him everything. Emma had been right. I was foolish. The more I thought about it the more I became convinced he had planned it for that night, so he could do it and escape to California the next day. I didn't want to believe it. It didn't seem like Eli, not the Eli I had grown to know, but it sure looked that way.

I was angry. I hated him. But I didn't. I wanted to yell at him and I wanted to rush into his arms. I wanted him to give me some logical explanation for why he hadn't written. If he had been playing a game I wanted to make him regret it, to see how wonderful I was and change his mind. I just wanted to see him, to hear his voice, and Ann was only making it worse.

Every day I was receiving updates from her. The smiles had continued and increased. Then she got a hello, followed by another and after that a compliment one afternoon as Thomas passed her on the stairs, "You look nice today, almost radiant." He had said to her, with *the* smile of course. I still wasn't sure if Ann was lying or not. Radiant? It seemed like a bit much to me. She couldn't even focus to eat that night. She would go to put her fork up to her mouth and stop before she completed the task, pausing, then smiling and putting it back down again. Everyone in the kitchen with her that evening found all of it very amusing though it escaped her notice, she might as well have not been in the same room as the rest of us. It was only about a week and a half after that, after more reports of smiles and hellos and compliments that she stopped reporting to me at all. I didn't know if I had done something to upset her or if perhaps Thomas had. When I finally asked her, she simply said no and told me that she just didn't want to bore me with it any longer. I was happy that she had stopped. I liked Ann just fine, but details about the man she was obsessed with simply wasn't what I wanted to hear all things considering. It reminded me too much of the days I had spent in the same consuming, though private, state.

Finally it happened, Mrs. Casserly received a telegram from Mrs. Sarrington. All was going well in California. They were wrapping everything up and would need Stanley to pick them up at the train station the next Friday. The news sent my mind into a tailspin of what ifs.

The following week was a flurry of activity as we all raced to get the house in order. Mrs. Casserly was in top form; this was the stuff she lived for. I went to bed most nights exhausted and sleeping soundly until morning, but as that Friday approached, bit by bit it became harder to do so. By the time the Thursday before Eli's arrival came around I couldn't sleep at all.

I tossed and turned. I tried counting sheep. I tried naming sheep. I tried focusing on my breath and moving the air in and out of my body slowly. After a while I finally just gave up and decided to walk down to the river. It was a warm night and the sky was clear.

As I crossed through the garden I was startled by a voice.
"Hey! Hey you!" The voice slurred just the slightest bit.
My heart raced as I scanned the area. My eyes came to rest on the figure of a man sitting on one of the benches.
"You!" It said again. "What are you doing? Come over here."
I didn't know what to do, so I turned to go back towards the house.
"Come over here. I won't bite you. I just want some company."
"Who are you?" I asked, trying not to sound afraid. It was silly to be I told myself. After all, I knew everybody who worked there didn't I.
"Thomas. James. Sarrington." The voice answered.
I turned towards the bench and made my way over. Thomas Sarrington sat on the bench leaning forward with his elbows resting on his legs and his hands together holding a bottle of some kind. I couldn't make out what kind of bottle; it was of a good size and oddly shaped. Though I couldn't see the label I had a good idea of what it contained.
"What's your name?" Thomas asked.
"Constance." I replied.

"Constance." He repeated. "Well, come sit down beside me Constance."

"Do you need something Mr. Sarrington?" I asked, trying to avoid having to sit.

"Just company. I have everything else I need right here." He replied holding up the bottle in his right hand before returning it to its previous position.

"I should really be getting back inside. It's very late." I said.

"You didn't look like you were in a hurry to get inside just a minute ago. You looked like you were headed down to the river. I've seen you walking down there before." He shifted as if he were preparing to stand. "Would you like to go there? I'll walk with you."

"No." I replied sitting down beside him. "Here is good."

Thomas laughed. "You're scared. It's alright. I don't blame you. It's the middle of the night, you just wanted to take a walk and suddenly a man calls out to you from nowhere, one that has been drinking no less. But I'm not going to hurt you." He paused. "So why are you out here in the middle of the night Constance?"

"I couldn't sleep Mr. Sarrington and decided to try to walk. You?" I could only see his form, not his eyes or expressions. The night sky was clear, but not bright.

"My name is Tom. You can call me that. No need for Mr. Sarrington just yet." Tom laughed, then he mumbled, "Maybe never."

"Okay Tom." I said. "Why are you out here in the middle of the night?"

"Just drinkin' and thinkin' I suppose."

"What are you thinking about?" I asked.

"Life." He replied. "What else is there to think about?"

"I don't know. What about life then?"

"Why it is the way it is. Can it be changed?" Tom said gesturing up at the sky. "Was William Henley right? Are we the captains of our souls? Are we *truly* the rulers of our own destinies or is everything fated, or even if it's not fated are we still not the rulers because someone else holds the scepter."

"I don't follow you." I replied.

"Think about it Constance. Do you think that your life is in your hands? I mean really. Do you think that if you wanted you could do anything or be anything? Or are you just stuck where you are forever, bending to the will of society or your station or your parents, or whatever it may be?"

I thought for a moment. "I don't know. I guess I've always believed that you just are what you are and you should just accept it. I mean that's what I've always seen. It's what I've always been told. But that's me and my reality, not you and yours. You're a Sarrington. You have the means to do whatever you want, so I guess for you, you could be in charge of your own life."

"Do you think so, really?" Tom said. "I don't know. Sometimes I think so but sometimes I don't. You say I have the means to be anything. I guess what you're saying is that I'm rich and can do what I want and you're not and have to take what life gives you."

I nodded though I doubted he could see me.

Tom continued. "But you see my means are my chains. The name, the expectations, the allowance. They're all links in the chains that bind me to the will of the one who controls it all, who has it all, my father. He has his plans for my life, not just mine; Jane's, Robert's. They seem to be fine with it. I'm not so sure."

"Are his plans so bad? I asked.

"No, not at all. I think most people would find them reasonable. Law school, politics. It's what's expected from …." he trailed off, lost I supposed in his own thoughts.

"What do you want then if not law and politics? Will he not consider your own ideas and feelings?" I asked.

"I don't know what I want. I struggle with it. I want freedom, but I want security. I think to myself that it's my life to do with as I please; whether I want to go to law school or travel across Asia and Africa or whether I want to join a carnie side show." He laughed short and bitter. "But it's easier to just go along with it."

"A lot of people want to just go off and do things that seem exciting, but most people can't, rich or poor, legacy or not. Most people have their own set of chains; money, duty, there's tons of them and they're all as valid as any other." I replied, surprised at my own audacity.

"So don't have a pity party is what you are saying."

"I didn't say that. I was just saying that you're not the only one with those feelings, but I guess some people are more stuck than you. I don't know what it's like to have a name and legacy you're expected to uphold but I know that some folks have children to feed, or old folks to take care of and that's why they can't follow their dreams or their whims; not because someone might be upset with them, or they might have to earn their own way, but because actual lives depend on them. Sometimes you have to do the responsible thing, and the world is made up of people doing just that."

"It might not even matter anyway." Tom said after a long pause.

"Why is that?" I asked.

"I screwed it all up. I didn't think I was doing it on purpose but maybe I was."

"Was what?"

"Failing my classes. I just didn't care I guess. I thought I was just having fun, but I guess maybe I was, somewhere in the back of my head, aware of what I was doing and what the consequences would be and I was welcoming it, hell, I was courting it. Now my father will be back tomorrow and he'll find out and who knows what he'll do. Maybe he'll rant and rave and call up the dean and get me a second chance, maybe he'll send me packing, a lost cause, maybe he won't do anything and leave it all up to me. He could do any of it and I'm scared of all of the possibilities and yet hoping for all of them at the same time."

"I guess," I finally said after a while "that when the time comes you'll know if you're the ruler or if you're the slave. Maybe in life you're both, and maybe you never know which part you're playing at any given time until the last moment. "

With that I stood up. "But I don't know. I do know that I have to get up for work early and should go back to the house and go to bed. It was nice to meet you Tom."

"Yes. You probably should go then. It was nice to meet you too Constance. Thank you for sitting with me my dear."

I looked at him not sure how to respond. I couldn't see his face and hoped that he couldn't see mine. The encounter was an odd one. I had never had someone of his stature condescend to have a conversation with me and I had been bold with him. As I turned away and headed towards the house I hoped he was now at ease, because I sure wasn't.

7

Morning came early after my long night, and while I would have expected my first thought to be Eli, it wasn't. It was Tom. Like me he would be spending his day in a state of agitation wondering what good or bad might lie ahead with the arrival of the train from California.

When the car finally did pull up I could hear the commotion that rippled its way through the house, but I was determined to stay in the laundry room no matter how hard a feat that might be.

"Don't cha wanna go out n see Eli?" Darla asked.

"Hmmm?" I looked up at her from the ironing board. I had heard her but I didn't know how to answer. Of course I wanted to go, but I wouldn't.

"*I said*, don't cha wanna go out n see Eli. He's here now."

"Um. No." I turned back to my ironing. "I'll see him later just like everybody else."

"Jus' like 'erybody else huh. Hmmm." Darla picked up another towel. "Alright then."

But I didn't see him later just like everybody else. I avoided him. I did want to see him. I wanted to hear his voice and see his face. I wanted to rush into his arms. I wanted to ask him why he didn't write me. I wanted to walk into the kitchen just to see how he would react to the sight of me. Would he smile or would he look away? I wanted answers to all the questions I had mulled over for the past month, but then again, I didn't want them. If the answers were good I wanted them, but if they weren't I wanted to hold them off just a little bit longer. I also knew that more than just Eli would await in that kitchen, so would a dozen or more pairs of eyes, watching and analyzing every look, every word and every movement, both mine and his. No, our first meeting would have to wait. No matter what it held, I knew I didn't want to share it.

I waited in my room while the first run of dinner took place in the kitchen. I knew Eli had to be there and I strained to hear him, catching words here and there over the din of pots and pans. "California." "Rocky cliff." "Train ride back." Now and then I would hear Eli's laugh rise up over the commotion and in those moments like no other I struggled not to open the door and join him in the kitchen. I could picture him leaning against the counter with a plate in one hand, fork in another, sleeves rolled half way up his forearms and one foot crossed over the top of the other, his golden head bent forward and moving side to side as he laughed.

When the talking finally died away and nothing remained but the sounds of the last of the dinner preparations for the Sarringtons, I laid back on my bed and waited to be called down to my own dinner later while wondering how the next dinner in the lineup would go, Tom's. Would it be tense, full of anxious worry and the sting of angry words or would it be cheerful, all forgiven and repaired? I wanted to sneak out and see the answer almost as much as I had wanted to sneak out and see Eli.

Finally Susan's voice came from down the hall to come eat and I rose, pausing only briefly at the door to wonder if I should just stay and suffer through my hunger. I looked around the kitchen to make sure Eli wasn't there. He wasn't, filling me with a mixture of relief and disappointment. I stood away from everyone against the wall next to the door that led to the pantry, listening as Paul and the rest of the kitchen staff relayed bits of Eli's story from earlier and tried to look away when one of them seemed to be trying to gauge my expression.

I was almost finished and ready to retreat again to my room when Eli appeared at the open backdoor. He didn't enter the kitchen, he simply leaned in, hands on either side of the door frame.

"Telling stories Paul?" Eli said. Though he had addressed Paul, it was me he was looking at.

"Me, Eli? Never! I was just telling everyone what you said about how the place they're building out in California runs almost right to a cliff that just drops off into the ocean." Paul answered, though as he finished he followed Eli's eyes. Everyone did.

I couldn't read Eli's expression. It was neither happy nor angry, loving nor uncomfortable, but his eyes looked at me with fierce intensity and I was held by them.

"That it does." Eli finally responded. "Well I was just looking for something. Y'all get back to eatin'."

"Aw, come on Eli." Eloise said, trying to sound playful but instead it came across like a whine. "You won't tell us about your trip, we have to hear it second hand from Paul."

Paul opened his mouth feigning offense.

"Nah, like I said, I just needed to see something." Eli answered.

"That ain't what you said." Darla piped in, ever sharp. "You said you was lookin' for somethin'. Was you lookin' or needin', cause theys two different things."

"Not in this case they aren't." Eli answered before tipping his head in farewell and walking away.

"I don't think it matters what he needed, it was nice to see him again after all this time." Emma said.

Helen nodded her head in agreement.

"Well, think what ya want. I think we all knowed what he wanted ta see or needed ta see, however you wanna say it." Darla said as she looked at me and everyone else followed suit.

I turned my head up to look at the ceiling in a pathetic attempt to appear ignorant.

Joan started to laugh and I turned my head to look at her. "Girl," she said, "why don't you just follow the man outside and give him a big old kiss. Myrna ain't here and we ain't blind."

My mouth dropped open and though I tried to close it, it only fell open again. The room erupted in laughter and I couldn't help but to join them, my face prickled with heat, a sure sign it had gone red which only served to make them laugh all the harder. Shoving my plate at Joan and smiling, I crossed the kitchen and walked out the door.

The night air was hot and sticky, enough to make anyone sweat. As my eyes adjusted to the darkness I looked for Eli, but he was nowhere to be seen. I wondered if I should go knock on the door to the men's quarters over the garage, but quickly decided against it. There would be good odds Frank would answer the door and dealing with him was something I always wanted to avoid if possible, his cockiness irritated me and the way he looked at me made my skin crawl. No, the best plan was to go towards the river. It was after all, one of the many places we liked to walk together and the place where our mutual desire was revealed and surrendered to.

I reached the river but Eli wasn't there. I found myself alone with nothing but the sounds of water rippling gently over rocks and field crickets searching for their own mates. I didn't know if I should go left or right or if I should turn back. He could be in any direction and while part of me longed to find him there was still the same struggle to put it off raging within me that had been taking place all day. After considering the options I decided to sit where I was and wait. If Eli was walking along the river in either direction then he would have to pass this way again. If he wasn't then he might eventually make it down this way before the night was through.

The warm air and chirping insects wove their magic spell and soon I felt compelled to lie down on the soft grass. Looking up at the distant stars the feeling of peace that was beginning to envelop me grew heavier and heavier like a soft blanket until my eyes no longer had the will to stay open despite the beauty that stretched out above them.

I was walking down a street in New York City holding the hand of a little girl of about five years old. Men and women stood in one long continuous line, silent and downcast, all along the sidewalk in front of the tall gray buildings on either side of the street. There were no cars, no sounds, not even a single bird flying above. The world was made up of various shades of gray and white like a photograph. The only color that could be found lay in the large round hazel eyes of the child who walked beside me. I wanted to get off of the street which filled me with unease. I led us down an alleyway hoping to escape the oppression that began to overwhelm me but it was a dead end. We turned back and tried another, but it too led only to a similar gray brick wall. Trying again and meeting with the same I began to run, holding tight to the child's hand, trying alley after alley but they were all dead ends.

My heart raced as I opened my eyes. A sound had woken me and though I knew immediately that I was lying on the grass in close proximity to the river I felt ill at ease and something inside me knew it wasn't just the dream or the unsettling feeling that always accompanies waking up somewhere other than one's own bed. It was something else, something was not right. It was a primal feeling that had its source in my gut. I slowly raised myself up a little on my elbows to survey my surroundings.

Immediately every muscle in my body tensed and my breath stopped in my throat. Not twenty feet away at the water's edge walked a black bear. It was big and bulky, a huge black shadow amidst the starlit landscape. I could see that it was moving its head back and forth as if searching for something and I hoped it couldn't smell or hear me. I had spent weeks wishing for such a sight and now that I was experiencing it the possible danger of such an encounter was suddenly occurring to me.

The bear turned its head towards me and its body followed. My mind raced as my body froze. The voice in my head sped through options. Run. Lie down. Crawl towards the trees. But it was no use. I have heard the often used admonition to do something as if your life depended on it. My life may very well have been depending on action but my body was apparently suicidal.

As the bear slowly inched its way closer, I heard a yell come from behind me. The sound was enough to loosen fear's grip on my body and I turned to see Eli, running towards me and the bear, yelling loudly and waving his hands in the air.

I turned back towards the bear and saw that it was running across the river where the rocks served to make a path. I let out my breath and turned again to Eli who now almost upon me, was slowing to a walk, panting.

Eli held out his hand to me and pulled me up to him taking me firmly in his arms. I could hear his heart rapidly pounding in his chest as my head lay against it. He didn't say a word nor did I, both of us still trying to recover from what had just transpired. There was no time to stand long though, Eli released me and we began to walk quickly back towards the house lest we find ourselves once again facing a bear that had changed its mind about being run off by a creature half its size.

"What were you thinking being down there alone at night?!" Eli asked. Collecting himself he let out a long breath. "Are you okay?"

"Yes." I answered. "I think so. I couldn't move, I didn't know what to do. I've never been so scared."

"Me either."

"You said you've seen plenty of bears before growing up as you did in the mountains."

"Yes, I have and it has always been an experience that made my heart race and my hair stand on end, but this was worse than other times."

My throat tightened in fear. What had I just escaped?

"Why Eli," I asked hesitantly. "What was it that made this time worse?"

"You." he answered.

We continued on in silence until we came to the garden.

"We should be fine here." Eli said. "Would you like to sit down on the bench with me or would you like to go inside and be left alone?"

I could see his face and eyes in the light from the house. He looked vulnerable, like a little boy. I had never seen him look that way before.

"To sit down please." I answered.

"You didn't come out to see me when I got back today." Eli said. "I thought maybe you couldn't get away, but then when I came to eat you didn't come out either even though when I asked, Nellie told me you were in your room."

"You didn't write." I replied.

"Of course not. You couldn't have actually expected me to. How would I have managed it and even if I did, what would Myrna have thought about it? We both need our jobs. I couldn't have risked it. I figured you knew better."

I felt stupid. No, it was worse than that. I felt childish.

"I know, you're right and I thought of that, but then..." I was tempted to say but then Emma, but I didn't want to bring her into it.

"But then what?"

"But then I wondered if maybe, I don't know."

"Maybe what?"

"If maybe you were...." I fought to find the right words. Ones that wouldn't make me look worse.

"Glad to be away from you?" Eli finished my sentence.

"Yes." I answered.

"I see." Eli stood up and walked away from the bench. I was afraid I had made him angry enough to leave, but after taking a few steps he turned around and walked back to stand directly in front of me.

'You thought that I had only been after one thing and since I got it I was done with you."

"I wasn't sure." I replied. I didn't want to look up at him. I felt ashamed.

"Is that what you think of me?" he asked. "That everything has just been an act? You think I'm like Frank?!"

"No! No, please. It wasn't like that." I reached up and took his hands, rough with work. I liked the feel of them. "Please Eli. I didn't know. It wasn't something I really believed of you, but you have to understand, that's all I've been warned of all my life. I couldn't help but wonder. Then when you got here I was scared that maybe I had been less to you than you were to me after all and I couldn't bear the humiliation. I thought I would wait and see what you would do and then just follow your lead. If you ignored me, I would try my best to do the same and if you were happy to see me I could let myself relax and be happy too."

"I wanted so badly to see you." Eli said.

"I wanted to see you too. It was hard to stay away."

"I missed you. I missed your smile and your voice. I missed the way you rest your hand at the bottom of your throat when you're thinking." He smiled out of the side of his mouth, then lowering his voice and leaning in towards me he said "And though I didn't get to spend as much time enjoying them as I would have liked, I missed other things about you too." His grin widened and I turned away sure I was blushing, though I knew he couldn't see it. "But I missed all of you Connie, just you."

Eli smiled and sat down beside me again.

I looked at him and felt contented.

"You don't have anything to say to me?" Eli asked.

"I do." I replied. "But you know I've never been good with words. I don't ever know the right ones to say what I feel like you do. It may not be beautiful or eloquent but, I love you, and I missed you, and now that you're here with me again the world is good and I am happy."

Eli leaned in and kissed me. The first kiss was delicate, a whisper of love and devotion. The second was hard and frantic, a silent scream of long frustrated desire. The passion in his kiss called up my own that had laid dormant in me all this time. It sent of ripple of longing up from my loins through my stomach, aching into my chest and catching in my throat. I reached out my hand and grabbed his arm, wanting to pull him closer to me. His hand was on the outside of my dress, moving up my thigh towards my waist as his other hand found its way from my face to the back of my head and gripped my hair tightly.

"I'm sure she's fine." Emma's voice washed over us like cold water. I straightened up, running a hand over my dress and then another over my hair. I saw Eli reach to smooth his own as he stood and faced the house.
"I don't know what she's doing staying out like this, but I don't like it and I mean to find out exactly what's going on."
"Myrna." Eli whispered looking down at me over his shoulder. I nodded in reply.
Within seconds the two women appeared over the hill.
"There you are Connie!" Emma said. There was a hint of anxiety in her voice as her eyes darted from Eli to me and back but it wasn't enough for Mrs. Casserly to notice, at least I hoped not. "And look Eli is with you. Isn't that nice. See Mrs. Casserly, she wasn't far."
"Yes I can see that she wasn't far. I can also see that she is here with Eli and that it is very late. I can see a lot of things, what I would like to hear, is an explanation."
"It's a frightening story actually." Eli responded casually. "You know that Connie and I are friends." Mrs. Casserly nodded though she looked like suspicion personified. Eli continued. "I hadn't had the chance to say hello to her since I got back today and when I went into the house they said she had left for a walk, so I went to look for her. It was a good thing I did too. When I almost got to the river I saw her sitting on the ground and a black bear headed right for her."
Emma gasped. Mrs. Casserly's expression remained unchanged except for a single cocked eyebrow.
"Dear Lord!" Emma came over to me. "Are you alright? What happened?"
"I'm alright." I answered. "I went down to the river and laid down on the grass to look at the stars, but I feel asleep and when I woke up I saw the bear right at the water's edge. It was the most terrifying moment of my life. Then it turned towards me and I froze. I couldn't move and I didn't know

what to do. Then I heard Eli yelling behind me and I turned and saw him running towards me and the bear and the bear took off. After that Eli helped to steady me and we walked back here as quickly as we could, but when we reached the garden I wanted to sit down and try to gather myself. I don't know what would have happened if Eli hadn't come looking for me when he did."

Emma shook her head and took me in her arms.

"It's true. You may want to spread the word. Someone else may not be so lucky." Eli said.

"Well that is quite a story indeed." Mrs. Casserly said. "Okay. I will let everyone know. Shall we all head back towards the house? I am sure after a scare like that you will be happy to lie down."

"Yes Ma'am, I would." I replied.

Emma and I stood up. She linked her arm within mine and we followed Eli and Mrs. Casserly back to the house. The two of them were talking about the probability of the bear coming up into the gardens. Emma and I stayed silent, listening to their conversation. Not a sound escaped Emma lips but every time she heard the word bear she patted my arm, though whether to reassure me or herself is anyone's guess.

Reaching the garage our good byes were simple and necessarily platonic. Still following Mrs. Casserly, I turned my head as I continued to walk forward, arm in arm with Emma, to watch for a moment as Eli made his way up the stairs to the men's quarters above. Seeing me he smiled and nodded before disappearing through the door and into the sound of male laughter. Mrs. Casserly turned around and looked towards the garage at the sound of it, but didn't say a word.

It was later than I had realized. When we entered the house the kitchen was completely empty.

"Do you think you'll be okay?" Mrs. Casserly asked as we headed towards the hall.

"Yes." I answered. "I was pretty shook up at first, but I'm alright now."

"Understandable. Alright, good night." Mrs. Casserly made no sign of moving and I soon realized she intended to watch until I was secure in my room.

I wished her a good night in return and turning to Emma wished her good night as well, receiving her testimony to the goodness of God and thanks to him in sending Eli at just the right moment. She too stood waiting for me to enter my room, as if it was the most normal thing in the world to do so. I looked at the two older women and felt as if I had been transported back to my youth and was once again 6 years old and in need of an ever watchful eye. Were they simply being reassuring after a trying ordeal or were they worried I might try to sneak something from the cookie jar?

I spent Saturday under the constant gaze of Mrs. Casserly. She was in fact so suspicious that rather than have me in the kitchen or laundry as usual, she had me in the common areas, where it would be much harder for Eli and I to run into each other. She even took it a step further by having me up on a ladder cleaning the chandeliers. Perhaps she thought it would keep me from sneaking back and forth to the kitchen, though I don't know why she would have, it wasn't my style, perhaps the chandeliers simply needed cleaning and I was being paranoid.

If keeping me away from Eli was the goal as I assumed, she did a good job. With me out of my usual spots Eli couldn't sneak in and speak to me and I wouldn't be around during his meal times, though there was a possibility he might find a way to step into the kitchen during mine but I doubted he would. He was smarter than that. Surely he would realize that I, that we, were under observation and wouldn't give Mrs. Casserly more opportunity for suspicion than absolutely necessary. It seemed cruel to me that she should seek to keep us apart and I couldn't help but look after her in disdain when she would pass my way. But it didn't matter. Tomorrow was Sunday.

I spent my day thinking about Eli and hating Mrs. Casserly, no, Myrna. It made me feel better even thinking it. Myrna, she would be Mrs. Casserly no more. I laughed to, and at myself.

I was right; Eli didn't show up during my lunch, or during dinner. As I had suspected, Myrna decided to sit in on both. There was no pretense. She didn't try to pretend she was going to eat with us. She didn't try to act as if she was polishing or organizing. She just sat, watching me, watching the door and making everyone tense and miserable. At lunch a few people had attempted small talk, but by dinner no one tried to speak, not even Darla. Emma fidgeted, Paul tried to look everywhere in the room except Myrna's direction, Joan looked as if she were in danger of boiling over and Ann looked on the verge of panic.

Although I barely touched my dinner I had had enough of the entire thing and decided it was time to remove myself from the kitchen and Myrna, then maybe everyone could enjoy their evening as they were accustomed. I stood up, grabbing my plate and turned to take it to the sink.

"I hope you're not planning on going out tonight." Myrna said.

"I hadn't decided yet why?" I asked.

"I would be surprised if you did after your ordeal last night."

"Oh. Yes. If I did I would stay near the house. Believe me, I don't want to have that experience again." I actually had not thought of the bear since breakfast when everyone was grilling me over the details.

"I think it would be better if you just stayed inside. Perhaps read in your room or write a letter."

My mind and will balked at the suggestion. What was this? Was I now truly a child, told what I could and could not do *after* work? I tried to keep my expression in check, though I could feel my eyebrows knit together. The already unusually quiet kitchen became pin drop silent, even the sounds of forks and plates withholding their din.

"Of course I can't stop you from sitting outside. I would just," Myrna paused, though it was obvious by the look on her face that she had not forgotten what she wanted to say but rather that she wanted to make a point. "Strongly advise against it."

Myrna held my eyes and I returned her stare. I don't know why I felt strong enough to do such a thing. I had always been quiet and timid, but for some reason I did, though my defiance ended there. Still looking in Myrna's eyes I slightly bowed my head to her and in silence made my way to my room.

Once there I paced the short distance between the nightstand and the door. Within a few minutes I could hear voices coming from the kitchen, low but constant. Myrna must have left shortly after I did. Even so she had won. I was too angry to leave.

After a while my anger subsided a little, I was still too upset to read and I wouldn't even try to write a letter, that would have felt like I had given in completely, but I was at least able to stop pacing and sit down on the bed. My anger was slowly replaced with worry. How would Eli and I be able to be together if Myrna was determined to keep us apart? For all my offense at her assuming to have more power over me that what I myself willed, I had to admit that she did indeed have just that. Eli had his plans, they couldn't happen without the Sarringtons and I had a family to support. Myrna had the upper hand and I knew it and while it worried me, somehow too I knew that it didn't matter. Eli would find a way.

I heard a timid knock on the door. I waited for the door to open but when it didn't I crossed over and opened it myself. Ann stood before me wringing her hands.
"Hi Ann." I said.
"Hi Connie. Can I come in for a second?" She asked.

I nodded and stood aside allowing her to enter the room, then motioned for her to sit on the bed as I closed the door and took a place beside her.

"So?" I said. I had not spoken to Ann much in the past weeks and couldn't think of what she could possibly want.

She looked anxious. She fidgeted and would only look at me for a moment before turning her eyes away.

"Myrna was acting odd tonight, don't you think?" She finally asked.

"I guess." I answered. I really didn't want to talk about Myrna.

"She acts like she knows about you and Eli? Do you think she does?"

"I don't know. She might have her suspicions but I don't know what she could actually know."

"What do you think she would do to you if she found out?"

"Found out what?"

"I don't know." Ann said obviously flustered.

"I don't know what you're thinking but I guess if she thought Eli and I were having a relationship and she found out that she was right then she would do like she did with Joan and Doyle, tell us to end it or get fired."

"But if you were really in love?"

"But what? You see yourself how Doyle and Joan look at each other. They're as in love as I guess anyone could be, but it doesn't seem to matter to her."

"If Eli were different though, if he were above her, then she would have to just leave you alone."

"I guess she would, but he's not and I don't know that he ever will be." I replied wondering what kind of help she thought she was providing.

"But it's true." She said standing up. "Good night Connie."

"Good night." I said watching as she left the room though I got the feeling she didn't hear me.

I woke late the next morning. It was my off day and I wanted to try to get out of the house before Myrna spotted me, but I didn't know if I would manage it now. On my way towards the kitchen Joan passed by me, shoving something in my hand as she went. It felt like paper. I returned to my room before opening my hand and taking a look.

I leaned against the door and opened my hand. It was a note but I didn't know who it was from. Joan didn't say anything as she passed and it wasn't signed. I knew only Emma's handwriting and it wasn't hers. It was short and said only, '*Ask to go to town with Stanley.*' I folded the note back up and placed it in my pocket and walked back out the door to the kitchen.

Paul nodded to me as I fixed a plate of eggs and bacon. Everyone who wasn't off today was already working and from the looks of it even those who weren't were already off to enjoy their day.
I had planned on avoiding Myrna but now I would have to see her. Myrna ran the house and if Stanley was headed to town she would know and if he was off today and I was going to get him to drive me to town, we would have to get her permission to take the car.

As I was contemplating this, Myrna walked through the door. She stopped when she saw me at the table.
"Good." She began "I was on my way to find you. I have spoken to Mr. Sarrington and he agrees that no one should be walking the grounds until we know more about this bear situation. Even the grounds men will be working in pairs for now. So if your plan was to take off on one of your hikes today you better make a new one"

I was momentarily dumbstruck. I looked up at this woman in total disbelief. Why was she so cruel? Now it was more than just my time with the man I loved she was depriving me of, it was the nature I loved as well. My disdain was fixed and I could not imagine it would ever relent. She turned to leave and I remembered the note.
"Well since I can't go out walking today maybe I can go to town and look for a new book. Are one of the drivers headed out and if not, can one of the ones who have the day

off take me? That is if he agrees?" I asked trying to sound as if the thought had just occurred to me.

Myrna had turned to look at me when I spoke and now she looked up towards the ceiling thinking about my request. Making up her mind, she looked at me once again.

"Yes. I suppose you can. Stanley is headed to town sometime today, though I don't know when. He has the day off as well but he needed to get some things and has agreed to pick up a few items for some of the others as well, but I guess he can't necessarily pick out a book for you. Go ahead and see if you can find him." Myrna turned abruptly and left the kitchen.

I looked over at Paul and grinned. I felt triumphant though I wasn't exactly sure why.

"Stanley is above the garage. I think he is planning on leaving soon." Paul leaned towards me and lowered his voice "As soon as you're ready that is." He straightened himself back up and gave me a wink.

I hurried back to my room and grabbed my purse before heading to the garage. It was a large building. It held five cars, which considering my family, not to mention every other family I knew, owned exactly zero, it seemed almost unreal to me, but five cars fit in with this world of portrait galleries and private swimming pools.

Going up the far side of the garage was a metal staircase. I had never been on the stairs let alone up to the men's quarters and I knew as I climbed them that I had to remember not to enter the building. I knocked on the door and soon found myself face to face with Frank.

He wore the same cocky leering expression he always did, accompanied by a pair of tan slacks and a white tee shirt, the sleeves rolled up almost to his shoulders.

"Hello there Connie." He brought an apple up to his mouth and took a bite out of it as he leaned his arm against the door frame, "Here for Eli?" he asked, then he leaned in towards me and lowered his voice "Or are you here for me?"

"Neither." I said. "I'm here for Stanley. Is he around?"

"Stanley huh?" Frank said looking surprised but recovering quickly. "Sure."
Frank turned his body at the waist while continuing to block the door and hollered for Stanley. "Stanley! Connie is here for you my man."
From the back I could hear Stanley call out in answer. "Okay, just a second."

Frank turned back towards me and took another bite of his apple as he looked me over slowly from bottom to top, the look in his eyes as he did made the hair on the back of my neck stand on end. Then shaking his head, he walked away from the door.

I could see inside just a little bit. The view afforded to me seemed to be that of a living room. A number of the men were gathered around a low coffee table and appeared to be playing cards, though what game it was I didn't have time to find out; within seconds Stanley appeared at the door.
"Ready to go?" Stanley asked.
"Yes, thanks." I answered.
"Good, come on."
I turned and headed back down the stairs then followed him as he opened the garage. I felt like I was being watched and looked over towards the house to find Myrna looking out of one of the second floor windows.
I entered the garage behind Stanley and walked towards the same Packard that I had arrived to the estate in.
"Ready?" Eli's voice came from the back of the garage somewhere, though I couldn't see him.
"Yep" Stanley answered as he looked at me and smiled.
I searched the area where Eli's voice had come from and saw him emerge from the shadows. He smiled big and crossing over to the car opened the back door for me. I climbed in and Eli closed the door before getting into the front seat beside Stanley.
I wondered how much Stanley knew and whether or not I should just act naïve. I quickly decided he must know enough.

"What is Myrna going to say?" I asked, knowing she may still be at the window.

We drove out of the garage and I couldn't bring myself to look up to find out if she was. I did see Eli look that way however, but if she was there he didn't let on.

"What can she say?" Eli replied. "I already spoke to Mr. Sarrington and told him I needed to go to town today to pick up some things. The fact that you just so happened to ask Stanley for a ride to town as well, well, that's just a coincidence. After all you didn't know I was headed to town when you asked did you?"

"Hmm. No, I didn't." I said, though I was still unsure how this scheme would pan out. "But it's anything but coincidence."

Eli laughed. "Did you hear that Stanley? I'm shocked that she would even imply such a thing."

"I agree." said Stanley. "Next thing you know she going to be claiming someone handed her a note."

Because it was a Sunday in a small town most of the stores were closed. Going to town and seeing that many of its inhabitants were observing the Lord's Day, reminded me of the fact that I had not been to church even once since I had arrived at the estate. I had not been to mass. I had not been to confession. I had not done the rosary. I had been reading more than I ever had in my life, many inspiring, wonderful books, but none of them holy writ, not of the usual kind anyway.

The same tinges of guilt came up as they always did only this time they were magnified since I was not only not spending any part of my Sunday off in church or even adhering to a single tenant of faith, but I was not spending it there with my lover and though I couldn't be sure entirely, I knew that I might not end up honoring the Sabbath and keeping it holy at all, in fact, I thought to myself, I might end up keeping it decidedly unholy at some point.

I wrapped my arm within Eli's and looked up at him as we walked. His face was freshly shaven and his golden hair was combed back. I didn't often get to see him like this. Usually he was dirty and sweaty from a day's work or from a day of hiking, though I didn't mind it, I liked him that way. But I liked this too. I felt a sense of pride swelling in me as we passed people on the sidewalk. He was mine. He may have had me, but I had also had him. As my eyes followed his neck down to his chest I let pride mingle with another of the seven deadly sins, lust. My chest began to grow hot and I could feel my breasts begin to tingle under my dress. I couldn't help but wonder, a smile forming on my face, if sin is so very bad, then why does it make you feel so very good?

Stanley had taken off to run his errands and though they were very similar to ours and could have been done together he let us have our time. I had always liked Stanley. He reminded me of my eldest brother Eoghan, tall with dark brown hair and eyes. He was usually smiling and quiet. When he did speak it was often short and to the point, much like Myrna, but the delivery was altogether different. When he was with Eli he loosened up a bit, sometimes making little jokes that would take you by surprise. The closeness between the two of them was obvious and I wondered if there was a story behind it or if it was simply a case of meeting a kindred soul in a place far from home.

As we approached Miller's Five and Dime on the corner of Main and 1st Street, Eli began to slow. He had been quiet, which was usual, we both tended to be quiet, but we also were usually out hiking somewhere, here it made me curious. We still hadn't spoken much in the short time we had been together since his return.

We reached the store and as I began to turn to go inside, Eli took me by the elbow and directed us across the street to the city park. It was small, not even as big as the main garden of the estate and it wasn't as well landscaped but it was lovely in its humbleness.

"No reason to rush through our errands." Eli said. "I can't see any reason we should be in a hurry to be back where we can be kept from each other do you?"

"No, absolutely not, if I could figure out a way to take all day I would." I replied.

There were many couples in the park, some picnicking, some walking arm in arm just as we were. I found myself wondering what their lives were like. Were they free to eat together, holding hands across the table? Were they able to look at each other in the company of others and not monitor themselves? Were they free to let their love express itself however it may or were they like us, hiding, stealing moments whenever it was safe to do so? Were they able to enjoy their love in all its glorious fullness with nothing to dampen it or was theirs a love, true and hot and fierce as any other, yet tainted by fear and guilt and necessary deception.

I suddenly became aware that Eli was watching me.
"What are you thinking about?" he asked. "You seem to be off in another world."
I laughed. "I'm thinking about a lot of things. I'm wondering if any of the other couples here are like us. I'm wondering what kind of future we could possibly have. I'm wondering if a love that has to hide itself can survive or will the worries that accompany such a situation dampen its flame until it goes out and can't be revived."
"You can't think of it that way Connie. You have to think only that we love each other. That's all that matters. Everything else will work out."
"Will it? " I sighed. "What hope do we have Eli? You and I, we're stuck, bound as if in chains by the world we find ourselves in. We have to live the lives that were set before us. You a groundskeeper, me a maid. People like us; what more can we do? What more can we hope for than to survive? To have enough for bread, to have enough for shelter, to work forevermore for just enough. Maybe we can have some moments of happiness in the midst of all of it, but if those

who hold our livelihood say no then they have that choice, they have that power. It's sad and it's not fair. It's not and I hate it, but it's life, and for people like us it's all we can have." Eli stopped and turned to me.

"Why? Tell me why Connie?" Eli's stare was intense. I wanted to shrink under it as he continued. "Who says we can't have whatever we want as we are willing to work for it, as long as we are willing to take a chance for it? By what law is it written that I should always be just what I am now? I've told you my plans. I aim to make them a reality. Why should I set my future in the hands of someone else to do with as they please?" Eli's voice began to rise and he paused bringing it back under control, before beginning again. "I have but one life. This is it. I have no guarantee of another. I have no guarantee that I can make it all I envision it to be and I have no guarantee that you and I will ever be more than what we are now. I don't know if we will go our separate ways or if the day will come when we can hold each other without fear and never let go. I don't know any of it and there is no way I can know, but does that mean I have no right to try for it, or that I would be a fool to do so?"

Eli took my arm once more and we began to walk again. He spoke softer. "The only things gained in life are the things fought for; the things man has been willing to strive for. Maybe I am wrong. Maybe we can only be what we came to the world as, but I've heard the stories of men who would not submit, those who believed in their own abilities and sovereignty and I've seen what they've done. And maybe I won't ever climb so high or achieve even a tenth of what I dream, but I refuse to come to old age saying 'What if?' I will not come to the end saying 'I could have been'. I will come to the end knowing that succeed or fail I had the courage to try and that by my own will and strength I stood."

We continued on a short way in silence. This time it was me who stopped.

"I don't mean it like that Eli." I said, trying to reassure him. "I know that you're smart and you're a hard worker. I know that when you want to do something you find a way, just as you found a way for us to be together today despite Myrna. I'm not trying to upset you. That's the last thing I want to do. It's just, I don't know, maybe you have what it takes to do everything you want, maybe you can do it, but if we've seen anything these past few years hasn't it been what chasing after dreams can do? So many people, that couldn't just be happy, they had to have more and why, why Eli? Why couldn't they be happy with what they had? Why did they have to risk everything? For a bigger house? For a car? So their wives could walk around in mink? I don't get it. I'm sorry but I don't." I paused trying to collect myself but failing as the image of my father pulling wood from the wall in order to heat the apartment one day last winter when no one had managed to scrounge the coal needed to heat the building came flooding into my head.

"It's us Eli, we're the ones who are hurt by dreams, we're the ones who have everything to lose and often do. People like the Sarringtons, they don't care, they can dream and dare all they want and for whatever reason they want. If they lose it doesn't matter, not like it does to us. If we lose we die, we *die* Eli, we starve, if they lose it's no different than if they lost a game of poker, it's all fun to them because there is no risk. There is none, none at all and maybe it's just how the cards are set up. Maybe they're always supposed to win and we're always supposed to lose. Look at it now. Who lost everything Eli? Who? Tell me! The people like us. The people who didn't know their place, the people who couldn't just be happy, and what happen to the people like them? They got richer Eli! That's what happened. It's always the people that have that end up having more and the people that don't have that end up having less. The powers that be don't like when we mess with their plan Eli, they won't let us win. You can't buck God, you can't buck Fate, you have to deal with what's put before you and maybe, just maybe you can have something; something that makes life worth living, love or a family, and you can hold onto it and be grateful for what you were given. Maybe all we can do is accept how things are and find the peace that comes with that. I don't know, but I know what I've seen." I looked at him, my voice calmer, but pleading. "I've heard stories too, but of a far different kind, the kind that start with a dream and end with an empty pair of shoes on the side of a bridge."

Eli's brow furrowed. I could see that I had upset him. "I've heard those stories Connie. I know the risks. I won't pretend there are none. You talk of the people who lost everything and it's true, many people did. Some of them were good hard working people, smart and dedicated and they didn't deserve it, but they can't be faulted for trying and maybe some of them were good people who just didn't take the time to learn. They were gullible and trusted in the words of someone else, maybe they deserved it and maybe they didn't, and then there were some who were lazy, who just wanted a quick buck without knowledge and without work and they deserve exactly what they got, but it wasn't the fact that they dreamed that caused the hardship for any of them. It was chance or laziness but it wasn't the dream. And what happened to those who didn't dream? What happened to those who knew their place? Did they fare any better or are they standing in the same bread line as everyone else? I'll take my chance Connie. Right or wrong, believe in me or not, but I'll take my chance."

Eli turned from me and began to walk away. This wasn't what I wanted but what could I possibly do? I watched as he crossed the street and went into Miller's. I walked over to a wooden bench and sat down. Was it so bad that Eli wanted more? He was right, my family had always stayed in their place and in the end it didn't do us any good. It may have delayed the inevitable but that was all. I stood and made my way to Miller's and Eli. I didn't know what the future held, but I knew I didn't want to sacrifice my present to it.

Eli was in the men's aisle picking up bottles of cologne then putting them back without really looking at them. I walked up to him slowly and quietly. As he reached for a bottle shaped like a horse reared back on its hind legs, I purposely reached up for it too, taking care to make sure our hands touched. He didn't look at me, but he didn't move his hand away either.

"I'm sorry." I said quietly. "I do believe in you and I do want you to go after the things you want. Please forgive me Eli."

Eli took my hand in his and gave me a halfhearted smile. "I don't want to spend our time together like this." He said. "Let's go get something to eat and we'll come back here to get our stuff when we're done okay." I nodded and we headed out the door.

No matter what I said the hurt that I had obviously caused Eli would not be undone so quickly. He had only been home for three days and yet we had spent more time in such states as these than in enjoying each other's company and it pained me. We had lunch and did our shopping in relative silence, only speaking in common niceties. As the afternoon wore down and the time to return to the estate drew closer I began to feel a sense of panic. I had to do something, before we returned and were surrounded by the eyes and ears of the curious or suspicious.

"Are you ready to head back to the car?" Eli asked after I finished paying for my purchase, a leather bound journal; there had been no books that interested me, but I had to come back with something. "Stanley is probably already there waiting."

I nodded and followed Eli out of the store. He began to walk towards the car but I stayed still, standing just outside of the door looking down at the sidewalk. I looked up just in time to see Eli turn and look at me. He jerked his head, motioning for me to come to him, but I didn't move. Although I didn't say a word inside I was crying, 'Please come back before we get too far apart, before it's too late.' I looked at him and waited to see what his move would be. It would be everything, salvation or damnation, would all be determined in his next step.

Eli looked away from me and down the sidewalk towards the car, my heart sank and once again I looked down. I couldn't bear to watch him walk away. A shadow appeared on the ground in front of me and I looked up to see Eli within a few feet. I looked into his eyes feeling vulnerable and desperate but now hopeful as well. He reached out his hand to me and smiled. It wasn't a big smile. It was small and hurt, but it was also kind. I dropped my bag and reached up grabbing his face and drew him down towards me, kissing him hard and deep, and not caring who was around or what they would think.

I felt Eli's arms wrap around my waist as he lifted me off the ground holding me tight against his body. It was only a moment, but it was all we needed. Eli slowly lowered me back to the sidewalk and I reluctantly let my hands drop from his face. He looked down at me and smiled with eyes wide. Eli bent down and picked up my bag, then taking my hand in his, we made our way back to the car and a grinning Stanley.

As on the ride to town I was mostly quiet on the way back. Stanley had been kind enough not to mention the kiss and he and Eli had once again begun to discuss things I really didn't care about. I was glad to not have to make conversation; my mind was busy enough with its own thoughts. With the rift between Eli and I mended my thoughts turned to Myrna. Surely by now she realized that it had not just been Stanley and I that had made the trip to town and she would see it as outright deceptive and insubordinate and in a way she would be correct, it was necessarily deceptive, she had made it so. But as I thought on it more I realized she had not truly forbid Eli and I to be together. She had tried to be deceptive in her own way and accomplish her goal through round about means. The fact that Eli was smart enough to see the loopholes, and liked enough by the staff to get help in taking advantage of them, was something she couldn't really take umbrage with could she? The only rule she had laid down had been obeyed had it not? Yes, it had indeed. I tried to rest in the thought.

As we pulled into the garage Stanley announced that it was ten til six and both he and Eli laughed. At first I didn't understand but it quickly dawned on me that it was almost dinner time for the Sarringtons and as such Myrna would not be at liberty to leave to come to the garage and it also meant that I would have a chance to make it back to my room without having to answer to her. I began to realize the extent to which Eli had gone to make sure every detail was planned, and if he was willing to do all this just for an afternoon outing, maybe he was right to believe that if anyone could try to change the rules of the game of life it was him.

Eli opened the door and took my hand to help me out of the car. "Myrna should be busy right now as you probably already guessed, and we recently ate, so, as far as I can tell you shouldn't have to leave your room for the rest of the night unless you want to. With the new ban on walking the grounds, I can't see any reason for me to leave mine unless you plan on eating with the rest of the staff later, if so maybe I can think of a few things I may need from the kitchen after all."

"No. I'll stay put. We don't know what Myrna knows or how she will react. No reason to fan any sparks into a flame." I answered.

'I agree." Eli said. "You go on in and I will stay here for a little while, just in case."

Eli brought my hand which he still held up to his lips and took a depth slow breath as he kissed it.

"These past few days are not how I envisioned my return." He said.

"I know." I replied.

As I walked away I could feel Eli's eyes on me. I looked over my shoulder and caught him staring at me as I walked, though he didn't seem to be looking at the way my hair bounced on my shoulders. He looked up into my eyes, caught, and I shook my head and laughed. The poor man.

8

The following weeks were a mixture of frustration and excitement. I was frustrated by my prolonged confinement. I had come to need the outdoors and to be kept from my enjoyment of them drained my spirit. I felt as if I were being suffocated by the silver and the linens and the rugs. I needed to hear the sound of twigs and pine needles crunching underfoot and to feel the rough scratchiness of the bark as I slid my hands along the tree trunks in passing. And I was frustrated by Myrna's increasing watchfulness and need to monitor my every word and action. She seemed to grow more tense with each day sensing perhaps that she was failing in her endeavor to separate Eli and I and yet unable to know for certain, or how.

However the game we had begun was exciting, with its hidden notes and the surprisingly frequent adrenalin filled rendezvous. I never knew what or when to expect either and as such my days and nights were filled with a constant sense of anticipation. With the help of a few of the staff who were close to Eli and his own ingenuity, we managed to meet in a variety of places that I would not have considered, under different, and I thought, clever, ruses. "Stanley needs lemon to clean the chrome on the cars, could you please bring it to him?" Joan said, or from Paul "Will rang up from the guard house, says his throat is killing him. Take him this tea and honey for me." Our time together was not long but it was passionate and cherished, we sucked the marrow out of every moment, taking nourishment from each touch and whispered word.

Our friends proved to be not only indispensable but loyal. Except for the handful, the rest of the staff remained unaware of our little trysts. They knew that Eli and I had feelings for each other, but as far as they could tell Myrna had succeeded in her efforts to keep us apart just as she had with

Doyle and Joan. Some of the more observant of them, Darla or Emma for instance, would look at me quizzically from time to time, when catching me with a satisfied smile or when I was lost in a recently made memory, but there was nothing more that they could do except guess. My smile may have been worth a thousand questions but questions they safely remained.

After the first week the small notes were joined by letters. Eli and I had very little time to discuss anything when we were together –we had other, more pressing matters to attend to- so we began exchanging letters during our encounters. This amused me greatly considering that we were corresponding thus while only a couple dozen yards away and yet had not exchanged a single line when we were a country apart.

Eli's letters were much longer than mine. I had very little to say really where as he could talk at length about his plans to become a landscape architect. He talked about which steps he needed to take and how he thought he might accomplish them. He talked about his heroes, such as Andrew Jackson Downing, the founder of Horticulture magazine and father of modern landscape architecture, and Calvert Vaux and Fredrick Law Olmstead who together designed Central Park, Prospect Park and many others I had never even heard of. He always made a point to talk about us too because what is a love letter without words of praise and passion and promises, though sharing ones most precious and private dreams would have to be counted as a great act of love too I would think.

I mostly wrote in encouragement to whatever he had written previously and asked questions about things I didn't understand that I had read in them, but I also spoke about Eli and I, my mother and brothers and of course my father. I had thought of writing to him of my own ideas and thoughts that had begun to form in my head during my long nights alone in my room, but I couldn't do it. They were still fragile like the wings of a butterfly freshly emerged from its cocoon, and I felt a strong instinct to protect them from even the most gentle touch.

I had begun to think about the conversation I had had with Eli, and the one I had had with Tom Sarrington. To ponder the questions of Fate and free will and whether they can both exist simultaneously. I was beginning to believe that they indeed did and always had, though neither in the way I had supposed them to be. Perhaps free will is only available to those willing to take it, those willing to fight for the right to self-determination, and perhaps Fate was simply the explanation we give to lives lived in a state of continuous default by those who for whatever reason, refuse.

I could see this. I could see it in Eli. I could see it in Emerson and others like them, brave, intelligent and strong. They could do anything. But could I see it in me? It was almost easy to believe others could map out their own lives and succeed at it. Not just to want it and wish it, but to be capable of attaining it. Could I be capable? Dare I even think of what I might want to do with my life if I could do and be anything? Did I have the courage to ask myself such a question?

I was lying on my bed thinking about these questions which kept me from restful sleep on more than one occasion, when I heard a low voice coming from the hall. I couldn't make out the words; they seemed to be rolling together in one long strain. I got up and went over to the door putting my ear against it. The voice would get softer and then louder, at times seeming as if it was coming from right outside my door. I couldn't figure out who would be up, it had to be well past midnight. Surely, I figured, sometimes one of the other women would get up and go to the bathroom, after all I sometimes did, but why would they be talking as they went? It didn't make sense.

I opened up my door just a crack and peered out into the hall. The bathroom light was always left on to illuminate the hallway and in it I could see Ann from behind walking towards the bathroom, her long fiery hair was loose and messy, and oddly she was in a dress, not a robe. She neared the bathroom door and rather than go in she turned and headed back up the hall. With Ann facing me, I could see that she was rubbing her arms and her chest in a frantic motion as if they were bothering her. As she neared my door I could hear her mumbling but I couldn't make out the words which were like the slurs of a drunkard. But she wasn't drunk, at least I didn't think she was. She came closer and I prepared for her to notice that my door was cracked and maybe even see the sliver of my face brightened by the light from the bathroom, but she didn't even look in my direction, she continued to walk past, her eyes large and her gaze distant. She seemed confused, and frightened.

I had heard that when people walk in their sleep they do it with their eyes open, not closed like you would expect. I thought maybe that was what was going on, maybe Ann was a sleepwalker. I had also heard of people doing crazy things in such states like setting fires and decided that it would be best if I tried to wake Ann up or at least try to steer her back to her room.

I quietly slipped out of my room and tiptoed towards Ann. Right before I reached her she turned around and we both let out a tiny scream. I held my breath waiting to hear a door open, sure we must have woken someone up, but there was nothing except silence.

Ann looked at me, quiet now, her eyes darting around wildly as she continued to rub at her arms.

"Ann," I whispered. "are you okay? Were you sleepwalking?"

Ann continued to look at me but she didn't reply. It was odd and uneasiness began to settle in my stomach.

"Ann." I said again. "Are you alright? Why are you out here?"

Ann rubbed at her chest and whispered almost in a cry "It burns! My skin burns!"

"Okay, okay." I said "Did you do something to it? Do you need a lotion or maybe to wash?"

Ann's green eyes widened further almost crazed as she looked into mine.

"It's God." She said. "He's punishing me. He's burning me. That's what he's doing. I know it. He's burning me! He wants me to know what waits for me!"

"Shh. Shh. Calm down Ann. Why would God do such a thing?" I asked.

Ann began to cry uncontrollably. "It burns. Please help me Connie. I can't stop it. Ask him to stop. Please Connie! Ask him to stop!" Her voice began to rise and I worried soon it would be loud enough to wake someone else.

"Okay." I said as I put my arm around her and began to lead her towards her bedroom. "I'll ask him. Don't worry Ann. I'll ask."

Ann began to calm a little bit, rubbing her arms with less intensity as the tears continued to roll down her cheeks. I opened her bedroom door and helped her to her bed. She didn't resist me as I gently pushed her down to a lying position and helped her lift her legs placing them under the covers. I leaned over her and smoothed her hair along her temple.

"Shhhh." I whispered. "It's okay Ann. You're safe now."

Ann nodded.

"Try to go to sleep alright." I said, straightening myself up.

Ann nodded again but she looked with eyes still wide from me to the ceiling without a word, she had stopped rubbing her arms and chest and her crying had stopped as well. I didn't know what else I could do, but at least now she was safe in bed; that had to be better than roaming the hallway talking to herself. I looked at Ann one more time as I backed out of her room. She lay in her bed, the moon shining in through the window, making her eyes glisten as she stared straight ahead, her hands clutching the blanket tightly to her chest. A shiver ran through me as I closed the door and returned to my room. Sleep would not be coming so easily for me either.

I fell asleep after an hour or more of tossing and turning, fighting an increasingly sick feeling in my stomach, but the sleep that finally came was anything but sound.

I found myself once again standing in the middle of an indistinct street in New York City, lines of people on both sides. The little girl was holding my hand tightly looking up at me, waiting for me to make a decision. Looking over my shoulder, the street and the lines seemed to go on forever. I looked ahead and it was the same. Out of the corner of my eye I saw something familiar in one of the lines, my family. They were all there, my mother, my brothers, even my father, all standing as if entranced. I called out to them, but they didn't answer, they didn't even seem to hear me, they just continued to look on. I started to step towards them and the little girl held fast to my hand refusing to budge. I urged her to come, but she only looked at me and shook her head. With all of my strength I pulled her and she lost her firm footing, but still she didn't let go of my hand. We stumbled with the momentum of my pull. Regaining our balance, we made our way towards my father. As we got closer I could see him better. His skin was taunt with a dull sheen to it, giving him the appearance of a wax figure. I glanced towards the others and saw the same, but I kept moving forward. My father's face was downcast and though I called to him as I got closer he still didn't seem to hear me. Once I reached him I wrapped my free arm around him from the side, happy and relieved to see him safe and back where he belonged. Almost immediately, yet slowly, I could feel him move, but he wasn't trying to return my hug, he seemed to be trying to turn me, to put me in line. I straightened up, looking into his face for the first time and gasped. His lips were grey and cracked and his eyes were milky white like those of one long since dead. He pushed on me harder and I could feel his nails digging into my skin. The girl beside me pulled trying to get us back to the center of the street but my feet wouldn't move. I felt other hands pulling at me and looked around to see my mother and brothers all pulling, staring straight ahead, unblinking, with the same milky white eyes. I wanted desperately to escape yet part of me wanted to just give up. It would be easier to just let them pull me along, to get in line just as they were. I could feel my resistance fading. The little girl grabbed me with both hands and using all her strength pulled me along with her back to the middle of the street. I looked back at my family, my father and brothers had already resumed their trance like state, facing ahead as if I had never been there, my mother alone still faced me with outstretched arms, cracked lips forming into a smile on her waxen face. I went to take a step towards her and the little girl dug her heels in once more. I looked down at her and she shook her head as before, then raising her little arm, she pointed down the road in the opposite direction.

I woke in a cold sweat to the sound of pots and pans clanking together in the kitchen. Glad to turn on the little lamp beside my bed with its welcoming light that chased away the darkness, I dressed quickly, in a hurry to join the company of others and leave the strange night behind me.

At breakfast Ann seemed to be fine. She was quiet, but she had often been lately. She looked at me once or twice, offering a weak, apologetic smile before turning away. She ate quickly as if ready to be anywhere else. I understood the feeling and couldn't fault her in it. She obviously remembered something of the previous night, how much was anyone's guess but apparently enough to feel embarrassed.

I was to work with Joan in the gallery. Each of the portraits needed to be dusted thoroughly. The assignment was welcome. I enjoyed opportunities to get out of the laundry room and the gallery had always interested me. I liked to look at the faces of generations of Sarringtons and wonder what their stories were. Not the story everyone knew of a noble, old money family stretching back to English aristocracy that now in the New World had its hand in every industry imaginable, but the hidden stories, the loves, the passions, the fears. What had they thought as they sat for their portraits? Did they feel pride, knowing it would hang over the heads of future generations, reminding them of all those who stood behind them, or did they feel as if each brush stroke imprisoned them just a little more to the obligations that stretched out before them as one of their descendants now did? I could only guess, but sometimes, with some of them at least, it seemed so obvious.

It was not Myrna's kind heart that had sent me to the gallery. Eli was working close to the kitchen and as such Myrna didn't want us to be close enough for close encounters. I knew I could expect other such assignments within the main house as he would be there for a few days at least. Mrs. Sarrington had decided that seeing the kitchen garden on her way to the main garden was more than she was willing to tolerate any longer and had requested that a wall, preferably a living one, be placed around the small plot's perimeter. It was, in my opinion, a ridiculous example of snobbery and in others' opinion just plain foolishness. A wall would undoubtedly block the sun from reaching parts of the garden, effecting the harvest of the vegetables and herbs therein, but Eli saw it as a challenge and welcomed it as he did any other.

Joan and I started at the top row of portraits. The ones so high up we needed a ladder to reach them. I stood on top with dust rag in hand while Joan stood at the bottom steadying the ladder. Occasionally she would try to dust a lower hanging portrait while still holding the ladder for me, but we found this made us both nervous and quickly gave up. We didn't talk unless necessary, not only was it distracting but no one dared more than a word or two in any volume higher than a whisper when they were outside of the servant areas and though we were not a great distance apart, we were far enough that whispering was of little use.

After lunch we were down to the bottom row and able to enjoy each other's company. I liked Joan from the very beginning. She was funny and self-assured. She knew what she thought and was unwilling to let anyone else's opinion of how things should be affect her own. She was not conventionally pretty. Her shoulder length dark brown hair was course with tight curls that spun in on themselves. Her eyes were brown, simple, except when she laughed, then they would shine, or maybe it was just her. Though only in her

late twenties lines had begun to etch themselves into the skin on either side of her eyes. To someone passing her on the street, she may have seemed like any other woman, blending into the surroundings, but to those who knew her and observed her she couldn't possibly. To me, she was beautiful.
"Thank you." I said as I ran a soft rag over a young Jane Sarrington's yellow ringlets.
Joan looked me. She understood. "You're welcome."
"If I may Joan, what happened with you and Doyle?" I had wanted to know for a long time but had been too embarrassed to ask.

 Joan sighed. "Doyle and I have both worked here for a long time. I came to the estate when I was just a little bit younger than you, actually to fill the same position you're in now. Doyle was already here. He had been here maybe five or six months before I arrived and worked in the kitchen. He was 21." She paused and smiled. I imagine she must have been seeing the two of them as they were then. "We became friends, but that was all. Like most young girls I had a crush, but not on him."
"On who?" I had already asked one rude, personal question, I may as well stay the course.
"John Sarrington." Joan's face turned red and she hid it in her rag laughing at herself.
"No!"
"Yes. I really did. He was rich and sophisticated and remember, he, and I for that matter, were younger then. I use to sneak up to his dressing room just so I could touch his combs and things."
I laughed along with her. I could hardly believe it, but I knew Joan well enough to know if she was saying it, then it must be true.
"Anyway," she continued, "as I said, Doyle and I were friends. I think he may have had his eye on someone else at the time as well, yes, Marie, that was her name, but she left within the first year. Over the years the feelings of friendship deepen into something more. I began to realize that when I

was near him I would become nervous and my palms would sweat. I would spend our time together just studying him. I didn't just want to be there with him, I wanted to take him in. I didn't know it, but he had begun to feel the same way. I don't know, to think about it now, maybe it wasn't so much passion but familiarity." Joan paused, face momentarily falling. "Then one day we were outside talking. I was leaning with my back against the side of the house and he was standing beside me leaning on his arm. I don't know now what we were talking about but the wind picked up a whirligig. Do you know what those are; maple seeds that spin as they fall?"

I nodded.

"The wind blew one into my hair and Doyle leaned in close to remove it. We looked into each other's eyes and we knew. He kissed me. My first kiss ever by the way. It was soft and sweet. Then he handed me the whirligig. I still have it stuffed inside my Bible." Joan took a deep breath before continuing. "I don't need to tell you what all followed. I'm sure you already know a thing or two about the process, but sufficed to say we moved along the most obvious path, stopping to enjoy all the milestones as it were."

Joan gave me a knowing look and I quickly looked down at the floor causing her to laugh again.

"Then Myrna found out. Maybe she knew already. I always got the feeling she did, but the point came where she wouldn't tolerate it any longer and we were given a choice, end it or leave. I would have left. I would have gone with Doyle anywhere, but he chose otherwise and in doing so chose for both of us. So I stayed. I had a job and couldn't see any reason to lose it too. I still have feelings for him. I won't lie and say I don't, and he does for me too, but he gave up. He didn't even try." She grew sad for a minute but quickly pulled herself back together, pushing it down to wherever it was she had to in order to get on with her life as it was. "Not like Eli. He's not giving up. Sure Myrna hasn't come out and said anything yet, but he knows what she's up to, just like the rest of us, and he's fighting it. I respect that."

"Ugh. Myrna." I said. "She's evil. How can she be so hateful?"

Joan smiled. "She's just hurt that's all. Like a person whose eyes have been damaged so that the light hurts them. It ain't the sun's fault and they don't hate it, but they still can't bear it. It's the same thing. She doesn't hate you or me or what we have, she just can't be around anything that makes the pain come back that's all."

Joan went on to tell me about Myrna's husband and daughter. I felt horrible for having wished her ill and I said so.

"It's not just that." Joan said. "I think she still could have tolerated being around other people in love if it hadn't been for Frank."

"I have noticed there is something there for her when it comes to him." I said.

"Yep. Frank started working here about a year after I did. Doyle and I hadn't moved beyond friendship at the time so I was paying closer attention to what was going on around me then. Frank is a, well, to call him a flirt would be putting it mildly. I've seen him try to work on you and I'm sure you have seen him put the moves on Ann and Eloise and pretty much any woman in the house. He's been that way from the beginning. Sometimes he would succeed with one of the girls, have 'em for a little while, then cast them aside but they usually didn't stay around long after that; though I will say his luck with the ladies seems to have run out the past couple years. I don't know what it is, he can't seem to help himself. It's not that he's bad, I don't think he is anyway, he did raise his two little brothers when his parents died. He was only a kid himself, fourteen I think he said he was. Joan paused for a moment before returning to her original thought. "But anyway, it was only a matter of time until he put the moves on Myrna. It had been so long for her since a man had paid her any attention. At first she ignored him. He didn't have any effect on her, all his little ploys just rolled right off of her like rain that won't penetrate ground that's been dry too long, but then just the same, if it continues it softens the ground little by little until the soil can't help but soak it up. That's how it was with Myrna. Who knows maybe he really did have a thing for her and he's just too fickle to sustain it, maybe his pride wouldn't let him give up on her until he had won, but for whatever reason he just came on stronger and stronger until she was hooked. She would have done anything for him. I think he knew it too. Then he just withdrew it all, all his light and he began to shine it elsewhere, anywhere, everywhere, except on her. It crushed her. Despite all her hope, once again she wasn't good enough. She was hurt, and I think humiliated, and he won't let her heal either. He throws her crumbs now and then, who knows why, and even though you can see that she hates herself for it, she's starving so she eats them all the same."

As I headed back to my room I decided my days of hating Myrna were over. No matter what she did from then on I would remind myself of everything she had been through and just let it slide. I wondered if Eli knew about it all, but I didn't want to ask him. I didn't want to seem like a gossip and if he didn't know I didn't want to add to Myrna's humiliation by letting yet another person in on it. Frank however, I hated entirely. He had always seemed cocky to me, too cocky, a man with an over inflated opinion of himself, something common enough, but nothing to get worked up over, but now I knew that he was more than that; he was a man ready and willing to trample over someone else for ego's sake or the pure fun of it, just because he could.

The next day I worked in the foyer cleaning the baseboards. It was a boring job as most housework is but mindless work gives a person plenty of time to think and as usual I had plenty to think about. The sun was shining in through the large windows, shadows of swaying trees and flying birds danced across the floors migrating to the walls as the day wore on. I had to do something about this ban Myrna had us under. I couldn't stay in the house much longer. I needed to be out again. As I began to clean the stairs, climbing along the edge of them it came to me. Climbing, that was the answer. When I finished with the stairs I went to find Myrna. Tomorrow was Sunday, and I had the day off.

I found Myrna in the far pantry on the men servants' side of the house. Unlike the pantry on our side that held food stuff, this one held the other things needed to make a house run smoothly such as soap and hanging hooks. She was taking inventory.

"Excuse me, Mrs. Casserly." I said, knocking lightly on the door.

Myrna looked over at me briefly. "Yes Connie?"

"I wanted to ask you something, about tomorrow." I said.

Myrna put her clipboard down on the shelf in front of her and turned to face me, taking off her reading glasses. "Are you going to ask me if you can go to town again?" Her eyebrows rose, not in question, but in the form of a dare.

"Um, no, no Ma'am." I stammered at the mention of town and hoped the subject of it would be easily dropped. "It's just that you know how much I enjoy being outside in nature, hiking and all…"

"I've already made it clear to you that you won't be hiking. It's too dangerous and as you know Mr. Sarrington agrees." Myrna interrupted.

"Yes, yes Ma'am you did, but it's just that I miss it so much. I don't know if I can go much longer without it. "

Myrna didn't say a word; rather she just stood and stared at me with a look that said '*Are you serious?*'

I continued on determined not to lose my nerve. "I know that you feel it's dangerous for me to be out there alone, or for even Eli and I to be out there alone." I looked away briefly. "But what if we all went? I mean one big hike and picnic, everyone who's off and wants to go. So many people would make a lot of noise; no bear would come within five miles of them. You could come too if you wanted to get away for a little bit. We could hike up to this one spot on top of one of the ridges behind the house. It's beautiful. I'm sure you would like it." I smiled as I finished, wanting her to realize the invitation was sincere.

Myrna thought about it for a minute. Her eyes showed suspicion and I was ready for defeat.

"Okay." She said. "If you can get at least seven people to go with you, you can do it, no less. Maybe I will join you. Go around and ask and let me know."

"Thank you so much Mrs. Casserly." I said. "I really do hope that if we go you will come along." I turned to leave when I heard Myrna call after me.

"Be sure to discuss it with Paul to see what you can take for the picnic."

I smiled and nodded.

Within half an hour I had spoken with almost everyone in the house. Joan, Doyle, Peter, Eli, Paul, Helen, Stephen, Alan and Susan all agreed to go. I needed seven. I got ten, including myself, and just maybe it would turn out to be eleven.

Paul said I could make some sandwiches out of leftover turkey and that there were cucumbers too if I wanted to slice them up as well and also plenty of blackberries. Helen helped me prepare everything since Paul and Susan were busy trying to get dinner ready for us. Once everything was set I went and found Mrs. Casserly to tell her the news. She congratulated me and said again that she might come along after I asked a second time. When night came I felt like I was a child on the night before my birthday.

We were ready to leave early and the day was starting out clear and bright. Everyone wanted to get going but I said we needed to wait to see if Myrna was going to come. Helen smiled sweetly but everyone else just laughed.

"Myrna's not coming." Eli said. He and Joan both stood outside of the kitchen door with me but the others began walking.

"She said she might." I replied. "More than once in fact."

"It's really sweet of you to invite her," Joan said "but Eli's right, she's not going to come. There's no reason for us to wait."

I peeked inside the kitchen door, even though I already knew she wasn't there.

"Okay," I sighed "if you say so then I guess we can go."

"Why won't she go along with us?" I asked as we turned to leave.

Joan laughed. "Connie, you should know better. You're smarter than that. Myrna's not going to go anywhere with us; she's the housekeeper, she's above us. It's just not done."

"Joan's right." Eli said. "The only reason she would even consider it would be to watch us but I don't think even that is a big enough incentive for her to break station for an entire day."

"Well I thought she might and I know it's not likely but sometimes people will do it. Break station I mean." I said.

"Who, I've never seen it?" Joan asked.

"The Sarringtons do sometimes don't they? It seemed like they were nice to Eli on the California trip and Tom has spoken to me, and Ann too." I said.

"Tom?" Eli asked turning his head to face me dead on.

"Thomas Sarrington." I said.

"Yes I got that." Eli replied. "When did *Tom* talk to you?"

"While you were gone." I said, but I already regretted bringing it up. "It wasn't a big deal. I'm just saying he was nice to me, polite. He told me to call him Tom in fact, and Ann has told me he sometimes talks to her too. It's not a hike along or anything but my point is he is definitely higher than Myrna could ever hope to be, yet he still condescends to speak with the help so I don't think it would be too shocking to imagine Myrna might like to join us."

Eli looked at me funny but we had reached the rest of the group so he let it drop. I had the feeling that that wouldn't be the end of it though. Joan gave me a *'What were you thinking?'* look before striking up a conversation with Helen about her sister in Newark. I agreed. What had I been thinking?

Despite the awkward start Eli and I had a good time together. We had more than just Joan and Paul with us so we minded our interactions carefully but we were having fun just like at the beginning. It was nice to spend time together without the physical part taking center stage.

Just as he had done with me, Eli pointed out various animal tracks as we would come across them and he named the different trees and plants though Helen knew even more of them. She and Eli would get caught up in detail filled conversations about this plant or that tree and I would watch amused as Eli's excitement grew with each new thing he learned. That wasn't the only surprise. Peter, who I had never spent time with at all -actually we had probably not said more than ten words to each other in my entire employment- was surprisingly interesting. He knew a great deal about birds and could identify them by their calls and even tell us what the calls signified as we went along. His mother was an avid bird watcher and he had been listening to them as keenly as one would listen to another person all his life. By the time the day was over I knew the difference between a robin's call and a blue jay's, but that was unfortunately it, though not through any fault of Peter's.

For everyone except Eli and I it was their first time on top of the ridge and their first view of the valley below in all its splendor. They gasped and ohh'd and ahh'd. I understood what they were feeling and hoped that maybe now they would understand why Eli and I, or even just I, longed to be there.

We ate our lunch on the boulders and talked. That was different. Eli and I, while we did talk to each other quite a bit, also spent great amounts of time in silence. I was beginning to realize that that was not something that was possible for everyone. I had not noticed it as we had made our way up the mountain but as we sat eating and taking in the view and especially during our descent it became very evident and the sound of voices, which usually didn't matter to me much one way or the other began to grate on my nerves. A minute couldn't pass without someone needing to come up with something to say, not Eli and not Helen, who was quiet by nature, but the rest seemed determined to not let the silence touch them. I wondered why. Were they so scared of the voice in their head, or perhaps they were scared of what the voice may be saying in the heads of everyone else. Maybe they had just grown so accustomed to the noise of everyday that it seemed out of place for it not to be there. I remembered my own experiences when I first came into the woods and was greeted by what was then deafening silence, but I had grown use to it, refreshed by it and their constant need for chatter was like sacrilege.

When we reached the level manicured lawn Eli came up along beside me. Within a few seconds he slowed his step and I took my cue to do the same.
"Be careful of Thomas Sarrington." He said.
"Why? Is there something I should know?" I asked.
"No, not that I know of." Eli replied. "But I know men. I don't know many rich ones, but they can't be that different."
"Okay." I said, holding back the urge to laugh. "I'll watch out."

That night for the first time in weeks I was able to fall asleep easily and wake up feeling as if I were truly rested. At breakfast everyone was talking about our hike and I was happy that it was a success; perhaps Myrna would let us do it again if the restrictions continued. Hiking with a group was not exactly what I preferred. But it was far better than nothing and I did like these people, and wanted them to find whatever happiness they could in life. If such an outing could bring them any, whether for an hour or a day or many days, then I was glad of it.

Monday came and I was to clean the servant bathrooms then afterwards work in the library all day by myself. It was by far the most excited I had ever been about a duty I had been given. The library was a large room with white book covered shelves that ran along three of the four walls. On two of the walls the shelves ran from the floor to the ceiling but on the wall directly opposite the windows, the shelves did not. That wall contained a centered fireplace with prerequisite portrait above, and on the rest of the wall three quarters of the way down the shelves stopped and were replaced by white painted cabinets. There were multiple seating areas with accompanying side tables situated throughout the room but the largest was in the center around a large circular wool rug and invitingly placed in front of the fireplace. When I had first come to the estate the library had been nothing more than just another room and an odd one at that. Reading, though I had enjoyed it when I had done it, had not been even a mildly important pastime within my family and the idea of owning walls and walls of books had seemed absurd. How could you possibly read them all? Why would you want to, and even if you did, why own them? Surely you wouldn't want to read them again?! Now that I had discovered the magic that a book could possess, it had become, in my eyes, the most exquisite room in the house by far.

I made my way to the library excited to have an opportunity to take as much time as I needed getting a good look at the inventory. When I got there I saw that if there was a Fate she certainly has a sense of humor seeing as in a chair in the far corner leafing distractedly through a small but thick book with a blue cover sat Tom Sarrington. He was slouched down in the chair with one of his legs draped over the arm looking bored. When I entered the room he saw me almost as quickly as I had seen him and straightened immediately.

"I apologize Sir. I didn't know anyone was in here, I'll come back later." I said and turned to leave.

"No," came Tom's voice "it's okay, don't leave, please. I would like to have the company."

"I'm not really company Sir, I would just be cleaning." I replied.

"Alright fine, I would like having someone else in the room even if they are only cleaning. How is that?"

I made a slight bow and headed over to the corner farthest from him.

"I heard you had a run in with a bear Constance."

He surprised me by using my name. I would not have thought that he remembered much, if anything, about our encounter, least of all the name of a servant.

"Yes Sir. I did."

"Hmm, must have been frightening."

"Yes Sir it was." I wanted to get back to cleaning and for him to get back to his book. Myrna would not be too pleased if she walked in on such an exchange, and better to not even think about what Eli would have to say about it.

"And I thought I told you to call me Tom."

"Yes Sir, you did." I replied, feeling my face heat as I realized immediately what I had done.

Tom laughed. "Orders well followed. I hear *you* are called Connie, but you told me Constance. I guess perhaps you didn't feel as comfortable with me as I did with you. I can't blame you, a drunken man in the dark, not much to feel confident about in that."

I didn't know what to say. He had left me in an awkward position, having to choose between rudeness and inappropriate familiarity. Neither seemed to be a good option.

"Yes that's true. I'm sorry." I answered deciding to avoid Tom and Sir altogether at least circumventing that choice. "My name is Constance and it's how I introduce myself to unfamiliar people, but those who know me call me Connie. You may call me whichever pleases you best."

"Which pleases you best?" he asked.

No one had ever asked me what I preferred to be called and I hesitated even though I knew the answer. I had always known.

"I prefer Constance."

"From me or from everybody?" Tom asked.

"Everybody, though I have never been asked by anyone besides you. I like the name. I think it sounds soothing, not at all like Connie which has always sounded too forward in my own ears."

"Then I will call you Constance." He replied, smiling in his charmingly boyish way which I had seen in pictures and in his portraits, but not in person. It had been too dark the one time we had talked.

"Thank you," I said returning his smile, with one perhaps not as perfect but sincere, "Tom."

"So back to this bear." He said. "You were outside, alone, at night."

"Yes."

"That seems familiar." Tom smiled and I nodded. "Why are you walking alone to the river at night? Are you making moonshine?"

We both laughed as I shook my head.

"No? Hmm. I was sure that was it and had planned on scolding you for not offering some to someone who was so obviously a lover of spirits."

"Well that's it." I answered. "Spirits. That's what I do by the river. I converse with them as I dance under the moon in dark pagan rituals."

I stared at him, determined to keep my face serious. I didn't know what had come over me but it was fun and made me feel energized. I felt like I was back in Brooklyn teasing the neighborhood boys. Tom was silent for a moment. He seemed to realize I was joking, but he looked as if he couldn't figure out how to respond.

"I thought you were supposed to summon a goat footed god, not a bear." He said finally.

"Yes," I tried to sound solemn, "I need more practice."

We both laughed again.

"So you were out alone, again, and you fell asleep and the groundskeeper rescued you."

"Yes. That's right."

"How lucky that he was there." Tom said, his eyes looking directly into mine. I wanted to turn away, but that would be too obvious.

"Yes, it was lucky, I was lucky." I replied.

"And now no one can go out alone." He said.

I shook my head though I knew it wasn't a question.

"But you never did tell me why you were out there. I was thinking about it. I thought maybe it had something to do with the groundskeeper, Eli," he paused watching me at the mention of the name, "and maybe it does, sometimes, but the night I saw you headed down that same way he wasn't here; he hadn't returned from his trip to California with my parents yet. And I have seen you headed that way at other times too, during the day."

I thought about the time he had been swimming with friends in the pool and how I had felt someone watching me.

"So are you going to solve the riddle for me Constance? I'm sincerely intrigued."

"There is no riddle." I answered. "I just like being outside."

"A lot of people like being outside, but they don't go for walks in the middle of the night."

"That may be true I suppose but that's really all there is to it. There is no secret, no mystery; it's just where I want to be."

"Enough to risk your life?"

"I hadn't thought about it like that until after the bear. I had never had an encounter with one and so it wasn't even in my mind when I went down there. Of course the thoughts are there now, but I can't say that the knowledge would keep me from the woods." I paused to consider it. "No, I'm certain it wouldn't. I know more now and would be more careful and alert."

"This worries me Constance. It really does. I like you, I don't want to wake up one day to find out you've been turned into bear fodder." Tom paused, "You love being outdoors that much?"

"I do."

"Why?"

"I don't know how to explain it to you. All my life, as much as I have enjoyed it, there was something missing, and it was a vague something. Maybe I didn't even realize it, but I think I did. I think I knew somewhere in the back of my head that," I couldn't grasp the words. I knew I could feel it, the trueness of what I was saying but it was true deep inside of me where words wouldn't suffice. "something wasn't right or maybe I didn't know, maybe I am just remembering it from what I know now and assuming it was there, but I know that when I first came here, even on the way, peering out of the car window as we drove, that I sensed the world I was seeing was important to me. Then I began walking on my off days, spending time in the woods and it filled me up and made me whole in a way that made me realize I had never been whole, not ever, not anytime that I could remember. And now I need it. Now it's a necessary part of me, like my heart or my lungs. Apart from nature, I would die."

"Death is a strong sentiment." Tom said. "Is it the land here or just nature in general?"

"Nature in general I guess, but I don't know, aside from city parks this is all I've experienced."

"So then, now that you have realized all this, are your plans to stay here or to go work in the hinterlands somewhere?" Tom asked, and though he sounded sincere, a voice crept up in my head whispering that he must be mocking me.

"What do you mean?" I asked not knowing whether I should be curious or offended.

"What do you think I mean?" he laughed, "Do you want to stay here working as a maid and enjoying your days roaming the surrounding land or has your love affair with the natural world caused you to set your sights on something else?"

"What else could there be for me? I'm just a maid." I answered.

"There are other things you could do if you wanted. You could be a naturalist or a park ranger."

I thought about this for a moment and my heart leapt in my chest. I had seen pictures of some of the more famous parks like Yellowstone and they were beautiful, like the mountains and woods surrounding the estate, but magnified. As I thought of myself in such a place reality quickly set in.

"I was born to be a maid Tom, and I'll die a maid. My mother has always been one, my grandmother was one; it's what there is for people like me."

"But you would enjoy doing something like that wouldn't you? Not just going out on your off days but doing it every day; walking the hills as your job. Wouldn't that be better?"

"Yes, it sounds wonderful, but it's just not reality."

"Why not, because you're a maid, a woman? You could do it. Women have done it."

"Who?"

"Just a couple years ago I remember hearing about a woman that was appointed as a temporary ranger at the Grand Canyon National Park. I don't remember her name, but still, she was, or is; I don't know. And once when we went out to Yosemite when I was younger I remember seeing a woman ranger then too. I think they called her a rangerette."

"Was she temporary as well?" I asked.

"I don't know but that isn't the point. The point is that women rangers have existed. Maybe they still exist, maybe there are dozens of them and you just don't know it." He paused letting it sink in. "Maybe some of them are permanent."

"But, I'm a maid." I answered slowly, though my mind was already reeling with this new possibility.

Tom sat quietly watching me, then he stood to leave. The change in his position brought me back to the present and I felt rude.

"I'm sorry." I said "I didn't mean to drift off like that."

"It's okay." Tom replied. "I'm glad to see I may have given you something to think about, something perhaps, to dream about."

"What about you Tom?" I asked.

"Pardon?"

"The last time we talked. What happened with your father?" It was a bold question but he had handed me what felt like a gift and I wanted to know that he had something to look forward to too.

"Oh that. He made a phone call. I'm headed back to school. Soon in fact, right back on track." Tom smiled, but it was contrived. "Have a good day Constance."

"You too Tom" I returned, but he was already gone.

Throughout the rest of the day and night my mind was going nonstop through the same round of questions. Could a woman really be a park ranger? Obviously they could, Tom had told me so and I had no reason to think he didn't know what he was talking about. The bigger question, the real question, was could I? And if I could, then how? This would bring on the next set of questions. How could I find out what steps to take? Did I need a degree? Experience? And if I did needed either of them or both of them for that matter, how would I get them? I was still just lower class of little or no means. There had been others who had been poor; I began to think to myself as I lay in my bed that evening. Carnegie had been poor. Lincoln had been poor. Da Vinci had been poor. But they were also men. Was it possible to surmount any obstacle if you were poor *and* a woman? Some women had made real strides, done great things, but the only ones I had heard of had come from families who sent them to college, who had means to put them where they needed to be. No doubt where my family thought I needed to be was right here. I could only imagine what my mother would think of my entertaining such an idea. She wasn't fond of ambitious men let alone women. Men needed to work hard and risk nothing; women needed to love their men and raise babies. Anything else was a gamble and the house had the odds. Stability, that was the only game worth playing.

Still I couldn't shake the thought. A little dream couldn't hurt could it? A little hope is a good thing, right?

I began to listen to what Eli was saying even more intently than before. Eli had no doubt. He knew he would do exactly what he planned and that nothing could ever really stop it. Delay him perhaps, make him come up with a different approach possibly, but he knew that the only thing that could ever truly stop him was himself. I wanted that same faith.

I wished I could talk to Tom again as well. Maybe he would know more or have some ideas at least, but it was more than just that. I found I enjoyed Tom's company and after the way our last encounter had ended I was concerned about him. He wasn't happy. Everything may have been right back on track but from the look on his face you would have thought the track lead straight off a cliff.

After a week I was back in the laundry room with Darla and it was harder to hold on to the hope I had felt elsewhere. I have heard that our environment shapes and affects us and I think that's true. I knew that when I was in the woods I felt different than in the garden and more different still than in the house, but I noticed that even within the house there was variation. In the grand rooms of the family it seemed that ideas could be just as grand, and great deeds could be accomplished by the hand of man. In my room I felt a peace and comfort. Not as much optimism, nor complete pessimism, but balance. In the laundry however, especially with Darla there spilling out her gossip and opinions, or trying to wrench mine from me, it felt as if hope was nothing more than a mirage faintly flickering in and out of focus in the washer steam.

I wished Fate, if she was there, would give me a sign, something to let me know which path to choose. I wanted a pointing arrow complete with the words. "Head towards your dreams. There lies your destiny and all will fall into place." Or for a voice to come from the sky saying "Stay put, it's a fool's journey." I longed to be released from the fear that comes when one is set before a choice and no matter what rationalization or what omens, the choice can only be yours alone. No one can make it for you; no one can guarantee you the end result. You have to bear the responsibility for your own life, to face all consequences and know that try or not, fail or succeed, it was you and only you all along, and that's all it ever could be. Your talent, your drive, your will. Your faith in *your*self. In the end either *you* could or *you* couldn't, end of story. Accepting that my life is in my own hands was the most frightening thing I have ever done and that revelation of freedom and burden brought with it great joy at the possibilities and great despair that in the end I might find, I simply wasn't enough.

One afternoon when I returned to my room from work I found an envelope on my nightstand. It was a crisp, heavy paper with "Constance" written along the front in perfect script. It wasn't from my mother or Eli, that was obvious, and I hoped it wasn't a letter of termination from Myrna, but I had a feeling I knew who it was from. Only two people had I ever told to call me Constance, and Frank had only obliged me the once.

I sat down on the bed and carefully opened the envelope. Inside was a piece of paper of the same type as the envelope. I unfolded it and read the note.

Dear Constance,
I hope you find the enclosed newspaper clipping useful. It took some work to find, but I believe it was worth it.
Sincerely,
Tom

I looked in the envelope to find a small newspaper clipping. It wasn't the size of a normal article, just a photo with an accompanying description. The photo was of a lone dark haired woman in camping clothes who looked to be about my age. The description underneath read, "Pauline 'Polly' Mead has been appointed as a temporary ranger-naturalist at Grand Canyon National Park." Beside the picture someone had written 1929 – 1931.

9

The newspaper clipping was on my mind throughout the evening. It was absolute proof that at least one woman had been a ranger, even if it was only on a temporary basis, which gave me hope. But it was also on my mind because I couldn't help but feel touched that Tom had went through the trouble to find it for me. There was also one question that simply wouldn't go away, how had he delivered it to my room? He couldn't have snuck down without being noticed, someone was always around and no one would have let such an incident as a Sarrington setting foot in the servants quarters slide. Talk would have consisted of nothing else, yet no one had mentioned any such thing. That could only mean that he had someone else deliver the note. It couldn't have been Peter, Tom's valet, his being in the women's quarters would have been equally odd and he would have to ask where my room was, which once again would have been brought up almost immediately in the nightly gossip if not sooner. The only other option was that he had had a female servant deliver it, but who? No one had said anything to me or anyone else as far as I knew, and it bothered me not to know. I needed to know who had been in my room, clear up whatever they must be thinking, and more importantly find out whether or not they would say something to Eli.

Though I sent Eli a letter before dinner I hadn't mentioned it to him, and I felt guilty about it and yet defiant. The note was innocent, and I was not Eli's wife, actually I wasn't Eli's anything. He had made no formal claim on me despite declarations of love and talk of future plans, but it was still all just talk and realizing this upset me and made me feel even more that I had every right to Tom's friendship and was under no obligation to say anything to anyone. Still keeping it from Eli made me feel dirty, as secrets often do, especially since I knew he wouldn't like it and would read more into it than what was actually there. I had to admit that that would be somewhat understandable. The wealthy don't typically go to great lengths for their servants, not without a good reason, and let's face it, there's one that comes to mind first.

At least one of my questions was answered fairly quickly. Late that night after everyone else had went to bed I heard a knock on my door. It was very faint and had I not already been awake, it would have never sufficed. I walked over and opened the door. Standing before me once again was Ann, though she was not worried nor was she hysterical. This time she looked dangerous. It wasn't anything obvious, there was no knife or fist being shaken before me, but it was something in her eyes. They flashed as she greeted me before quickly settling into a concentrated half squint, like a cat watching its prey. I invited her in and shut the door behind her. Even her walk was different. Before it could only be described as nervous, but this time she practically sauntered over to the nightstand. She picked up the book I had been reading, *Leaves of Grass* -I was still struggling to get through it- and put it back down before with great care she turned to face me, beginning first with her head, then followed slowly by her shoulders, then waist, then finally her full body.

"Tom had me deliver a note to you. I wanted to make sure you saw it." Ann said. She was struggling to sound casual but everything about her was conveying the exact opposite.

"Yes I did. Thank you. I wondered how he got it here." I said.

"It was me." Ann plopped down on my bed. "So, a note from Thomas Sarrington, that's unusual."

"Yes. I didn't expect it." I said making my way to lean against my dresser so Ann and I could be face to face. I didn't know what she was up to, but I wanted to be square of her, to let her know that whatever it was I had nothing to hide and nothing to be afraid of, including her.

"Hmmm. Really? Well I have to admit it spiked my curiosity." Ann offered up a forced smile. "Is there something you want to share? Do you have two men vying for your attention?" she said laughing.

"No, nothing like that." I replied, laughing myself, except my laughter was sincere.

Ann raised her eyebrows as if to say *"Well?"*

"Ann," I said, "Is it bothering you that much? Do you want to see the note or hear what it was?"

"It's not bothering me. Like I said, I'm just curious." She replied

"It's fine Ann." I turned and took the note out from the top drawer of my dresser. "I saw him when I was cleaning the library while Eli was working right outside the kitchen on the garden and Myrna was trying to keep me away from him. Anyway, Tom had heard about the bear and from there we got into a discussion about female park rangers. I had never heard of one." I said handing Ann the envelope. "So he got a clipping concerning one he had told me about and that was what he had you deliver."

Ann opened the note and read it, her hands shaking. Despite its brevity she looked at it much longer than it should have taken for her to read it. Next she took out the clipping and looked at it briefly before putting it and the note back in the envelope and returning them to me.

"Well, that was nice of him." Ann said as she rose and went to the door. She reached out and grabbed the doorknob and pausing yet without turning to face me, she continued "Interesting that he went through all that trouble."

I had no reply. Ann opened the door and walked away.

I laid in the dark unable to sleep. Once again Ann was causing me to be restless. I couldn't figure out why she was acting like she was. I knew she had a crush on Tom, she had made that clear, but she had had a crush on Eli and from what I had heard, at one point Stanley, so was it really that big of a deal? She hadn't acted strange when she realized Eli and I were together, so why would a casual encounter with this current crush cause her to react so strongly? It didn't make sense, but one thing was clear to me; whatever she thought was going on, she didn't like it and that would mean trouble. I could feel it in the pit of my stomach.

I thought about the possibilities. She could say something to Myrna, but that was unlikely. Ann may have had knowledge about Eli and I or suspicions about Tom and I, but nothing she could prove. No, the real threat was that she might tell Eli before I had a chance to. I sat up in bed and turned on my lamp. Reaching into the nightstand drawer I grabbed my pen, some stationary and the journal I had bought at Miller's to bear down on. I would have to write my own note.

First thing in the morning I sent my letter to Eli though Paul and quickly received a note telling me to meet him in the garage. Unlike previous notes, this one did not contain instructions on how I was going to accomplish that. Whatever ruse was to be employed would have to be my own. It worried me that Eli had not thought it out as usual or worse that he perhaps had, but decided to leave me to my own devices. Whatever he thought, he was obviously not pleased.

There was a table we used for folding in the laundry room but it had one bad leg. If you pressed on it hard it would tilt the table, but usually it was fine for our purposes. I told Darla that I thought it would be good for me to go see if I could find a small chunk of wood left over from Eli's project that might fit under the table leg. At first she looked at me sideways, asking me what had made me think of that, but almost immediately after the words left her mouth a light seemed to switch on in her head and she smiled and told me to make sure I took my time and found the perfect piece.

When I got to the garage Eli was pacing. He stopped suddenly and turned to face me. He was angry, but it was a different anger from what I had experienced with him before, there was no hurt to it, rather, it was more like the look a parent gives to a disobedient child, but even that is not right because it was mixed with something else.

"I thought I told you not to talk to Thomas Sarrington." Eli said.

"You told me to be careful of him." I replied trying to appear calm.

"You knew what I meant." He said.

"How am I supposed to not speak to him when he speaks to me?"

"Avoid him. You don't need to be where he is. You work in the servant areas, he doesn't come there. Did you seek him out?" Eli stepped closer to me.

"No! Why would I do that? Myrna sent me to work in the library last week. She was trying to keep me away from you and when I got there he was already there."

"Last week? You spoke to him last week and just now told me! When last week?"

"Monday." I replied knowing it looked bad.

"Monday?!"

"I didn't see any reason to tell you. It was just an innocent conversation. It wasn't until he sent me the note that I thought I should tell you. Not that it was a big deal or that he meant anything by it, but just so that you would know."

"Why didn't you just leave when you saw him in the library and why the hell would he send you a newspaper clipping?"

"I was going to leave but he told me to stay." I answered.

"He told you to stay even though you wanted to leave and you did. You just do whatever he says?"

"Yes. I'm a maid Eli. If the boss says stay and clean the library you stay."

"I wonder what you would have done if he asked you to clean his bedroom."

"What is that supposed to mean?" I asked though I knew perfectly well what he was implying.

"Forget it."

"I don't want to forget it."

"Well I do. Why did he send you the clipping?"

"We had talked about rangers and I guess he thought he would send me a newspaper clipping about one of them."

"Why would he go through the trouble of finding an old newspaper article, cutting it out and sending it to you? That's a lot of work for someone like him. I doubt it was done out of the kindness of his heart."

"I don't know why he would have done it other than kindness Eli. Do you know him so well that you can say for certain that he isn't the type of person that would do such a thing for no other reason? He seems nice enough to me."

"Does he?" Eli widened his eyes in mock surprise. "I know him well enough. I don't need to know him any better. You're naïve Connie." Eli tilted his head toward me and looked at me from under his brow. "I told you already that I love you. I told you that I want a future for us, a good future, and I'm going to work to make that happen. But let me tell you this too. I will not be made a fool of. Stay away from Sarrington."

Eli walked past me leaving the garage without another word. I wiped away the tears that had formed in my eyes with shaking hands and quickly looked around the garage for a piece of wood.

10

I did not receive a letter from Eli that night, nor did I the next day. There was no note to arrange even a casual meeting. He didn't even come to the kitchen for his meals; instead he had someone else bring them to him. Everyone watched. No one said a word to me about it but they didn't have to. The way they avoided my face said enough. Whether or not they knew of the note from Tom I didn't know, but they knew that Eli was avoiding me, that was obvious. I wanted to go to him and patch things up, but I didn't know what to say. I was still unsure of what I had done that was so wrong.

I was hurt and scared and angry, but mostly I was confused. Life had been so simple at one time. I would work in a simple job then I would fall for a dependable Irish man, probably close to Greenpoint, if not an actual neighbor. We would marry, have children, and live near our families. We would work at our meager employment until we were too old to be of much use, then we would move in with one of our children. Our life would not be grand, or exciting, but it would be stable and most likely happy. This was the way it was supposed to be. It wasn't necessarily a plan, because a plan wasn't necessary, just as it isn't necessary for a fish to plan to swim or a bird to plan to fly. But now everything was upside down. The life my mother had banked on was gone, though she clung to it dearly. The nation was in turmoil and no one knew for certain what the future held. I had found Eli and Tom and between the two of them they had shown me a different view and I had begun to believe it possible for even me to tread a new path. I had done more than just believe. I had begun to hope and think and work out solutions. I had begun to feel myself uplifted by possibility, but now I seemed to be plummeting towards the ground. Eli was my strength and faith. He didn't know it, but he was.

Knowing he would be beside me gave me courage, but now I didn't know and my fear and doubt tore at me.

Once again I decided to seek solace in the only place I knew I could find it. When Sunday rolled around I rose early in the morning. Earlier than I ever had and snuck out of the house. As I walked past the garage for a moment I was tempted to leave a note for Eli, but I quickly overcame the urge and continued on. Usually I headed towards the river or left to the mountains, but not today. I was already breaking the rules but Myrna, Eli, and bear be damned. Today I did not want to be found. It would be mine alone as no day had been for far too long.

For a long time the landscape looked the same as it did everywhere else I had been, green grass poking through old leaves and needles from the previous fall, trees and bramble constantly forcing me to weave one way than another, but after a few hours I came to something different. The land was covered in water. It was shallow, not more than six inches at most, just enough to cover the grass and leaves and the roots of the trees. The trees standing tall in the midst of the water reminded me of pictures I had seen of swamps in the southern states, though it wasn't any such thing. I couldn't see where the water had come from or make any guesses as to how long it had been there, but there was something ethereal about it, this place that appeared out of nowhere, out of the ordinary and without reason. I sat down on the ground and leaned against a tree facing the water. It was still and quiet. No wind, no birds, no squirrels, just peace. My mind had raced around for the first hour of my walk, by the second it was working out details sensibly, but by the time I reached this place it was ready to just be. No questions, no answers, just a heart beating and breath going in and out, in and out.

But humankind cannot tolerate a perfect moment, one of happiness, or peace, or pleasure, for too long. They are states that suspend the mind, and as such they frighten us and we must bring back the inane chatter that both tires and pacifies. Without the constant drumming in our heads we lose who we are and we panic or we come too close to finding out and it frightens us. I am no different and the peace that I had longed for and happily surrendered to soon became overwhelming. I began to feel that to continue in it would be to court madness. Perhaps we are bound to a life were it is our burdens that keep us sane, though I hate to believe it, but I have seen all too often that for sadness and doubt and worry, we have all the time in the world, but for bliss, in whatever form it takes, more than a few fleeting moments is too much to bear.

I rose and turned to head back. I wished there was somewhere else to go, but there wasn't. With no other distraction to be had, my mind was already charging full steam ahead to the possibility of what would lay in wait for me when I returned to the estate, happy to be back where it belonged, where it was comfortable and most importantly, where it was in control.

As I drew closer to my usual spot at the river, the one I always ran to, I heard voices. I couldn't make them out clearly. I only knew that one was female and two were male. As I came closer they became recognizable. It was the Sarrington children, Tom, Robert and Jane.
"You can't be serious Tom." Jane said laughing, though it sounded nervous rather than amused.
"Why not?" Tom asked.
"What do you mean why not?!" Robert said. "It's simply not possible! It's not done! Have her if you want, privately, you wouldn't be the first to do such a thing, but for Christ's sake leave it at that!"
"I don't even see why privately." Jane added. "There are plenty of other more appropriate girls who gladly concede to whatever you want, why even bother with her? It's beneath you. *She* is beneath you."
I didn't want to ease drop, though the conversation admittedly intrigued me, but it was no great morality that

made me step into plain sight. I didn't want to ease drop because I didn't want to hear anymore. I didn't want to know who they were talking about.

"Constance!" Tom said when he saw me emerge from the woods, a nervous look settling on his face. "What are you doing here?"

Jane and Robert turned towards me, looking me over with obvious disdain and suspicion.

 "I went for a hike and was headed back to the house." I replied.

"How long have you been there?" Robert asked.

"I just walked up, a few seconds I guess." I answered.

"You're alone." Tom said regaining his composure. "But the rule on walking the grounds has not been lifted."

"No you're right, it hasn't. I probably will no longer have a job when I get back, but I couldn't stay in the house another day. I needed to be out." I said.

"Enough to risk unemployment and possible mauling?" Tom laughed.

"Yes. " I answered, laughing at how silly it must seem to them.

"Then I guess we have no choice but to escort you back. You managed to avoid becoming bear food, maybe we can tempt Fate a little more and keep you from being fired as well." Tom said.

   Jane looked at Tom and shook her head. Sighing, she and Robert turned towards the house and started back ahead of us. Tom had no idea how much we really would be tempting Fate by showing up at the house together. I thought that I would rather risk going it alone.

"It's not necessary Tom. Why don't you go ahead and catch up to your brother and sister. "I said.

"Nonsense. I would much rather talk to you anyway." He replied. "So did you get my newspaper clipping?"

"Yes! Oh Tom, I'm sorry. Yes I did. Thank you so much. You didn't have to go through all that trouble."

"I know I didn't, but I wanted to." Tom smiled wide. He really was quite handsome, and charming too. I could see how what his sister had said was more than likely an undeniable fact. He probably could get any number of girls to do whatever he wanted. "Did it make you happy?" he asked.

"Yes. It did." I smiled back. It was true. It had indeed.

"Good." Tom said, though it seemed as if his mind was already somewhere else. "Good."

We walked on in silence. It would have been very nice had I not been thinking of what would happen when Eli found out I was with Tom again, and he would find out. Either he would see us himself or someone would tell him. Something like this would not just be overlooked.

"Are you glad to be headed back to school soon?" I asked, trying to force my mind to focus elsewhere.

"Sure. It'll be nice to get back. See everybody. Start back on the right track, full steam ahead." Tom chuckled. "But I hate to leave here too." Tom looked at me and smiled again. "I will miss the company."

I returned Tom's smile not knowing what the proper response was. But I didn't have the opportunity to dwell on it long. At the top of the hill I saw a figure come to an abrupt stop, then turn and run away. Within minutes it returned with three others besides. Now that we were closer I could see that the first figure had been Teddy, one of the grounds men and didn't matter much, but the other three were Myrna, Emma, and Eli. I watched as Myrna turned to face Emma; almost immediately Emma turned to leave. Myrna then turned to Teddy and he left also. I continued watching to see if Myrna would turn to face Eli as she had with the others but she didn't. I could feel Tom looking at me and then he did the unthinkable. He took my arm in his. I gasped and pulled away.

"It's okay Constance." He said.

"I know. I'm sorry. I didn't mean to do that, you just startled me." I said. "I know you are just being a gentleman, but I'm fine, really."

"Alright." Tom said looking uncomfortable.

I turned my eyes back to the top of the hill. There stood Myrna. Alone.

"Myrna!" Tom said brightly.

"Sir." She answered, slightly bowing as all of us did, not a true bow, more of a slight tilt of the head. Her eyes went immediately to me.

"Constance was down at the river with us and since she is, I assume, off today and was following father's rule about being with someone while out, I am surprised to see you standing here." Tom said.

Myrna looked back at Tom.

"Yes Sir. It was just that we didn't realize she was with someone so we were in a bit of a fright when no one knew where she was." Myrna looked back at me, holding my eyes.

"As long as it's cleared up now. I would *hate* to hear that Constance was in any trouble." Tom said, his voice firm and meaning unmistakable. He turned to me. "Good afternoon Constance. It was a pleasure as always."

I gave a quick nod and walked swiftly to my room without responding to the many questions that rose up around me as I made my way through the kitchen and down the hall. I sat down on the bed and waited with my hands clenched in my lap for the inevitable knock on the door.

I sat there for a long time and still no one came. Soon my eyes felt tired and I laid down, ready for a reprieve from the anxiousness.

I was standing in the street with the child at my side looking up at me in expectation. I looked to the side at the line of people facing forward unaware of anything around them. Holding the little girl's hand I began to walk forward. We walked until the lines of people disappeared. I turned and could still see them, they were close, but they had ended. Now there was nothing but empty sidewalks and closed doors. I stopped and looked to my left, watching as a door opened and a man stepped out. His features were blurry but he stood tall and projected awareness unlike those in the lines. He held out his hand, offering it to me. I then turned to look to my right and saw another door open and another man step out. He too was faceless, hand extended. I looked down at the girl. She made no signs of moving, neither towards nor away from the men. She simply watched me. Both men stepped away from the doors and began to walk towards me at an identical pace. I felt frightened of them and yet I wanted to go with them both, to see what lay beyond the doors. Their pace quickened and soon they were almost upon me, hands outstretched. Only a few steps left, here they came, turning their hands from an open gesture they looked as if they were ready to grab me. Any second now. They lunged.

A knock came at the door hard and rapid. I looked around the room quickly trying to get my bearings, my heart racing and chest heaving. The knock came again and I rose, quickly crossing over to open the door.
"Connie," Myrna said flatly, "I want you to take a walk with me."
Myrna turned and I followed, past a kitchen filled with people who quickly grew silent, their eyes boring into me. We turned into the prep room, then the breakfast room, through the dining room, the hallway, then foyer and out the front door. We walked down the front steps, past the fountain and began down the drive way.

We continued walking until the house grew further behind us, the setting sun glistening off the windows creating what looked like portals to another world. If only they were.

We walked for quite some time before Myrna finally spoke. "I don't know what to make of you Connie. Everything was fine at first. You liked Eli, that was obvious, but you were only friends, that was obvious too. Then you became more." She looked at me waiting for a reply but I didn't dare answer. "I know you did. I have no proof, but I know it. I understood that, it happens. I don't condone it and I want it to end as I am sure you realize, but I do understand it. But now, there is Thomas Sarrington and this I am having trouble with. When you went missing today I thought you were with Eli, but I soon realized you weren't. As far as I could tell you had not gone off with anybody and I was ready to fire you when you returned. But you showed up with the Sarringtons and Thomas has made it clear that you are not to be fired. I can go to his father naturally, but I won't. I know my place, what the Sarringtons want done, no matter which of them it is, is done. Now of course I know you didn't leave with Thomas. He, Robert and Jane left the house well after you went missing. My real question is why he would walk back with you, why he would talk to you, and why he would protect you. This is what puzzles me. I don't know what you have done to cause his interest Miss Moore and I don't know what your goal is, but I'm going to be very clear. Men like Thomas Sarrington do not fall in love with women like you. Cinderella stays in the kitchen, sleeping in the fireplace, after the ball and the romance are over. You are not living a fairytale Miss Moore; you are playing a game and a stupid one at that, and I don't like games. I don't like people who don't know their place, and I don't like people who trample on the feelings of others." I remained silent though I wanted desperately to explain.

"You need to think about whether or not this is a game you really want to play. It's not just you that you are rolling the dice with. You have a family who depends on you and you have Emma who recommended you. If you continue to play, you will lose." Myrna paused as we came to an abrupt halt within a few feet of the main gate. "And then there will only be one path left for you to take. Make your next move wisely."

Myrna turned and began to walk back towards the house leaving me staring out through the iron bars onto the road ahead.

I stood there for a while until Will poked his head out of the guard house and asked if I was alright. I laughed at the question. Was I? I didn't know. I nodded and turned to head back to the house. I had been thinking as I stood there staring at the tempting open road behind metal bars, of how much I felt trapped. I was being attacked for something that was not even a reality, by three different people. It was ridiculous, and what could I do about it if they had each already made up their minds as they seemed to have done. I was frustrated and hurt. Why did these people think this way of me? Ann I really didn't care about, and Myrna, I kept trying to remind myself of all she had been through, but that Eli, with whom I had shared so much, would just decide that my character was so lacking, that was truly a blow.

At first I had wanted to run to Eli and explain everything; reassure him yet again of my loyalty, but as I walked further I found, I didn't care. He could come to me and apologize, until then I didn't want to see him. I didn't want to see anyone. I had started the day alone and I wanted to end it that way.

Alone. I laughed as it occurred to me that Myrna had left me to walk back by myself and she had done the same. If I had had any doubts as to the insincerity of her bear concerns previously, they were doubts no longer.

I should have known that the very fact that I did not want to see Eli would draw him like a magnet. It wasn't long before I saw him striding towards me. I didn't know whether he wanted to see if Myrna had put me out or if he wanted to confront me? Either way I wasn't in the mood to be meek and apologetic.

I waited for him to say something as we approached one another. He stopped when I was no more than twenty feet from him but still he said nothing. I slowed, but I didn't stop and as I passed him, I didn't say a word either.

"Connie!" Eli yelled.

I didn't respond. There was silence then the sound of him running up behind me. He grabbed me by the arm and I stopped. I looked down at his hand, not at his face, not because I was ashamed as I had often done before, but

because I was mad. I raised my eyes to his. My look was not an "I'm sorry." It was a "Get your damn hand off of me."
Eli let me go. I turned away from him and began to walk.
"Connie!" Eli called after me. "Are you not going to talk to me?! I don't deserve an explanation?!"
I don't know if I had simply had enough or if the stars were aligning a certain way, giving me the courage I normally lacked, but the fire that had been growing in me as I walked unleashed itself on him. I turned to face him.
"No." I said, my eyes fixed and back straight. I was in the right here and it was time he realized it. "No, you don't deserve anything. Repeatedly I have humbled myself and apologized to you. For what?! For having a different opinion? For having a fear? For having a friend? None of them transgressions yet I would plead with you like a sinner before God hoping for absolution. But not this time. What you implied in the garage, how dare you! I have been nothing but loyal to you. I have given you all of me and this insult is how you repay me? Is that what you think of me?! You would assume the worst of me so easily. I have been faithful to you, in every way, you can believe it or not, but if you don't then don't chase after me and don't stand here and demand that I answer to you, because if that's the case then I have no answer for you other than to say leave me alone. If you think so little of me, I don't want to hear it. I'm not going to justify my actions to you. My interactions with Tom have been completely unplanned and my conversations innocent. My conscious is clear and I'm content in that. "

I turned away from him and resumed my walk back to the house. I was shaking, but I had done it. I stood up for myself and I was proud. When I reached the half way mark I heard footsteps coming up fast behind me. It had been more than ten minutes by my estimate since I had turned away from Eli and I had stopped wondering if he would run after me, not that I had planned on him to, but I wanted to be prepared if he did.

Once more I felt his hand grab hold of my arm. I stopped and looked down at his hand once again, though this time I didn't turn to face him.

"I'm sorry Connie." He said. "You're right. You're absolutely right. You haven't given me any reason to doubt you, and I don't, not really. I just get scared. I worry that you'll realize that you're too good for me and you'll cast me aside for someone more worthy of you. Now with the way I've acted and the things I've said, it just proves my fears are justified. You should cast me aside, but I hope you won't. Please forgive me Connie. You can't understand how much you mean to me, how much I love you. It makes me feel out of control and it scares me, the intensity of it. "

Tears filled my eyes as I turned my body to be enveloped by Eli's arms. "How could someone always so sure of themselves say such things?" I asked. "If anything you have it backwards."

"You're so beautiful." He said, wiping a tear from my cheek. "Even when you cry."

Scooping me up, he carried me into the woods before setting me back on my feet. I met his mouth with my own, eager to taste his lips. Without thinking I jumped back into his arms wrapping my legs around his waist. He stumbled backwards a few steps before regaining his footing and stepped towards a nearby tree, pressed my back against it. His hands searched frantically under my dress and pressing his fingertips against the outside of my underwear caused me to moan, the sensitive area between my legs swelling and pulsating. Using a finger he pulled the underwear aside exposing my sex. Moving his hands away he fumbled to release his own as I tightened my grip on his waist. Slowly guiding himself into me he moved his hands to my hips taking me firmly in his grasp. I liked the feeling of his hands on my hips. It made me feel lush and womanly and I ground into him, arching my back to escape the rough bark of the tree that tormented me. I leaned in resting my head on Eli's shoulder and he backed up wrapping his arms around my back, pulling me tight against him as he thrust into me deeper and faster. My face and chest grew hotter as tension built up in my sex. The sensation increased more and more until it seemed to burst, a sudden release. Ripples of pleasure coursed through me, beginning in my sex and rising up in waves through my belly before fading into my chest. I let out my breath and felt Eli pulsate inside me, his own pleasure coming to fruition.

 Slowly I withdrew my legs and slid from him, standing wobbly on the ground, Eli's arms steadying me. He leaned in and kissed my forehead. I blushed. I didn't know how to explain what had just happened to me. It was nothing I had ever heard of before, but whatever it was, I hoped it would happen again.

11

Things went back to normal. Myrna, though still watchful, seemed to relent once she thought Eli had done away with me. Ann was acting oddly, but I had grown use to that. Tom was staying out of sight and Eli and I had resumed our secret meetings. Unfortunately it didn't last.

Late Thursday afternoon a telegram arrived for Eli. His mother who had been sick for some time was not expected to last much longer and had asked that he come home. Everything happened so fast. Within an hour Eli was backed and ready to go. Ken would drive him to the station where he would board the first train of his journey. He had to take two and even then it wasn't enough to get him there. It would get him to Nashville where his brother would be waiting to pick him up if all went according to plan. Eli didn't want to waste a minute waiting to formulate a plan through telegrams, so he had begun making phone calls to stations, came up with a route and sprang to put it into action immediately, he wouldn't wait to hear that they would be there, who knew how long that could take. He would simply send out a telegram with the details and hope it worked out.

I wanted to go with Eli, but we both knew that wasn't possible. We barely had time to speak privately at all, but we managed to take a moment behind the garage. I was grateful for it. It had taken what seemed like forever to get and I was on the verge of throwing everything to the wind and going to him right out in the open.

The orange light of the setting sun framed Eli's body making it appear to glow. I watched him climb into the Packard and as the last rays of sunlight disappeared from the horizon, so did he.

My sleep was restless that night. Tired of tossing and turning, I got up and went to the kitchen to get a glass of warm milk. I sat at the table in the dark wondering how Eli's trip was going and whether or not he was having trouble sleeping as well. Finishing the milk, I rose to take the glass over to the sink when the kitchen door opened slowly, the light from beyond casting an ever widening beam across the floor. Peter quietly walked through the door and began to make his way towards our hall. He hadn't seen me standing there, which caused him to jump when I whispered his name. He looked relieved and made his way over.

"Connie!" He whispered. "I was coming to find you. I need you to come with me."

"Why? Where are we going?" I asked.

"Upstairs." He whispered pointing with his finger.

I followed behind him as quietly as I could.

"What is it Peter? Why do you need me?" I asked as we began to climb the stairs. It was the first time I had ever left the main floor and I was disappointed that it was too dark to make out much. Peter didn't answer, he simply "shushed" me, waving his hands in irritation.

We made our way down a long, wide hall. In the dim light I could see someone huddled on the floor in the corner. It was Ann. She was rocking, her arms wrapped around her legs and hair falling loose over her face. One eye peeked out from behind the red strands. It had the same wild look I had seen before.

I crouched down on the floor in front of her.

"Ann." I said softly. "Are you okay?"

She looked right through me as if I wasn't even there. I asked again and still she wouldn't look me in eyes, but she did begin to whisper something, whether it was in reply or not I couldn't tell. It wasn't coherent, just a low rumble of words spoken too softly and too close together to be recognizable.

"We have to pick her up and take her downstairs to her room." Peter said.

"What's wrong with her? Why is she up here?" I asked.

Peter looked beyond me to a closed door and then back at Ann.

"Please Connie, just help me lift her up." He said.

We positioned ourselves on either side of Ann and pulled her to her feet. Placing her arms over our shoulders we led her down the stairs. It was slow moving, but otherwise easy. Ann was not in enough of her right mind to either help or resist. Within ten minutes we had her in her bed. I leaned over to pull up her blanket when she seemed to realize who I was. She looked in my eyes.

"You'll see." She said. Then she laughed and looked up at the ceiling as if I had never been there.

I straightened up and looked at Peter who was backing out of the room. I followed him out to the prep room.

"Peter, what is going on?" I asked.

"Don't worry about it Connie. It doesn't matter now." Peter answered.

I opened my mouth to demand he tell me when he cut me off.

"Thanks, really." He said, walking out of the room before I could get another word out.

I walked back to my room. As I reached my door I heard the sound of humming, very low, coming from Ann's room. I listened for a second, trying to make out the tune, a manic laugh cut in suddenly, sending chills down my back. I opened my door quickly as the humming resumed. Shutting the door I leaned against it, trying to make sense of what had just happened. I began to walk to my bed, but turned around halfway. For the first time, I locked my door.

When I arrived at breakfast the next morning Ann was already there. She smiled in greeting, looking as normal as I had ever seen her. Actually she seemed more normal. She had a calmness about her.

"Good morning Connie." Ann said. "Did you sleep well last night?"

I didn't know how to respond. Was she mocking me or did she not remember what had happened just a few hours earlier?

"I wouldn't say that exactly." I replied, grapping my breakfast and leaning back against the counter.

"Hmmm." She said, rising to take her plate to the sink. Ann placed it in the sink very gently so it didn't make even the slightest sound. She turned to me and smiled wide, her white teeth flashing. "What a pity."

With that she left the kitchen.

"She seems different today doesn't she?' Paul said. "Better than she has in a while. Whatever it is I hope it keeps up."

I nodded in reply. I couldn't exactly tell Paul that I found her more frightening with each passing night.

I went about my day as usual, spending it in the laundry with Darla. The day was dragging on. It had not even reached lunch yet when I heard a shrill scream. It sounded like a word, but I couldn't make it out. Darla and I looked at each other and ran out of the laundry room. The others had heard the scream as well and we all ran into the main area of the house. The scream came again.

"Connie!"

It was Ann's voice. Almost everyone was standing at the bottom of the stairs, staring up them but not daring to ascend. They turned and looked at me.

"Connie!" she screamed again.

I ran past them all, taking the stairs two and three at a time. If she was in trouble I needed to get to her quickly. Jane and Robert along with Peter and some of the other servants were standing at the top of the stairs looking towards the hallway I had helped remove Ann from the previous night. They looked bewildered and of no inclination to be the ones to discover what was going on.

"Connie!" Myrna called out from somewhere behind me. "What is going on?"

I looked over my shoulder quickly, she was only half way up the stairs, and yelled back that I didn't know.

The closed door that Peter had glanced at now stood wide open and sunlight flooded into the hall from the room beyond. I slowed my pace within a few feet of the door. I had been in a hurry to get to Ann, but now I wasn't so sure if I wanted to find out why she was screaming, and especially why it was my name.

I cautiously crossed the threshold into the room. The first thing I saw was Tom. He was standing in front of what I later learned was his bed with his hands raised up in front of his chest as if he was trying to calm someone. His eyes immediately moved to mine. They were filled with fear. Tom looked away from me and I followed. Ann was standing between Tom and the interior wall. She looked composed, neat and in charge, holding a revolver makes you feel that way.

"Connie." She said, her voice sickeningly sweet. "You made it."

Myrna came running into the room, stopping so abruptly she almost lost her footing.

"Ann, what are you doing?" Myrna panted.

Ann smirked, moving the revolver in her hand from side to side. "I'm about to teach a lesson."

"What lesson?" Myrna asked. My eyes darted back and forth between the two women.

"An important one." She answered. "One about love, and fidelity." She looked at Tom who shook his head slowly. "One about conniving and backstabbing and consequences." Now she looked at me.

"I don't understand Ann." Myrna said. "Why don't you give me the gun and then you can explain it to me."

Ann laughed. "No. I will not be giving you this gun. I need it. I have plans. But I will explain it if you like. Good and loud" she raised her voice "so everyone at the end of the hall can hear it too."

"Ann don't. Please, don't." Tom pleaded. "Just give me the gun and we'll talk about it. Nobody else needs to be involved."

"But they are involved. Connie is involved." Ann replied.

"Ann, I don't know what's going on here, but we can figure it out. Just hand Tom the gun." I said.

"You don't know what's going on here?!" Ann shouted, before bringing her voice back to quiet calmness once more. "How dare you stand there and act like you're oblivious, like you're innocent. You have known about my feelings for Tom from the beginning."

"Yes. I have." I replied. "But I don't understand what that has to do with me or why you have a gun."

"You knew that I loved Tom and you knew he wanted me, and you were jealous. You had to have Tom and Eli. Why? Why couldn't you just be happy with Eli?" Ann was pleading, tears forming in her eyes.

"Ann I never went after Tom. Please, let's talk about this. It's all a misunderstanding." I said.

"And you!" Ann turned to Tom, the anger rising up again after its momentary hiatus. "You used me. You never cared about me at all. I gave myself to you and you turned me into a whore, and now I am damned! But you still don't care. You only care about your devilish, carnal lust. You mounted me like some animal, something bestial and beneath you and I still loved you. I still hoped one day you would see everything we could be together, but you cast me aside for a new pet."

Ann began to weep uncontrollably. I looked at Tom waiting for him to say something to her, but he remained silent.

Ann regained her composure quickly and steadied the revolver. "But it doesn't matter now." She said. "You made your choice, both of you," Ann looked at me quickly then back at Tom "and every choice has a consequence. And now I have a choice to make."

"Ann stop." Tom said. "Don't do this."

Ann pointed the gun at Tom. "Eenie."

Then at me. "Meanie."

Then at Tom again. "Minee"

Then once again she aimed the gun at me. My heart pounded in my chest as my throat tightened. I couldn't speak; the swooshing sound of blood coursing through veins filled my ears. Ann paused for a second and raised the revolver to her head. "Moe."

I closed my eyes, not wanting to witness what would follow. The loud blast as the gun went off caused me to involuntarily duck. I could feel plaster raining down from the ceiling and hitting the top of my head. I opened my eyes slowly, scared of what I might see. But there was no blood. Instead Tom was struggling with Ann on the floor. She screamed at him. I ran towards them, Myrna close behind me. I helped Tom hold Ann down as Myrna pried the gun from her hands.

Ann lay sobbing on the floor as Tom leaned over her, holding her tight, tears streaming down his face leaving wet dots on her black uniform.

Within seconds the room was filled with people, voices running over each other. Everyone was talking at once, everyone, but us four.

Finally Myrna spoke raising her voice above the others, bringing everyone to attention. "I would like everyone who just entered the room, with the exception of Robert and Jane to leave. Go back to what you were doing, as long as it wasn't on this level. If it was, go find something else to do."
Once the room cleared Robert was the first one to speak.
"What happened here?" he demanded.
"Nothing." Tom said. "Just an accident."
'Don't bullshit me Tom." Robert snapped. "I know what happened. I was down the hall. I heard everything. I know this little bitch just tried to shoot somebody. What I want is details. And while you give them, Myrna you telephone the police and also our parents at the townhouse in the city. Tell them what happened but tell them I am dealing with it so they don't need to cut their trip short."
"No." Tom said. "Myrna, don't move."
"What?!" Robert asked. "Don't try to undermine me Tom! If you had just listened to me in the first place......"
"There is no reason to call the police Robert. No one was hurt." Tom cut him off.

"Are you crazy Tom?!" Jane said her voice unsteady. "You cannot expect us to all pretend nothing happened. That girl needs to be in jail. I don't want her in this house one second longer than it takes for the police to come and haul her away. If we could drag her outside to wait for them it would be even better."

"I don't want the police involved. I don't want mother and father involved either. It was a misunderstanding, that's all. Don't ruin her life over a mistake. No real harm done." Tom said. His voice sounded calm, but his body was shaking.

"Like hell!" Robert replied. "She tried to kill one of you and you want us to just pretend nothing happened! We should just let her get back to her dusting!"

"No." Tom shook his head. "No, I realize that isn't possible, that isn't what I am saying, but don't ruin her life. It was my fault too. Constance and Myrna were just innocent bystanders, but I'm not blameless. We'll send her home, immediately. She won't spend another night in the house." Tom looked at his brother. "Robert, she's so young."

Robert looked down at Ann who stared back at him with frightened eyes, wet hair matted against her cheeks.

Robert sighed. "What about the ceiling? How are you going to explain that?"

"I'll think of something." Tom said.

Jane opened her mouth to protest but Robert shook his head and she closed it. Tom stood up and crossed over to his sister, kissing her on the cheek. "Lovely Jane," he said. "you know you couldn't really send her off to prison or a nut house. I know you. You're just upset right now because you care so much for me." Tom looked at Robert. "Take Jane to her room and sit with her for a while. I'll take care of everything."

Jane and Robert left the room and Tom turned his attention to Myrna and I. "Constance, are you alright?" I nodded my head in reply. "Myrna, what about you, are you okay?" he asked.

"Yes. I'm fine." She replied.

"Good." Tom said. "Constance, go down stairs and find Ken. Tell him to get the car ready. Then I want you to go to Ann's room and pack her things. Don't say anything to anyone if they ask you what happened. They probably heard enough. Just tell them that I will talk to them all later. When you're done come back up here and let us know."

When I got back to the room Ann's hair had been brushed and pulled back and her face had been washed. She was sitting on the foot of the bed next to Tom staring ahead motionless, Tom's hand resting on her thigh. Myrna was standing by the window looking outside.
"Ken is ready." I said as I set Ann's suitcase on the floor beside my feet.
"Okay. "Tom replied. "Myrna, will you take Ann's things down please and get her her pay for the month? Then tell Ken where he's headed. Constance, can you help me walk Ann to the car?"

Myrna and I passed each other. She picked up the suitcase and left the room without saying a word. Tom stood up and pulled Ann gently to her feet. I reached out taking her arm. Her pale white skin reminded me of porcelain; she looked just as fragile.

We slowly made our way out to the car. Within moments a crowd that contained almost every worker at the estate gathered around the perimeter of the driveway. I let go of Ann's arm and stepped back slightly to let Tom help her into the back seat. She looked down at her arm, registering the absence and turned her eyes to mine. She didn't say anything but she didn't need to. I could see the shame and hurt plainly. A chill swept over me, as I thought of something I had heard my grandmother say many times when I was growing up. *"There but for the grace of God go I."*

Tom got Ann situated in the car and leaned close to her, kissing her forehead. He held his lips to her for a moment, his eyes drawn shut, then he stood up and closed the car door.

No one made a sound as we watched the car drive away. All of us standing like dozens of stone statues until it was no longer in sight.

Tom turned to address us.

"I know you all have questions. I am sorry that your day has been interrupted by these unfortunate events. The gun shot you heard was me. I was cleaning one of the revolvers in my room when it accidently went off. Some of you may have heard some things that were said, but they are not your concern and when my parents return no one is to speak to them about anything that happened today or anything they may have heard otherwise you will find yourself quickly removed from our service. I will make sure of it. If they ask you, tell them what I just told you, a gun went off, due to my carelessness. Otherwise, a misjudgment was made, that's all you need to know. Please return to your work."

Tom looked at me, his voice became softer. "Are you okay Constance? Really?"

"I'm fine." I said.

"I'm sorry that you had to go through all that." He said. "I think you should take the rest of the day off. Myrna!" Myrna came over to us. "I think Constance should take the rest of the day off. Why don't you as well."

"It's not necessary for me. I would feel better if I got back to work, but I agree, Connie would probably do well to go rest in her room until dinner."

I felt weary and was glad to be told to go lie down. I needed to think about everything that had happened and try to make sense of it and anything that would keep me away from the questions that would surely flood in was welcome. I thanked them both and walked away, feeling their eyes on me as I went. Once in my room, I locked my door for the second time. I didn't want anyone coming in, not even Emma, though I knew she must be beside herself with worry, but I wanted time to process everything.

I flipped the switch, turning off the overhead light and walked the short distance to my bed. Crawling on top of the blanket I sat in the darkness with my back against the wall and let the tears flow out of me in rolling waves.

    I didn't leave my room for lunch, nor did I leave it for dinner. Knocks would come and questions but still I would lie on my bed, dismissing them quickly and with as few words as possible, and never, ever rising. I listened to the sounds of work. I listened to the voices, usually they were too low to understand but sometimes an audible word would float to me under the door along the thin line of light. I listened to the bathroom shower turn on and the doors open and close. I listened to the good nights and still I lay in bed. I would sleep and wake up by turns and cry by turns as well. I thought of Eli and how I wished he had been there. I replayed the events of the day over and over in my head. Ann's eyes when she screamed at Tom. The heightened sensation of every cell in my body as the revolver made its way toward me. The feel of the plaster hitting the top of my head. The look of Tom leaning over Ann with tears streaming from his face. Over and over, on and on. I thought again of my grandmother's phrase. Could that have been me? Could I find myself one day so desperate? So hurt? I thought of my life. I had escaped death twice since I had come to the estate and it came to my attention that the day would inevitably come when I would not and when it did, how would I feel about the life I was losing?

    I remained on the bed long after the house became quiet and still. Though I was hungry and thirsty, I did not want to venture out while there was still any possibility I might run into someone else. After what I figured must have been at least one in the morning, I finally made my way to the kitchen. It was dark, but I didn't turn on a light. I knew what I wanted and found it quickly, milk and bread, nothing more. I sat down at the table just as I had the night before. The thought made me shudder. Pushing the thought aside, I ate quickly, propelled by the hunger that was seizing me fully. When I finished I didn't know what to do. I wasn't tired and

I didn't want to go back to my room yet. I thought briefly of going outside, but decided against it. To tempt Fate twice in one day, even I was not that foolish. I chose to go to the library instead. I had snuck there many times and a new book would surely provide a distraction.

I walked quietly through the prep room, then the breakfast room and the dining room, as I entered the hall I saw light coming from the billiard room. I stopped for a moment and listened, but I couldn't hear any noise. Thinking someone must have simply left a light on, I walked to the room to turn it off, but the room was not empty as I had supposed.

When I entered, Tom, who was sitting in an oversized chestnut brown leather chair, looked up at me, his blue eyes rimmed with red, a half empty bottle in his hand. He smiled weakly.

"Constance." he said. "I should have known you would come."

He looked broken. I walked over to him and sat down in a matching chair, leaning forward; afraid I might be swallowed by it if I dared to lay back.

"Are you okay?" I asked.

"I didn't want to hurt her Constance. The things she said to me. I never thought them. I never intended any of it."

"Did you love Ann?" I asked.

"Yes, no, I don't know, maybe." Staring at the floor, Tom shook his head. "When I came back from school, I couldn't help myself. She was so lovely, so delicate. And the way she looked at me Constance, it was akin to worship. She was so innocent, so naïve. I was more than human to her. It was intoxicating. I didn't plan on it going as far as it did. I would pass her in the hall and stop to say something to her and she would light up, her green eyes would grow large and her face would flush, rosy against her pale freckled skin. Then I would touch her when we spoke, just her shoulder or her hand, causing desire to course through me like electricity, soon it went further and I was leaning in to whisper in her ear, then stealing kisses until finally I found myself in one of the guest rooms, undressing her with trembling hands. It happened so fast. Within no time we were in each other's arms almost daily." Tom paused and looked up at me but I didn't reply. He returned his gaze to the floor and began again.

"But did I love her? I don't know. I think I did, I think I do. I care for her, deeply in fact. I didn't want her hurt and even now I hate the thought of her in pain. I wasn't trying to use her. I just thought we were enjoying each other. Giving each other…….. something." He fidgeted with the bottle, frustrated. "I guess I do love her in some sense, but it's not the kind of love she wants. I have been with women before Constance and she was more to me than any of them ever were. I wanted to have a relationship with her, not marriage, but something more than just a summer fling. But now, seeing what my carelessness has done. My heart broke. I wish I had never begun any of it, that I could turn it all back and spare her fragile soul all the pain I caused her. I will never forgive myself."

I didn't know what to say. What words could there possibly be?

"I'm sorry Constance."

"I know Tom." I said. "It's okay." I reached out and patted his hand, smiling as best as I could. It wasn't his fault entirely. They came from different worlds.

"Tom," I asked "why did she break down, if everything was going so well?"

"She became suspicious when I had her deliver that newspaper clipping to you. She thought that you and I must have the same relationship that she and I shared. I was having a hard time convincing her otherwise and she would rage at me, though it was easily contained. I could simply take her in my arms and her defenses would drop. When you came upon Robert and Jane and I down by the river, I had told them I planned on continuing my relationship with Ann after I went back to school. They had known about it here. I had confided in them, we have always been close, though I admit, I find it easier to talk to you, you have no stock in any of my decisions, but they didn't like the idea. It was too much like courtship to them. Over the next few days they pressured me to end it with her, that there was no reason to go on with a relationship that had no future. Eventually I conceded and last night I told Ann. She dropped on her knees to the floor, stunned. She hadn't expected it. She had believed we would go on together forever. I tried to make her understand. To see that while I did care for her and did want to be with her, that it just wasn't reality. She cried and pleaded with me. I hated to see it. Then it was like a switch flipped and she stopped, sitting up straight. She felt it was all clear. It was you. You were to blame. I tried to reassure her that nothing had ever happened between the two of us. It took a long while, but again the switch would flip and she was back to crying and pleading and you were forgotten. Back and forth it would go. As the hours wore on I was exhausted and so was she. She just sat on the floor muttering to herself. I didn't know what to do, so I sat her outside of the door, hoping she would get up and go down to her room, but she didn't. It was cruel. I know it was, but I didn't know what else to do, and it didn't help, so I called for Peter and shut the door."

Tom took a drink from the bottle, then another. "I should have realized that she wouldn't be able to handle it. She had begun to act strange already. It started even before I had her deliver the note to you. She would burst into tears, filled with guilt or fear of what God was going to do to her, to us. Sometimes it wouldn't make any sense and it would scare me. I don't know. I guess I was just naïve myself, thinking I could be so cavalier and it would all be okay, but I've always been used to women who understood, or, maybe they just pretended to."

We sat in silence for a while, Tom lost in his thoughts and I having no words of wisdom or comfort to offer him.

"Do you hate me now?" Tom asked.

"No." I said. "I don't. You're kindhearted Tom. I don't think you meant to hurt Ann. I saw the way it hurt you. It was real. I know that. Time will heal it, that's all we can hope for. The past can't be changed. You're good, you are, you don't need to doubt it and Ann will be okay. She's young, and so are you, and so am I for that matter, and the young never mourn long. It'll be alright. You'll see."
"I'm glad you're here."
"Me too." I replied. "Now you should sleep if you can. You'll feel better in the morning. Everything looks better in the light of a new day." I stood up and helped Tom to his feet, taking the bottle from him and placing it on the small side table. He wobbled for a moment, but found his bearings.
"Your name suits you Constance." He said as he hugged me.

I got to bed late and the morning came early. I felt as if my body was made of lead as I pulled myself from bed and down to the bathroom. The hot water of the shower did little to help in waking me, rather the comfort of the water as it ran down my body and the warmth of the steam as it surrounded me like a blanket simply made me want to crawl right back to where I had come from and I decided to do just that. After I dressed, instead of going to the kitchen as I normally would I went back to my room and laid down once again, letting my eyes close in sweet surrender. I had no worries that I would be allowed to sleep away my day. If I didn't show up in the kitchen soon, someone would come for me. In that knowledge I let myself drift for what little I might be able.
A knock did come, just as I had assumed it would. It was rapid and purposeful, Myrna's knock.
"Come in." I called.
Myrna came into the room, closing the door behind her. I was already sitting up preparing to stand, but the fact that Myrna had actually come into the room, and what's more, shut the door, compelled me to keep my sitting position.

"Connie," Myrna said, fidgeting with her hands. The meekness of her demeanor was not something I was accustomed to and it made me feel awkward. "I wanted to tell you I'm sorry. I realize now that what I had assumed about you in regards to Tom Sarrington was false," she paused, "or at least it appears to be." There was the Myrna I was used to. "So I just wanted to apologize. I like to admit my mistakes, for my own conscience sake. "

"Thank you." I said.

"Are you feeling alright this morning?" she asked.

"Yes. Tired, but otherwise, fine." I replied.

"Good, good." Myrna let out a long breath. "I have decided that I would like you to go back to the city tomorrow to visit your family. In light of recent events I think it would be beneficial and I am sure you would like to see them all regardless. I know it is not your day off, but we'll make an exception."

"Thank you." I said again.

"I need to go to town tomorrow anyway. I need to get a girl to replace Ann, or rather you, since you will be moving up to take Ann's place. I have been making calls and think I have found just the girl and I need her here as soon as possible. The estate really should never be shorthanded but with Mr. and Mrs. Sarrington coming back from the city Monday and the children headed back out to their schools later in the week, now it is especially important that all run smoothly. So," Myrna offered up one of her rare smiles, "Your promotion starts today. No laundry room for you, instead you will be in the billiard room. It looks as if one of the boys spent some time in there last night. Tomorrow we will leave bright and early. I want to be on the road by seven."

"Okay." I said." Thank you again."

Myrna nodded and turned to leave, holding the door open for me.

I was grateful to Myrna for not only raising me up out of the laundry room, but also for doing it immediately. I would not have to endure Darla a second longer. Myrna continued to elicit my affection when she also remained in the kitchen during breakfast. I was able to eat in complete peace, without a single question or comment on the previous day's events and that was something to be thankful about.

After breakfast I made my way immediately to the billiard room. It was littered with cigarette butts and ashes everywhere, empty bottles. I didn't know why I hadn't noticed it the night before. I guess I was still trying to see as little as possible after seeing far too much. After lunch, which Myrna graciously joined us for as well, I made my way upstairs. I was to clean some of the guestrooms that were off the opposite hall to the one I had journeyed so many times the previous day. They were magnificent rooms, far grander than the ones I was used to seeing at the Clare Regency, though I had heard some of those were quite grand as well; I had just never set foot in them. Each room consisted of a large bed with an imposing wooden headboard with fabric paneling draped behind it and valanced above. There was a dressing table and a large bureau in each as well as individual sitting areas. What I found most intriguing was that each room had a different color scheme. One room was purple, another was green, another golden. It made me think of a story I had read when I was younger by Edgar Allen Poe in which the guests of a great ball make their way through many different colored rooms, but in the end they all succumb to death. The story had been quiet frightening, and as I thought of it another thought occurred to me. Tom had said that the flirtation he and Ann shared had culminated in one of the guest rooms. I wondered if it had taken place in one of the other rooms I had cleaned earlier or if it was in the deep red room that I occupied. I shuddered. Another story of ill-conceived revelry that did not end well.

When I entered the kitchen for dinner Myrna was not there, though it seemed as if everyone else was. Even a few of those who usually weren't at our dinner shift; Matilda, Frank, Greg. My stomach sank, all appetite gone. I took a plate of Shepard's Pie, but only for appearance sake, and leaned against the wall in the farthest corner of the kitchen, hoping vainly that I would blend into it. Darla wasted no time, making sure I wouldn't.

"Now ya gonna tell us what happ'n yes'r day straight out or ya gonna make us beg?"

"I wasn't planning on doing either." I replied. "I think Tom did a good job already."

"Tom is it?" Darla said. "Tom. Hmmph. Well, I think Tom didn't say nothing worth hearin' or believin' and I thinks we gots a right to ask."

"Well I think," Alan said, "You should button that mouth of yours Darla before Myrna walks through the door. She's done been in here breakfast and lunch and I'm not about to risk losing my job just to hear what we all already know."

"We don't all already know." Darla said. "I didn't know it was a *Tom*, involved. I thought it was Thomas."

I glared at Darla.

"She doesn't need to explain anything to you Darla." Emma said. "She's been through a lot and I don't blame her for not wanting to be questioned about it by you or me or anybody else."

"It's alright Emma." I said. "Darla, I call him Tom because he told me to call him Tom. There isn't anything in that. I met him on the grounds by chance; he introduced himself as Tom and told me to call him that, end of story. As to what happened yesterday, you can feign ignorance if you want but everybody was around. You ran to the foot of the stairs right alongside of me, you might not have climbed them, but I'm sure if anybody heard enough to figure out what it was all about it was you. *Tom* told you what he wanted done, you can risk it all, like Alan said, if you want, but I don't feel like talking about it with you. Not now and probably not ever, and I'm not going to."

I handed my plate to Emma and walked out the door. The cool August night air hit my face and arms, causing my skin to bump, but it was welcome. I stood at the end of the garage trying to decide where to go. I knew I couldn't go too far, even in light of recent events I couldn't be certain Myrna would be lenient if I ventured down to the river, but I still wanted to be outside in a place where I wouldn't be easily found. Somewhere close but secluded. The back side of the garage was too close, but it made me think of another such place. At the far side of the garden stood a building used for storage in close proximity to the pool. I could sit behind it and be shielded from anyone, no matter where they were headed, but I would still be close enough to hear if my name was called.

It took little time to get there. I lowered myself to sit on the grass and leaned my back against the cold stone wall. The sky was clear and the moon was low in the sky, casting little light. The stars stretched out above. I felt peaceful, for the first time in days. A white streak flashed across the sky, a shooting star. Some people believe that a falling star is an omen of ill, but others believe that they grant you a wish. I hoped it was the later who were right. A few minutes later, another star, though not as bright this time shot across the heavens.

I heard the sound of someone or something walking. My heart began to race as I thought of the bear. I looked in the direction of the sound, preparing to run if necessary. The sound grew closer. It was human footsteps I decided, no bear would walk with such short quick steps. I leaned back against the wall and waited to see if they would pass. The sound was right on top of me and within seconds, Frank Golden came around the corner of the building.
"Hello Connie." Frank said. "Out to watch the Persiads?"
"The what? No." I answered.
"The Persiads. It's a meteor shower." He explained, pointing at the sky with a lit cigarette, "Goes on the same time every year. Have you seen any shooting stars?"
"Yes actually, I have, two." I answered.
"Good. There should be more as the night goes on."

"I don't plan on being here much longer." I said. I hadn't liked Frank from the beginning and the more I was around him and the more I learned about him, the less I wanted to be in his presence.

"No? You just got here." Frank said flicking his cigarette off into the distance, making a little orange streak across the air, mimicking the ones I had seen above. He squatted down in front of me, almost hovering, mere inches from my face. "You don't like my company?"

"I'm ready to go back inside is all. I just wanted to get a little fresh air." I answered.

"I understand. I'm not good enough for you. I'm not Eli or *Tom*." He reached out and brushed my thigh. "Maybe I'm better and you just don't know it yet."

I pushed Frank's hand away and stood up, but he grabbed my arm and pulled me down to the ground hard.

'Let me go Frank." I said trying to twist myself out of his grasp.

"Just give me a chance Connie. That's all I'm asking. Take a little bit of time to get to know me. You might like it."

"I don't want to know you any better. Now let me go!"

"Don't act so high and mighty." He spat. "Eli, Thomas Sarrington and who knows who else. You're just playing hard to get, but I know what you really are and I know what you want."

I tried again to pull away from him, but he tightened his grip, using both hands, instead of one. I kicked at him, but it didn't do any good, he was pushing me down flat. He put his legs between mine to spread them. I let out a scream, but he cut it too short to do any good, quickly covering my mouth with his hand.

"Shut up you stupid bitch!" His eyes bore into mine. He looked like no man I had ever seen, his face red and veins pushing out in his forehead, pulsating, spittle foaming at the corners of his mouth.

   Tears welled up in my eyes as I tried to shake my head no, but his hand on my mouth was pressing my head too hard against the ground. I tried to move my legs and arms, but they did nothing, he was too strong. I scratched at what little bit of him I could reach with my fingers. He had both my arms pinned to my chest with one strong gripping hand. "Stay still goddamn it!" He said, but I refused to obey.

He leaned down close to my ear. "Scream again and I will snap your fucking neck." He whispered, then slowly he lifted his hand off my mouth. I looked at him, my eyes wide, but I didn't scream.

"Frank, please, stop." I pleaded. "Don't do this."

He laughed at me as he struggled to free himself from his pants. "Why? You want this."

"No, I don't, please. " I said.

"Of course you do. You'll enjoy it." He said, slowly running his hand down my cheek, "And so will I."

In an instant I turned and bit his hand hard; the taste of sweat and blood filling my mouth. He screamed and grabbed his hand. Taking my chance I pushed hard with my hands, sending him falling onto his back as I sprang to my feet and began to run. Within seconds he was closing in on me, but I was too close to the house, I had to be safe. I felt his hand grab my arm and he pulled me back into him. I started to scream but he twisted my arm hard behind me causing my breath to catch in my throat.

"Say a word." He panted into my ear." A single word, to anyone, and I will sneak into your room while you sleep and slit your throat. Not just yours, Emma's too." Releasing my arm he walked in front of me and grinned. "Nobody would believe you anyway, especially not Eli." He looked down at his bloody finger, then spitting on the ground in front of me walked to the stairs and above to his quarters.

I stood shaking for a moment, listening to him whistle as he ascended the stairs. The sound of the door shutting releasing my feet to move. I straightened my clothes and walked in the house.

"Are you okay Connie?" Emma asked.

"Yes." I said, quickly making my way through the kitchen to the hall. "I'm fine."

"Alright." Emma replied, though her look was a mixture of concern and confusion, matching the expressions of everyone around her.

I went into my room and locked the door. Then I pushed the dresser against it, then the nightstand against that. Walking over to the corner of my room opposite of the bed, I slid down the wall and brought my knees up tight to my chest, wrapping my arms around them. I didn't cry. I didn't scream. I just sat, staring at the floor directly in front of me, the marrow in my bones burning as a feeling of deep, penetrating cold settled over me.

I needed to warm up somehow, and I needed to get the stench of Frank off of my body, his spit, his sweat, I could smell stale cigarettes on my hands from when he had held them. I wanted to be clean, to wash him away and every image and word with him and I didn't want to be alone, anywhere, but I didn't want company. I got up and moved the furniture back where it belonged and headed to the bathroom. I needed to shower while everyone was still awake and in the kitchen, that way I would be safe.

I entered the bathroom and looked behind the shower curtain before closing the door and locking it. I knew it was a silly thing to do, he wouldn't be there, but I couldn't help myself. I began running the water, letting it heat up, very hot. I stepped into the shower and my feet burned causing me to jump back out, but I didn't turn it down. I eased my way back into it gently, the heat closing in around me. I felt as if I was suffocating. I began to scrub my body hard, crying and arguing with myself. "Just get over it. It's all done now" and "He didn't violate you, you got away, be thankful." And I was thankful if I thought about it, but penetration or not, I had been violated and I could not take away the fear and shame and weakness that I felt and replace it with actual feelings of gratitude, no matter how much I rationalized.

I wanted to stay in the shower and let the water wash me, scald me, if necessary, whatever it would take to restore me, but I couldn't stand to be there naked and vulnerable and my mind was in cautionary mode. I wanted to be back in my room again, with my door locked and my furniture back against it, before everyone went off to their rooms.

I turned off the water and stepped out of the shower, drying off and getting dressed, I opened the door slightly and peeked outside, making sure the coast was clear. I made my way quickly back to the room and just as in the bathroom, checked with the door open to make sure the room was empty, even getting down on my hands and knees and peeking under the bed, before locking and barricading the door once again.

I lay on the bed, the blanket to my chin, clinging to it like a child. I tried over and over to close my eyes and will sleep to come, but Frank's face, red and sweaty was always there in the blackness to greet me.

I tossed and turned, the physical pain in my face and body now surfacing and mixing with the rest, compounding my feeling of helplessness. I had faced sleepless nights before but I had always had an escape, I could go somewhere, distract myself until a time when the sleep would come swift and heavy, but I couldn't do that now. I didn't have the courage to roam the house alone. Finally I dozed off in shallow sleep, every sound, each creak and bump bringing me back to full attention, only to struggle my way back to momentary oblivion.

I ate my breakfast quickly, watching the door. I wanted to leave for the city as soon as possible and Myrna was pleased to find me ready before her allotted time. With ten minutes still to go before seven, Myrna and I climbed into the car and set off with Stanley. As we approached the main gate, my stomach knotted making me feel sick. The feeling only grew stronger as I looked ahead to see Frank walking out of the guard building to greet us.

Stanley rolled down his window. "Morning Frank."
"Morning Stanley" Frank replied. "Off to get the new girl?"
"Yep." Stanley answered.
Frank stopped in front of Myrna's window. She rolled it down, irritated. "What is it Frank?" She said.
"Nothing, nothing at all. Just saying good morning to you Myrna." Frank looked at me. His mouth was formed into a smile, but his eyes were cutting, "and to Connie."
I looked away.
"Fine. Good morning and good bye, we have a schedule." Myrna replied.
"I know just how you are Myrna. Have a safe trip. "Frank said, tapping the side of the car. "And bring us back a good girl. A pretty one this time."
Frank walked back to the side of the driveway and I transferred my gaze ahead to the back of Stanley's hat to avoid seeing him as we passed.

 After about an hour the sick feeling began to pass. When we first left after our encounter with Frank I was overwhelmed and felt like the slightest thing might cause me to unleash a torrent of tears, but the hum of the road and the safety I felt in the presence of Myrna and Stanley allowed it to pass without incident. I was glad that Myrna was not the type to try to make small talk. I only wanted to sit in their company, in sweet silence as I looked up at the sunlight through the tree leaves as we drove. The light seemed to dance, just as it had on the day I had come to the estate. It hinted of nothing but happiness and hope and I had found it, but I had been so mesmerized by the beauty of the light that I had not paid attention to the shadows, though, they found me still.

 Stanley dropped me off in front of my building. They would be back to pick me up at five o' clock after running some errands and picking up the new maid, a girl named Elena. It occurred to me as they drove off, that it was a fair possibility that the same journey had been enacted only months before. Had Myrna dropped off the previous girl at her own building, before coming for me and taking me around the city? Maybe it was always the same.

    I climbed the stairs and made my way to the apartment. I had stood before our door a million times but never really looked at it. It was painted a tan color years ago by the building's owner. He had decided to try to fix the building up a little at a time until he could kick us all out and raise the rent for higher end tenants, but it never happened. For whatever reason he gave up after only painting the doors on the first and second floors. From the top of the door, halfway down ran one long crack from where the wood split, having not been properly dried before being put to use. Around the brass knob the door was a black patina from hands turning the knob over and over throughout the years. Big hands, little hands, my hands, my father's hands. I knocked on the door and waited for someone to answer, but no one came. I sat down leaning my back against the door and waited.

"Connie?!" my mother's voice said, rousing me from sleep. I stood up quickly as she finished making her way up the stairs. "What are you doing here?" she smiled but her voice betrayed her fear.
"I'm just here for a visit Mama." I said giving her a hug. "The head housekeeper had to come into the city and she told me to come along and visit you."
"Well isn't that nice!" she said, relieved as she unlocked the door. "Come in and sit down. Your brothers are out as usual, still looking for work, well, all except Pat; he got a job in the stockyard. It's just day to day, we don't know from one to the other if he'll be there the next, but for now it's good."
We went into the kitchen where my mother set a kettle of water to boil for tea before joining me at the small round table.
"Have you had any leads on finding Da?" I asked.
"No. We haven't given up hope though." She replied.
"What about you? Are you doing alright?" I asked.

"Yes! You know I am. I write to you." My mother answered.

"Yes I know, but I'm just making sure. You wrote me that everything was fine for two months before I found out about Da." I said, unable to completely hide the hurt in my voice though I tried.

"Well, I don't know what to say about that. I'm sorry if I hurt ya, but I did what I thought was best." She said.

"I know." I said.

"So, how is Eli?" she asked, smiling.

"He's in Tennessee right now, visiting his mother. She's sick and not expected to live." I answered.

"I'm sorry to hear that. God be with her." She said. "But are you two still good?"

"Yes. We are. Everything between us is great."

"It's perfect is what it is." she replied. "You both working for the same rich family, two steady jobs. You could get married right now."

"Not exactly." I said. "Employees aren't supposed to court one another."

My mother raised her eyebrow and frowned. "You didn't tell me that."

"We're being careful." I said quickly. "There's no proof. It's fine."

"Don't matter. What's the point in it if you can't marry each other?" She said.

"The point is we enjoy each other's company." I said.

"I don't like it." She replied, "You need to end it."

"So what time are you headed back?" she asked, quickly changing the subject before I could object.

"They said they would pick me up at five. What time is it now?" I asked.

My mother looked at the clock. "Three twenty-seven." She answered. "That's plenty of time."

The kettle began to whistle. I got up and removed it from the stove and walking to the table poured the hot water into the cups on either side. My mind was full. I didn't know if I

should tell her about what happened the night before. I returned the kettle to the stove and sat down absentmindedly.
"What's wrong Connie?" my mother asked.
"I don't want to go back." I said.
"What do you mean, why?" she asked.
"I just don't." I said.
"Just don't isn't an answer worth hearing. Whatever it is you'll have to get over it." She said.
"What if I can't get over it?" I asked.
"You can. Whatever it is, you can."
"I don't think so." I said, beginning to cry.
"What's going on Connie?"
I quickly opened my mouth and let it all tumble out before I lost my nerve. I told her everything. Frank's hands on my mouth, on my thighs. His words, his threats. My fear and shame all laid out before her, tears running down both of our faces.

She rose up and came over to me when I was finished, holding me and cooing. I cried hard and long, safe in my mother's arms. When I couldn't cry anymore she ran her hand down my hair and returned to her seat.
"Feel better now?" She asked.
I nodded my head. "That's it. That's why I don't want to go back. I'll tell Myrna I'm quitting when she comes to get me."
"You can't Connie." She said. "You have to go back."
"What?" I said. "I just told you what happened. I told you what he said, what he did. How can I go back?"
"You have to. We need you to, me, your brothers, without your wages, we'll starve. We'll be on the streets."
"Mama, you can't." I pleaded." You can't ask me to go back."
"Then I will have to tell you to go back. It will be okay. Just don't go outside alone no more. He doesn't work in the house. Men are just like that sometimes and we just have to push it aside. It was hurtful and frightening but there was no real harm done. You'll be alright."
I stared at her in disbelief. How could she ask this of me?
"Do you not care at all?" I asked.

"Of course I do. I love you, and it hurts me to know what you went through, but it is what it is, and you can't be selfish Connie, you have to do what you have to do, for all of us, or do *you* not care?"

I looked down at the floor. I couldn't stomach what I was hearing.

"It'll be okay. You'll see. Eli will be back soon, maybe you don't need to end it with him immediately, in light of the situation, as long as you keep being careful that is. Now, drink your tea."

I took the cup into my hand and sipped the cold tea, not even bothering to add sugar. What did it matter? I felt numb. This is what it came down to. This is what I was worth, an "I love you, but not that much, not enough to disrupt up my life."

"Well let's get you cleaned up shall we." I heard my mother's voice say as if from a distance. "It's almost five."

Out of the corner of my eye I saw her pass by me. She returned with a wet washcloth and handed it to me. I washed my face as she brushed my hair. When she was done she came around in front of me and took my hands pulling me up. "There's a good girl." She said.

I walked down the stairs and onto the curb as if in a trance. The car was already waiting. My mother introduced herself and expressed her gratitude to Myrna for allowing me to come for the day. When she was finished she hugged me. "I love you Connie." She said, then she whispered in my ear, "You can't change what happened, it's in the past now, you have to try to forget about it. Just be a good girl and forgive him like God says and you'll see, everything will go back to the way it was."

Mustering all my strength I looked in her eyes and forced a smile. I would be a good girl, if that's what she wanted. I would force myself to forget, and work hard, and send money.

12

Forgetting is easier said than done and forgiving is even harder. I did want to forget. I wanted to sleep soundly at night, free of nightmares. I wanted to stop looking over my shoulder and jumping at noises. I wanted to stop feeling sick every time I would see Frank's smug face, or shivering when, despite my attempts to avoid it, our eyes would meet; when I would see the cold, and the threat that lay within them. Yes, I did want to forget.

Forgiving however, was another matter entirely. I had -as all inevitably do- heard the advice spouted from those who claim a higher path, that one must forgive others of whatever wrong they have done, even the most vile of acts, so one can move on, so it doesn't eat you up inside, but I was finding the advice erroneous. If you can't forget, then you can't move on; if you can't forget, then you are left with guilt that you are still angry and hurt when the memory comes. So you say it again. You tell yourself that you forgive them, but it's a lie, mere lip serve because that's what you are told you are supposed to do, but the core of yourself, the part of you that still believes you're worth something, balks at it. No matter what words you say, it remembers, and it isn't so easily appeased, leaving you at war with yourself. But why? Why should their forgiveness come at the cost of your own soul? Why should someone who hurt you so badly not deserve your anger and hate? Despising the bastard gives you something. It validates your feelings that they were wrong and you have worth. So I left words of forgiveness to God and liars, and I enjoyed my hatred.

But it wasn't just my loathing of Frank that consumed me. I realized on the ride home I had been so upset about Frank that I had forgotten to tell my mother about Ann, but I didn't even want to write her now. She was no longer the person I could turn to. I felt betrayed by her and no matter how much

I tried to push it down I couldn't. My dignity, my safety, had a monetary value and up until that day I had been blissfully unaware of that fact. I tried to make excuses for her, but none would suffice. No excuse could erase the fact that I was her daughter; I was supposed to mean more than a paycheck. I was common, working class, but I wasn't without dignity. I could work hard, do what was right and be able to hold my head high knowing I was good enough to deserve a certain respect, certain rights. I couldn't be bought and sold. Now that illusion crumbled down around me. Through Eli and Tom I had begun to believe that I might even be enough to pursue any course I desired, but now, I wasn't so sure, if I had not been enough for my own mother to choose me over convenience, than how could I be enough for anything else.

Tom left the estate a week after my visit to the city. I had not had an opportunity to see him, though the knowledge that he was in the house somewhere brought me a sort of comfort, but once he left, what little I had went with him. I watched from an upstairs window as he, Robert and Jane climbed into the Rolls. Before he entered the car he paused and looked around. Though he didn't notice me looking down from above, I flattered myself that I was the one he was searching for. Watching the car pull away I felt empty. I could only hope Eli would return soon.

After Tom left I found a package wrapped in brown paper lying on my bed along with a note. I carefully tore off the wrapping, opening it like an envelope, delicate and precise. Enclosed was a book about the national parks. It was full of stories and facts and pictures of mountains and canyons and geysers. I held it tightly to my chest as I read the note.

My Dear Constance,
I leave you to tread down the well-worn path of my predecessors. Life set before me a choice just as it sets before all of us and for better or worse I have made mine. I want to say thank you for being my friend and confidant. Your presence has enriched my life.

I hope this book will be a reminder that there is a magnificent world out there for those brave enough to take hold of it however it presents itself to them. If you should decide to walk the path others lay before you, I have faith in your wisdom and if you should decide to set out in a new direction, making a road as you go, I trust in your strength. Either way, I will always wish you well.
Warmest Regards,
Tom

    The book became my lifeline as I waited for Eli to return. Through it I could view nature even if I couldn't touch it. Through it I was able to resume dreaming.

    Eli did make it back to the estate, nearly a month after he had left. It was a testament to the high regard in which the Sarringtons held him that he had been able to stay away for so long and still have a position to return to.

This time we did not bother with the silliness of before. When Eli came in I made sure I was there with the others to greet him. We had come too far together to go back to our old doubts and we had both been through too much to deny ourselves a single moment of the comfort we might find in one another. Even Myrna did not deny us our time together that first night.

    As we made our way to the garden together, we passed Frank. The previous weeks he had eyed me, cocky and threatening; now he looked nervous and weak, and with Eli by my side, I didn't, though I knew I wouldn't tell Eli. The temptation was there. I knew that Eli was capable of making Frank regret every second and every word, and I knew that if given the choice Eli would want me to tell him. He would want the opportunity to avenge me, but I couldn't do it. Unlike my mother who was willing to put her own wellbeing in front of my own, I knew that Eli would risk his very future for me, and because I knew that he would, I couldn't ask him to. If I could bear it all in silence for money, how much more could I bear it for love. I just needed Eli to stay by me and perhaps as my mother said, everything really would be okay.

But he didn't stay. Within a few days Mr. Sarrington informed Eli that he and Mrs. Sarrington were going back to California and Eli was to join them. They had been wanting to go for a couple of weeks, but had been waiting for Eli; now that he was back, they would leave immediately.
"How long will you be gone?" I asked.
"I have no way of knowing." Eli answered.
"Is the California estate almost done? Maybe enough that they need servants there and I could go along?" I suggested.
"No, not yet. Soon perhaps. It depends on how much they got done since we've been gone. But, I don't believe they would bring servants from here out there, Myrna perhaps, to get things set up, but I would imagine they would hire people that are already in California." Eli paused. "I don't know if I will be able to come back. Mr. Sarrington talks as if he wants me to stay there"
"So what does this mean?" I asked as my heart sank. "I have no hope of going out there and you may not come back here. This is the end then?"
"I didn't say that." He answered. "How many times do I have to tell you that I am planning for *our* future? I don't know yet how to work it out. I will probably stay out there. There is so much happening in California now, it would be good to be around at the start of it all, and I don't think they'll bring you out. It wouldn't make sense, not from their point of view, but just because we don't know the answer now doesn't mean we have to give up. Stay here and work, just as you have been until we figure it out. That won't be too hard will it?"

I lied and shook my head. My eyes filled with tears. Eli thought it was from the thought of being separated from him, and it was, but not as he imagined. I had enjoyed a respite from the fear, now it would be back with a vengeance.

Eli left within two weeks' time. I was upset and afraid. I felt abandon and yet part of me was relieved as well. I had been unable to have any form of intimacy with Eli since he returned. My body would lock up at even the slightest caress. I didn't know how long it would go on and the thought of it made me sick. To have experienced the pleasure that a touch could bring and then have it gone was devastating. Frank had robbed me of my peace of mind, of my sense of self-worth and now even my physical abilities. It seemed insurmountable and I had no idea when if ever I would be back to my old self. Having Eli look at me, hurt evident in his face, confused and frustrated, only made matters worse. He thought I was simply being childish and selfish, angry at him for leaving and that in turn made him angry. As much as I needed him there, I needed him away so I could heal without any more complications than what I was already facing.

So it was done. Eli was gone and Frank had won, and he knew it. I hadn't told Eli and now I was alone and he had nothing to be afraid of. The threatening looks left his eyes and were replaced by ones of mocking. He would look over at me as he flirted with one of the maids. He was paying particular attention to Elena, though she seemed to want nothing to do with him. I didn't know if that would do any good. I had not wanted anything to do with him either, and Elena was much smaller than I was. What could she do if she found herself in the same position I had?

But he didn't stop with just the looks. He taunted me as well. "It's a lovely night tonight Connie, don't you want to go for a walk?"

"I heard there was a meteor shower last month, did you get to see it?"

I hated him with a seething, writhing hatred, that as time went on, began to burn away my fear. I hoped he could see it as I stopped running away when he came into a room. As when he spoke, I began to meet his eyes. I hoped that he could see that I was not broken by him. It may have hit me hard, but I would not be undone by it; I would be strengthened and my strength would one day lift me up. I hoped that he could feel my hate pouring from my eyes into his and filling his soul with a poison to eat away at him. I would use the black that he had birthed within me and turn it on him and destroy him with it somehow, and each word he spoke, each look he gave, would only serve to feed the blackness and make it stronger.

    I spent all of my free time in my room looking at the book Tom had given me and reading what books I could sneak out of the library during the day. I never left my room at night and I never went walking. I felt starved and trapped, cut off from all the things I loved most. An inmate in a lavish prison, with the twin guards of Frank and my mother blocking my escape. I had begun to hold back part of my wages when I sent them home. It did not slip my mother's notice. She worried that I had done something to displease Myrna and had been punished with a loss of wages as a result. I didn't correct her. Actually I had received the raise promised to me when I replaced Ann and Myrna was happier with me than she had ever been. With Tom and Eli gone and me staying put, there was nothing she could see that might upset her tightly run house. Honestly I had begun to hold back some of my pay out of spite and nothing more. If this was truly what mattered most to my mother, then let her make due with less of it.

    As I slowly watched the money accumulate however, I began instead to hold it back less from spite and more for myself. I still didn't know if I would ever do anything beyond what I was doing, but I felt calmer and hopeful in the simple act of setting something aside, just in case.

    I have found in life that we are never truly left alone, even when we most feel like it; there is always someone there to give us encouragement. With Eli and Tom departing, Fate gave me Elena. Elena was nothing like Ann. She was thin with long flaxen hair that she wore plaited down her back. Her eyes were blue like Eli's and her skin was pale with a blue undertone to it making it seem almost translucent in places. She had delicate features and was quiet, soft spoken and moved with great delicacy no matter what she was doing. Being near her had a peaceful effect on anyone who happened to find themselves in her company. Elena was also happy, not in Joan's boisterous way, but she was always smiling. You could see that she was happy within herself and because of that happiness radiated out of her and fed all of us like the rays of the sun feed flowers. On the days we spent together when Myrna would send her to me, I would tell her about the land around the estate and all of the things I was reading about the lands beyond. Soon I began to want to spend as much time with her as possible. We would walk, close to the house; we would sit together in one of our rooms and talk and laugh. She would listen with interest to all I had to say, no matter what it was, and as she did I began to open up more about my own thoughts and though I didn't dare to call them such, dreams. Eli had convinced me that a person could pursue their own path; Tom had shown me that possibilities existed, but it was Elena who gave me faith. As I would tell her how much I admired and envied the women I was reading about in various books, living lives I could only imagine; she would respond with absolute conviction that I could do the same. Not only could but would. That it was the most sure thing to ever have been spoken of.

I had never had many friends. I preferred to keep to myself. Though I had had what I considered to be my fair share. And most people seemed to like me well enough. They would speak with me and laugh with me, but I knew they would never really care about me. If I died their lives would go on as if I had never existed with little more than a "That's too bad." And that was fine. Tom had been a friend and Eli was more. Whether or not he was my friend I can't say, he was my lover. I felt safe around him. I wanted him near me. I wanted to feel his arms around me. I wanted to listen to him as he spoke of his passions and I wanted to see him happy, but I rarely shared my own thoughts with him. I certainly didn't share my hopes, my maybes. Why I held back, I don't know, but for some reason I did. Elena was something else. Not a lover, but yet somehow more than a friend. She seemed almost more than human to me, like an angel or perhaps even one of the ancient goddesses she would tell me stories about from her Russian homeland's heathen past. Whatever she was, flesh or spirit, I loved her.

It was Elena who finally pushed me over the edge to decision. Up until then, though I had accepted the fact that everything was in my own hands alone, I still wavered back and forth between thinking that maybe I could and believing that I couldn't. One day as we cleaned the windows in the breakfast room, Elena spoke the words that set me straight ahead. They were not profound, nor were they many, but they were what was most important, the right words at the right time.

"Connie, when are you going to finally leave here and go work at one of these parks you talk about so much?" Elena asked.

"I don't know if I ever will. You know that, I've told you before. It's just not that easy." I answered.

"Who said it had to be easy?" she replied. "You are lucky. You know what you really want. Most people do not even think about it, but you did, so why are you not doing what you need to do to do it?"

"I don't know that either. Sometimes I think I can and sometimes I think I can't. It's that simple."

"Yes it is that simple. Either you can or you cannot, but how will you know which one it is if you do not try?

"I don't know." I said again, laughing weakly. "It's what I want. I know that. It's fear that keeps me here, and obligation too I suppose. You know my mother and brothers depend on me"

"It is good for you to help your family, but you cannot be expected to be a slave to them forever and the only remedy for fear is action. Always has been, always will be."

"And knowledge." I corrected her.

"Yes, knowledge too, but for you, action." Elena laughed.

"Ugh! I just wish I could be there and done with it. Sitting on horseback, patrolling the trails in Yellowstone or Glacier, or even the Grand Canyon. There isn't a night I don't lay in my bed and wish it were possible." I said.

"Wish! Wish, wish, wish! But do the work too!"

As I lay on my bed that night, Elena's words came back to me and mixed with those of everyone who had come before; Eli, Tom, Emerson, even my own. What she said was true. I knew it and had known it. The time comes when you know in your heart that you have to make a choice, that's it, you don't have to make an announcement, you don't even have to put one foot in front of the other, not yet anyway, you just have to make a choice. Seemingly the easiest thing in the world, but anyone who has ever done it knows, it's one of the hardest, because a choice is a commitment, and commitments never come lightly. With this heavy on my mind, I drifted off to sleep.

I stood in the middle of the street. The people had gone, so had the two men, only the buildings and the little girl by my side remained. We looked at one another and began to walk forward. A growl suddenly came from behind. Looking over my shoulder I saw a monstrous black dog run towards us fast, eyes red and foam hanging from its mouth. I tightened my grip on the girl's hand and began to run, dragging her along as she struggled to keep up. The dog was gaining on us, so close I could hear more than its growls, I could hear its rapid shallow breaths. I looked over my shoulder once more just in time to see it leap into the air. Its large paws with their sharp black nails hung in the sky, suspended it seemed, as the moment stretched and slowed. Then it fell on us hard, causing us to hit the ground. The dog towered over us, snarling, foam from its mouth dripping onto our faces. I felt paralyzed by fear but the child fought, kicking against the animal, though she alone wasn't strong enough. She looked at me, eyes frantic and pleading. I pulled my knees to my chest and jutted my feet forward with all of my might, sending the dog hurling backwards. I heard it fall with a thud and a yelp. Slowly I sat up and looked at the dog, but there in its place lay a man, face down, sprawled on the pavement. I felt a rush of anger and hatred at what he had just done to us and I ran towards him, ready to finish the job of what my feet had started, but the little girl grabbed my hand firmly and held me in place. I looked down at her again, angry that she would try to keep me from my revenge, but she wouldn't relent, she simply shook her head and turned back in the direction we had been heading. But the road was blocked. My mother stood ahead of me smiling, shaking her head and pointing for me to turn around. I stopped, ready to comply but the child pulled me forward, simply walking around her as if it didn't matter. I waited to hear the chastisement that would undoubtedly follow, but when none came I looked back, both my mother and the man were gone.

We walked on and as we did the buildings began to close in on us, until it seemed as if we were walking down a long narrow alleyway. Soon a wall appeared before us in the distance. I tried to stop the girl so we could turn around, but she kept walking. As we got closer I saw a woman sitting in the corner quietly waiting. She was dressed all in white with long silver white hair that flowed in loose waves and pooled on the ground around her. Her skin was a soft ivory color and her lips pale pink like the velvety flesh of a rose. As we approached she stood and smiled at us, then reaching up she grabbed the edge of the brick wall and pulled at it, dropping it to the ground, as it became like the fabric of a painted theater curtain in her hands. In its place stood another wall, this one made of packed dirt and grass with an arched wooden door in the middle of it. The wood of the door had a reddish tint to it like mahogany and trees and vines were ornately carved into its surface; a large iron knob and lock sat in its far right center. The door filled me with longing. I wanted nothing more in life than to walk through it. I waited for the woman to open it but she didn't move, rather she looked at me expectantly. Taking what I thought was her cue I held out my hand, expecting her to give me the key but she smiled and shook her head. My heart sank and I bowed my head ready to cry at the despair that flooded into me with the knowledge that I would never see what lay beyond. I heard a giggle beside me and looked at the child who had until then remained silent. She gestured at the door and I shook my head in reply. She giggled again. What did she want me to do? I didn't have a key. She shook her head and gestured at the door again. She didn't understand. I would have to show her. Extending my hand, I reached for the knob and as I did a large iron key, matching the lock appeared in my hand. I looked at the woman and laughed in amazement. Then looking down at the girl I smiled and squeezed her hand. Pulling her close to my side, I slid the key into the lock.

    I woke with a rush of exhilaration. I knew what I had to do. I got out of my bed and tiptoed out of my room for the first time in months. I walked out of the house in an act of faith and continued until I was at the river's edge once again. The sky was dark, clouds covered the moon and the wind blew cold against my body, the first snow of winter lightly dusted the ground, freezing my feet even within their shoes. It seemed as if I was being tested. My body wanted to turn back to the warmth of my bed and my mind wanted to return to its safety, but my heart had courage and purpose. I looked out onto the black water, watching ripples create darker shadows on the dark, silver surface. Looking into the clouds appealing to God, Fate and nature herself, I spoke my resolution.
"I will no longer bow to what others say or think possible and I will not let someone else determine my worth, or my destiny. I have made my choice, from this moment onward I will walk towards it."
    As if on cue the clouds parted and the sliver of moon, still young, like my determination shown small but bright in the sky, the wind died down and all was calm, in the world and in my spirit. It didn't last long, only moments. The clouds hid the moon once more and the wind rose again, causing the skin on my face and hands to sting, but it had been enough. I was reborn.
    I made my way back to my room without incident. There was no Frank waiting by the garage and no Myrna tapping her foot in the kitchen; there wasn't even a bear rustling through the forest floor, not that I could hear anyway. I felt whole and sure as I drifted quickly back to sleep.

    I spent the next month doing research. I needed a plan. I needed to figure out what I should do, where I should go - though I figured I would go West- and I needed to figure out how much money I needed to set aside to live, it was the Great Depression after all. Once I knew where I was headed a job may not be easy to come by. It was such thoughts that would cause doubt and fear to seep into my mind, but I refused to succumb to them. I had made my decision, I had spoken my vow and I would see it through. Doubt though, as it does, tries to find a loophole. Its little voice would tell me to stay where I was or at least close by. Why even head out West? I could do it in New York, if I just toned it down a bit. It wouldn't be a huge adjustment to my dreams nor to my comfort, but I knew that was not the right answer. I needed to break away. If I stayed where I was, I would find myself doing what I had always done and soon the fire within me would smolder eventually leaving nothing but cold, dead ash in its place. If I stayed I would never break free from obligation and the vision of life others had for me. I had to go west, just as the pioneers had. Not in search of riches in its common forms but in search of it in its truest form. Freedom, peace, fulfillment. I would leave everything I knew, everything that was safe and known, just as my grandparents had done, not even half a century before.

For the first time in my life they were more to me than family. I felt a special bond with them that went beyond blood. I had grown up not disrespecting them, but not quite understanding them. It was unfathomable to me that they had chased the wind and suffered for it. That they had been willing to risk everything they were connected to on nothing stronger than hope and an idea. Now I knew what they felt. I knew why they were compelled to take whatever chance necessary and whatever consequence. That same spirit that was in them lay in me also and it rose up and strengthened me. I was not just the daughter of those who sought safety and comfort above all else, as if it were the holiest of all virtues. I was also the daughter of the dreamers, the risk takers. Their courage may not have been spoken of in books and ballads, it didn't make its way to the towering screen or the radio shows, but it was just as real, just as strong and it was mine to draw from. When I began to doubt, when I began to falter I would look to them, they would be my inspiration, my heroes.

Thanks to a lot of research mixed with help from Tom when he came home for the holidays, I was eventually able to formulate a plan. When the time was right, I would take a train to Whitefish, Montana and try to get a job as close as I could to Glacier National Park which I had decided was my favorite of them all. Once I reached Whitefish, I would immediately begin spending as much time as possible at the park, getting to know the rangers there. After a while I would try to work as a volunteer and find out what I needed to do experience and education wise to move beyond to fulltime employment and work towards those qualifications whatever they may be. I figured I needed at least ninety dollars, for the train and to support myself while I looked for a job. Depending on what kind of job I was able to procure I knew I needed to save for the possibility of food and lodging expenses. I could sleep and eat meagerly, but sleep and eat I must.

Once I had my plans set I wrote a letter to Eli, and another to my mother. I wanted Eli to know my plans so he could decide if they fit in with his own. Though it had been months since I had seen him, I still felt I loved him and would like to have a future with him, but I finally knew what I wanted my future to be for myself, and I knew that I must pursue it. I trusted that my path was the right one, and everything else would fall in with it or fall away as it must, and as it should. My mother deserved a warning. Although I had not overcome the hurt she had done me, I did not wish her to be blindsided as she had been by my father. I loved her and I knew that in her own way she loved me. I believed she was doing as she had always done, the best she could in the place she found herself. I wanted her to have peace of mind. I wanted her to be happy. I was just no longer willing to sacrifice myself to it.

Eli's feelings were mostly positive. Being the type of man that he was, he was happy that I had goals beyond servitude for the rest of my life. Eli admired ambition and vision and now that I was stepping out into my own it only served to strengthen his feelings for me. He was a little put off by the fact that I had been mulling around this idea for so long and had never told him. He felt hurt by it and perhaps he had a right to, but I had no explanation to offer him, at least none that would make him feel better rather than worse. He also said that he would rather I try for Yosemite or Sequoia, maybe even Lassen National Park as it would be closer to him. But just as I knew I needed to break away from my mother and the comfort of my small part of the known world, I knew too, that at least at first, I needed to do this somewhere separate from everyone I knew, including Eli. I needed to know that I had the strength within me to strike out on my own, truly on my own, with no one to hold me up or to hold me down. I couldn't tell Eli this either, so I simply told him of my growing desire to experience Glacier, which was by no means a lie, and reminded him that, did it really change much? I was already apart from him and until my letter, he had no reason to believe that we would not continue to remain apart for quite some time. My choice didn't really change anything in that regard except a mailing address. Soon he relented and simply expressed his support and suggestions both of which were welcome.

My mother was another matter entirely. She sent letter after letter, each with the same reoccurring theme, with slightly varying twists. Had I gone completely mad?! Was I playing a cruel joke?! Or she even asked, was I hiding an illicit pregnancy? When I finally was able to convince her that I was neither insane, joking, nor with bastard child, her letters took on a new theme. Guilt. I think that all mothers are masters when it comes to guilt, but I believe Irish Catholic mothers must be the wellspring. She quoted scripture naturally, she brought up my father of course, that I was surely his daughter that I would abandon my family in their time of need. I was a selfish, wicked girl, hell bent on their starvation. I was foolish without doubt she said, and would reap the harvest of my stupidity and callousness. The letters would alternate between angry accusations and desperate appeals. At times it was hard to not respond in kind, but I managed, reminding myself that it wasn't really me; she was simply letting her fear drive her, letting it trump all else, just as she had that afternoon in the kitchen of our apartment when it had trumped my pain and need for comfort in one of my darkest hours. She would be alright I responded, and there was still time for her to prepare if she would use it wisely. I wasn't abandoning her, that was why I had written in the first place, so she could take the necessary steps to be ready when the time came to stand without me. I wasn't doing what my father had done. I hoped one day when the dust settled she would realize that, perhaps even find it within herself to be proud of what I had set out to do and all that it took for me to even attempt it.

With time the letters stopped. I assumed she either grew tired or bitter, but I knew she had not grown to accept it whatever she was. Her letters may have stopped to me, but before long they began instead to Emma, and in turn Emma began where my mother had left off. I tried to explain, and when that didn't work, I simply tried to avoid her, thankful that she at least had not revealed my plans to Myrna.

The hardest part of all however was Frank. Eventually he grew tired of his taunts and I saw him rarely, but he was still there and I was still angry. I didn't like the fact that he was getting off scot free. He should have to pay for what he did and there should be some way to make sure he wouldn't do it to someone else, but if there was, I couldn't think of it. He had been right, partially anyway, I couldn't tell anyone. Who would believe me? A few perhaps, maybe even most if I really thought about it, but would Myrna? Probably not, and even if she did, would it only make matters worse? Were her feelings for him strong enough that it would only hurt me more and do nothing to punish or stop him? It was likely. I didn't know how likely, but I knew it was enough to not chance it. I would not let him steal my future from me.

From the beginning I had found myself plotting, envisioning all the ways I would like to see him tortured or even meet with an untimely end and I cannot say that those daydreams ended, but I tried to control them more. While I hated him and had no intention on stopping, I had already lost so much because of him. I did not want to add any additional time and energy to the list, especially since I had decided my course. When thoughts of him would creep in I would simply try to remind myself that cliché as it may be, we all eventually reap what we have sown. The tapestry of our lives is woven with the threads we ourselves provide and so it was with him just as it was with all of us. Frank would get his, if I was lucky, I thought, I might be able to participate in it, or at the very least, witness it, but if not, it would come to him all the same.

Still I wanted to say something to Elena. I wanted to make sure that she was on guard when she was around him. And a part of it too was that I wanted to tell someone what he had done. Someone who wouldn't do anything except listen and maybe offer some sort of comfort. But I didn't know how to go about it. How do you bring up something like that? How do you explain it and how would I make her understand why I had not said anything to anyone? I stalled, going back and forth within myself, wanting to lay it all out and yet wanting to put it off. I looked up to Elena and I knew she looked up to me. We were on equal footing, and I didn't want to become soiled goods in her eyes. In the end, I waited too long.

Roughly two months after my one year anniversary of employment and mere weeks before I was planning on leaving, a virus swept through the estate. It was early May, the elder Sarringtons were in California and the house was calm. It was still a couple weeks before Tom, Jane and Robert would return home and their parents not for a few weeks after that. I would be gone before Lily and John Sarrington ever set foot back in the house. Quickly and without warning servants began to grow ill. It began with Charles and soon progressed to Doyle, Nellie, and Stephen. Within days two thirds of the staff could hardly bear to sit up, let alone do any work. An early summer flu. Myrna called out a doctor but there was nothing he could do and soon she too grew pale and weak. True to form, she refused to relinquish her post, and commanded the few of us still standing from a chair in the kitchen each day.

All the guards except Frank were moaning from their beds, so too were the grounds men. Emma and Elena busily attended to the infirm barely taking time to eat. Joan and I tried to keep the house in order and keep up with the soiled linens that were coming from the sick beds. Even Emily was trying to help, the only one of the upper servants left to do so. Paul kept the meals coming to keep our strength up and light soups and crackers for the others. Next Emily and Joan fell and there were only the five of us left. Charles was beginning to improve rapidly but he still was not ready to resume work just yet.

Wednesday, night after finally getting Myrna to abandon her post and go off to bed, the four of us, excluding Frank - who thankfully was forced by Will and Greg's sickness to stay at his post twenty four hours a day- sat wearily around the kitchen table discussing the possibility that it was still days before anyone would be able to come to our aid and that any of us might fall in that time. Barely having the strength to stand and not wanting to think about such things I excused myself to take a shower. I was taking them more often than usual. Our schedule was irrelevant at that point and they had become my saving grace. I relished being able to let the hot water massage my aching muscles, knowing that for those few moments I could just relax, that while I was there, the calls for tea and the vomit covered bed sheets could wait.
When I made my way back to the kitchen Elena was gone.

"Where is Elena?" I asked. "Did she go to bed already? Is she sick?"

"No. Neither." Said Emma. "I asked her to take Frank down his dinner tonight. I'm too tired. I didn't think I could walk the distance to the guardhouse."

"What?!" I nearly shouted at her. "When? How long has she been gone?"

"I don't know. Right after you went to the shower I suppose. It's been a while. She'll probably be back any minute." Emma said, looking at me sideways.

I ran out of the kitchen and looked down the driveway. I couldn't see her anywhere.

"Elena!" I shouted as loudly as I could, causing my throat to hurt, but there was no answer. I began to run towards the guardhouse, but after a few steps turned around and went to the garage. I switched on the light and scanned the room. A crowbar was propped up near the door. Grabbing it, I began running again down the driveway. Elena was probably fine I told myself, but better to check and better to be prepared, just in case.

Halfway to the guardhouse I saw her, she was stumbling forward, her hands raised up in front of her.

"Elena!" I shouted.

She fell to the ground and I ran to her side, dropping the crowbar as I fell to my knees. Her hands were covered in blood. She looked at me, tears streaming down her face. Her lip was cracked and bleeding.

"Elena, what happened?" I asked, tears filling my eyes, but I already knew. She leaned her head against my chest but didn't answer.

"Did Frank do this to you Elena?" I asked.

She still didn't answer, but she began to shake violently at the question.

"Shhhh." I said. "It will be alright. It will be alright." I petted her hair, rocking her in my arms, a mixture of feelings flooding through me. Rage, guilt, fear, pity. It was all there and I didn't know which to let reign.

I gently removed myself from her and picked up the crowbar. Rage would reign. I stood up and told her to stay there and stay still, that I would be right back. She looked into my eyes and I followed them as they made their way down my arm and to the crowbar in my hands. I nodded at her and turned towards the guardhouse when I felt Elena's hand grab me. My decision seemed to change something in her, bringing her to attention.

"No." she said faintly.

I looked down at her. "Elena, he has to pay." I said.

"I know." She whispered. "But don't. Just help me up and help me back to the house Connie."

She didn't want to be alone right now I told myself. I understood that. He had probably threatened her, and he had most certainly hurt her. She probably wanted to clean herself from his filth as well. The most important thing was Elena, I would deal with Frank later.

I turned around and slowly helped her to her feet. She moaned with the pain and hobbled as we walked slowly towards the house. It was a long way still and I wished I was strong enough to carry her. She was covered front to back in blood, her dress ripped and hair failing out of its braid, most of it anyway, clumps attached themselves here and there on her dress where they had been ripped from her head.

"You're bleeding." I said.

"Yes." Elena replied. "I was," she paused. "I," her voice faltered and she couldn't go on, but she didn't need to. I understood. She had been a virgin. Still it seemed like a lot of blood, more than should be expected. She had endured great violence and I quickly prayed to God that she wouldn't die. My main concern was getting her to the house and calling a doctor. I couldn't lose her.

Elena had stopped crying. Though physically she looked completely broken, her face seemed resolute, as if she was in deep contemplation. I wondered if she was going into shock.

When we entered the kitchen Emma screamed. Paul seeing us dropped the pot he had been holding, sending soapy water and bits and pieces of chicken and vegetables cascading across the floor as he rushed over to us and took Elena from me.

"What happened?!" Emma cried.

'Frank," I began.

"Said thank you for dinner." Elena interrupted. "I tripped on a rock walking back."

"You tripped?" Emma repeated, but she was looking at me. Paul raised his eyes to me as well. They both knew as well as I did that what they saw before them was not the result of any fall.

"Yes." Elena said. "Can someone help me to the bathroom? I want to get cleaned up."

"I think maybe we should call a doctor to see you instead." Said Emma.

"No, I just need a shower, just a quick one, I'll be okay. Please, someone." Elena replied.

"I'll take you there." said Paul.

We followed Paul and Elena to the bathroom. He set her down gently on the seat of the toilet and turned and walked out.

"Do you need me to stay? "I asked.

"No." Elena answered. "I will be alright."

Emma and I returned to the kitchen. Paul was standing, his large arms crossed over his chest, waiting for us.

"What happened Connie?" he asked.

I stood for a moment trying to figure out the best way to say such a thing, but there wasn't one.

"I found her a little over halfway from the house." I answered. "She didn't say, but I'm sure it was Frank."

Emma put her hand over her mouth, her eyes welling up with tears. "That poor child." She said.

"Frank huh." Paul said. He headed for the door.

"Where are you going?" I asked.

"I'm going to pay Frank a little visit." Paul said his face turning red with anger.

"No Paul." Emma said. "As much as I would like to let you, you can't. "

"Like hell I can't!" Paul shouted. "I'm going to beat the shit out of him and if I'm lucky, I'll kill the bastard in the process!"

"Paul, he's in the guardhouse. That means he has a gun." Emma said. "Let's call the police. Let him rot in jail."

"Rot in jail?! She just told us she fell Emma! What makes you think she's going to tell the police anything different?" Paul said.

He was right. She had lied, why, I didn't know, but she had, and whatever her reason, it was unlikely that she would tell the police anything other than what she had told Emma and Paul.

"I will tell the police." I said.

"You weren't there; they aren't going to listen to anything you have to say." Paul replied.

"He tried to do it to me too. I will tell them that." I answered.

Emma's eyes grew wide. "No, Connie. Tell me you're lying, for Elena." She said.

I shook my head and looked down at the floor.

"When?" Emma asked.

"That night you came in, you looked like you had just been in a fight. Went almost straight to the shower, just like Elena." Paul said.

My eyes welled up with tears.

"That was nearly a year ago." said Emma. She came over and took me in her arms, but I pushed her away. I didn't want to be touched.

"Why didn't you say anything?" She asked.

"I should have. If I had," I trailed off, the tears falling freely as I thought of Elena, as I thought about what my cowardice had done. "I was scared." I said after a while. "He told me he would kill me," I looked at Emma, "and you. Besides he told me no one would believe me, especially not Eli."

"Eli would have killed him." Paul said. "And I *am* going to kill him."

"No." I said. "Emma is right. We'll call the police."

"No, we won't" a soft voice came from the hall. We turned to see Elena leaning against the wall for strength.

Paul ran over to her and helped her to a chair.

"Elena, you have to tell the police what he did." Paul said.

"If you call them, I will tell them I fell, and Connie can tell them her story, but that was so long ago, it won't matter." Elena said.

"Then I will take care of him myself." Paul said.

"No." Elena answered. "He has a gun."

"Elena, you have to let us call the police. I don't understand. Between the two of us, they will believe us." I said, desperate that she wouldn't listen.

"It wouldn't matter. I know the police." Elena stared off towards the door, growing silent for a moment. "The same thing happened to my sister, though for her it was worse. It was three men in an alleyway in Skorba. She was only fifteen. Her body," Elena began to cry, but quickly regained her composure, though how, I couldn't say. "Her body looked like someone had put it on a butcher's block, red and purple, torn, skin hanging. The blood…" Elena paused, looking as if she might break, but instead she began again, "We went to the police, but it didn't matter, one of the men was a cousin to the chief. They did nothing. My sister suffered, was shamed, beaten, raped. She had everything taken from her, and they did nothing. My Papa, he tried to go after them, but he was too old; they beat him and then had him arrested. My sister, Anoushka, she couldn't take it. Her spirit broken, her attackers walking free and her one defender sitting in a cold cell, she snuck outside in the middle of the night and hung herself from a tree. Fifteen, that's all and everything was gone. Papa went insane and turned to drink. Within a few months he was dead from alcohol poisoning. Mama packed me and my little brother up and moved us to New York, trying to run away from the pain and the memory of it all. It didn't work. Not for me, not for any of us. I was ten years old when it happened."

"I'm so sorry Elena." Emma said. She went to her and hugged her. Elena smiled back at her weakly, more for Emma's benefit than her own.

"I'm sorry Elena." I said. "I am. I'm sorry for your sister and I'm sorry for you, and I'm sorry I didn't say anything. I might have prevented this whole evil thing if I had been braver. I wish I could change it, but please Elena, let us call the police. This isn't Skorba."

"It doesn't matter. Police are police and he's a guard, they'll feel he's one of them and want to protect him. It would be the same thing all over again." Elena said.

"I can't believe this." Paul said. "I, *we*, are just supposed to sit here and pretend nothing happened? I can't do it! I can't! I will kill Frank the second I see him!"

"Paul," Elena looked at him, "Thank you. You are a good man, just like my Papa, but you will not suffer the same fate as him, and I will not suffer the same fate as my sister. Please, let all of us go to bed. It will all be alright, you will see. Just let us go to sleep now."

She reminded me of my mother. Would Elena just push it aside, as my mother had, as I had?

"Elena, he will just do it to someone else." I pleaded.

"Please Connie, I know you are hurt, for me and for yourself, but please. Maybe tomorrow we will talk about it more, maybe tomorrow I will change my mind, but right now I just want to sleep." Elena replied.

She raised herself up from the chair slowly and unsteady. Paul ran to her side again.

"Promise me." She said, looking at each of us. Hesitantly Emma and I nodded. Elena looked at Paul. Begrudgingly he mumbled the answer she wanted. I followed them to Elena's room, Paul stood at the door as I helped her get into bed. I kissed her forehead and she winced, a bruise would be visible there by morning.

"I love you Elena. I'm sorry." I whispered. "I am so very, very sorry.
"I love you too Connie." She replied. "It's not your fault. It'll be okay, you'll see, it will all be okay."
As I left I reached over to turn off the light. She asked if I would leave it on. I nodded, understanding, and closed the door behind me. I turned to see Paul looking at me, tears filling his eyes.

Though Elena had said everything would be okay, the next morning she did not look any better, though she tried to be as light and cheery as usual. Her skin was very pale, even more so than normal, set against the bruises that were staring to form, blue and purple, and coupling with the brown-red scab that ran down her bottom lip; she looked as something risen from the grave. Even when she smiled it did not ease the shock of it, instead it made it worse, out of place and frightening, like the images in the ghastly horror films that would appear at the opposite end of the century.

Seeing her, Myrna was left near speechless. When she finally stammered out an inquiry she seemed almost too grotesquely entranced to fully listen to the explanation. If she had, she surely would not have bought it.

Those of us who knew better were torn between wanting to dote on her in any way possible and wanting to turn away from the pain that the sight of her brought, but still she carried on as if nothing had changed, seeming to be more concerned with our pain than her own.

Throughout the morning we each went about trying to convince Elena to let us call the police, but she still refused, increasing our frustration. Paul slammed pots and threw utensils into the sink with deafening force, his anger threatening to boil over.

"I'm telling you," He said to me as we stood outside the kitchen for a moment's reprieve, "If she doesn't agree to call the cops by tonight, I will go down there and beat him until he's dead. Period. That's it. I can't know what I know and look at her, or you, and do nothing. What kind of a man does nothing while the women around him are raped and beaten?! I won't stand for it. Gun or no gun, it won't matter."

I had no reply. He was right.

We were standing in silent contemplation when Charles came across the drive. He was almost skipping he was so happy to be well and out of bed and his broad smile and bright eyes seemed offensive and out of place given the circumstances.

"Hiya Y'all!" Charles said as he approached. "So good to be up and about. I've been stuck in that bed, not able to move a muscle, now I feel like I could run across New York. It's funny how something can come on you so fast, without a warning, then leave the same way."

"I have a job for you then."

We turned at the sound of Emma's voice in time to see her emerge from the kitchen.

"I made a tray of food for Frank. We're all tired from watching over everybody and trying to keep up with the regular work too. Take it down to him for us will you? Emma asked, her voice annoyed.

"Sure I can do that." Charles said. "But, uh, I'm starving for some real food myself. How about I eat something first?"

Emma smiled faintly. "Thank you Charles. I appreciate it. All it is is vegetable soup, little different from what you've been having already. But I tell you what, if you'll take it down to Frank for me, maybe Paul can cook you up some real food while you're gone, something heavy and meaty."

"Sure I can do that." Paul said.

Charles agreed as we all walked back into the kitchen and grabbing the tray headed out the door quickly, ready to get back as soon as possible; guessing by the look on his face, he was already imagining what rich and heavy delights would be on the table waiting for him at his return.

"Emma," I whispered, careful to make sure Myrna couldn't hear me. "Why in the world did you make that miserable low life food?!"

Paul who was standing close enough to hear me chimed in. "We were more than ready to let him starve to death down there if possible," Paul held up a boning knife, "or force him up here to the kitchen where I could give him a present."

Emma shook her head. "It's not like I wanted to. He called up from the guardhouse. Myrna answered and he started yelling at her that we hadn't sent him down anything all day. What choice did I have?" Emma looked over at Myrna then lowered her voice further. "Have you had any luck with Elena?"

"No. Not yet." I answered. "I just don't understand. I wonder if maybe she's in shock. I've heard of such things. People kind of go into denial about something that happened to them when it's too much for their mind to handle."

"I don't know. She seemed to know fully well what had happened last night." Paul replied.

As evening approached Elena was still adamant that we carry on with life as usual, but with Paul's growing threats to make good on his promise, she finally made a deal with us. If, after Myrna went to bed for the night, we all still felt that it was necessary, she would let Paul drive she and I to the police department and would tell them everything.

We never did talk to the police. When Charles headed to the guardhouse a second time to take Frank down his dinner, he found him dead, lying face down on the floor beside his chair in a puddle of vomit and smelling of urine and excrement. Charles called up to the house, frantic, nearly screaming into the receiver. Within in seconds we jumped into the car; Myrna, Paul, Elena, Emma and I, and headed for the guardhouse.

The guardhouse was a small building, not even as big as a tool shed and not big enough for more than three people to fit in comfortably at a time. As I looked in through the door

I could see Charles standing over Frank's body. Myrna ran past us all and fell to the floor, lying her head on Frank's chest before beginning to sob uncontrollably.

Paul, Emma, Elena and I looked at each other, but didn't say a word. What could we possibly say? Certainly not what we were all surely thinking.

"He seemed alright when I brought him lunch." Charles said pushing his fingers into his eyes as he sat down in the one chair in the little building. "I mean, he did look tired, but he wasn't complaining about feeling sick or anything. When I came in, I thought maybe he had passed out, so I turned him over. I knew as soon as I touched him though that he was dead. Suppose he might have been sick this whole time and not stopping, well, it just pushed him too far?"

"That would be just like him." Myrna choked out, barely audible.

Emma took control of the situation as Myrna continued to wail on the floor from depths no one would have guessed she had.

"I need to head back to the main house and make some phone calls. The doctor I think and of course Frank's family. I don't think Myrna is up to the task." She said calmly.

"Myrna," Emma leaned into the guardhouse, "would you like to stay here or would you like to come back to the house?"

Myrna didn't answer.

"Okay. It's fine, we'll take care of it." Emma said quietly. "Charles, will you please stay here with Myrna?"

Charles shook his head and left the little room.

"I'd rather not." He said. "Dead body is bad enough, but I don't know what to do with Myrna on top of that. Can't somebody else do it?"

"I understand." Emma said, turning her gaze to Paul and I.

"I'll do it." I said. A strange part of me wanted to be there, to see for certain that Frank was truly gone and another part of me was afraid to leave Myrna alone with him, even if he was a corpse.

"Thank you." Emma said. Then she walked into the guardhouse, handed the dinner tray out to Paul and took the lunch tray in her own hands and the four of them, Paul, Elena, Charles and Emma, drove back to the house.

I have had many unique, even bizarre moments in my life. Moments that seemed larger than life, moments that seemed as if heaven or even hell had manifested here on Earth, some where time stood still and others where it flew by too fast to catch it, but as I sat in that little marble guardhouse, watching as this stoic, formidable woman poured out to this soulless fiend every bit of love and heartache, longing and admiration, frustration and hope that she had held through the years, as if nothing else in the world existed, it was the strangest moment of them all. To witness it would have been odd enough on its own, regardless of who was involved, but this was Myrna, and even more than that, this was Frank. She had had such passion, intensity, and deep loyalty all hidden within her for a man who mocked her, for a man who though unknown to her, was the lowest of them all, a man for which death, no matter how it had come, was surely too kind, and a man who would never, had he lived to be a hundred, be worthy of the depth of feeling that was coming from this woman.

I wanted to comfort her and yet I wanted to scream. "He's a monster! Foul and degenerate, unworthy of you! Get off the floor! Kick him, spit on him, beat him! That's what he deserves, not your tears! Never anyone's tears!" But I couldn't. So I simply sat in the chair, quiet and still, swimming in the surrealness of it all. The devil was dead, that was all that mattered, the devil was dead.

The doctor came as quickly as he could manage, he himself busy and tired from the epidemic that had swept the area. He quickly looked over Frank and pronounced him dead, the probable cause the same one that was taking the lives of many others across the county.

Frank's brothers were called, and he was transported back to his hometown of Fairview. No one from the estate went to the funeral, and while it could be said that it was sickness that kept some away, it probably wouldn't be entirely true. Myrna spent the day Frank was buried in her room only venturing out once to go down to the river for a while. Darla, who had been at the estate longer than anyone, said it was the first time she had ever seen Myrna miss work for any reason.

Emma, Paul, Elena and I never spoke of Frank. There wasn't a one of us who dared to. I am sure that they had found it as odd a coincidence as I did, but did it really matter? He was gone, and whether from God, sickness, drink or other, was of no consequence. We could rest in the knowledge that somehow justice had been served and he would never again darken the face of another woman.

I cannot say that ever forgave Frank, but with him gone the hatred I felt began to dissipate. The fact that he was not walking around unpunished in the world no longer fed it and he faded from my mind, only to return briefly on rare occasions. I hope it was the same for Elena, though I have a feeling it was not.

Many years later, long after Emma, Paul, even Myrna had passed from this life into the next, Elena confessed to me what I had at times, in the very back of my head suspected, she had killed Frank.

She told me the story a couple years before she would pass away from stomach cancer as we sat in her living room in the late hours of the night, two old, dear friends, reminiscing over decades long gone that had left only memories and wrinkles in their place. She had been in a state of shock almost when I first found her. Fear and pain were the only things that reality was made of, even I had seemed to be just an apparition. She could see my lips moving, but the only sound she heard was the pounding of her heart, all else was silence.

She didn't know how long the rape had lasted, she didn't know how long she had been walking, or how long we had been on the ground, her body, broken in my arms, but the moment I stood up and she saw the crowbar in my hands, it was if reality came flooding back to her clear and instantaneous and with it the memory of her sister and her father. She knew then that this time it would be different. This time the rapist would not escape, this time no one would fall for her sake, she would take everything into her hands and redeem the mistakes of the past. She vowed to herself that in the end there would be no victim, only victor.

All of this was clear to her in a matter of minutes, her mind working at breakneck speed. Frank would not escape punishment. She would kill him, her, no one else, but how could she do it? She had to be smart, so that he fell but she stood. As we approached the house the way to go about it flowed into her like the rain falls from the sky, so simple. It happened when she saw the water fountain that stood in front of the house. She remembered the Sunday outing a few of us had taken in late April, mere weeks before. It was the only one we had had since the previous fall, the cold and snow of upstate New York having kept us indoors until then and we chose that day to picnic down by the river. Emma, Helen, Elena, Peter, Paul, Joan, Doyle and I spent the day laughing and enjoying the shining sun, glad that the winter was finally behind us and warmer days beckoned. Elena had decided to pick some flowers and was amassing quite a large bouquet when she reached for a stem of jagged thin leaves, that watching from afar, I had assumed at the time to be Queen Anne's Lace that simply hadn't bloomed yet. Helen however was closer and knew better. She quickly stopped Elena from harvesting the Water Hemlock and went on to explain the difference in the two plants and the danger that the Hemlock held. She told Elena how the poison of the plant and especially the root, was extremely potent and would bring on craps, convulsions, and stop a person's breathing resulting in a horrid and painful death, and could even do it in a relatively short period of time if the person was small, weak or had ingested enough of it.

The knowledge had been little more than something interesting to Elena when Helen offered it, but by the time she stepped out of the shower, she had the plan entirely laid out in her head and in her heart the will to see it through to its end.

In the early dawn hours before anyone else had woken Elena snuck out of the house and walked down to the water, finding the Hemlock plant and digging up its roots. She harvest enough to fill her hand, then she threw the plant stalks into the river and watched for a moment as the current carried them away. Then kneeling down Elena rinsed the roots clean of dirt and tore away the small fine hairs that jetted from them in the clear freezing water before wrapping them up in a handkerchief she had brought along.

Elena quietly slipped back into the house and into her room and laid the roots on top of her dresser. Taking a pocket knife that had belonged to her father from the top drawer she began to chop the roots up into small pieces so that they might be mistaken for tiny bits of potato. When she had finished, she wrapped the Hemlock once again in the handkerchief and placed them in her pocket. She would slip the cut roots into Frank's soup when lunch time came around. She had become irritated when we seemed determined to make him starve, but then, he made his own death call and Myrna ordered his lunch made. She wasn't sure how to get the Hemlock into the soup Emma was preparing, she needed Emma out of the way and she was worried about how to get the soup to Frank. A concern Emma was muttering over herself as she ladled the soup into the bowl. Asking anyone of us to take the tray down was out of the question. Elena couldn't take it to him herself even if any of us would allow it, she knew she could not bear to see him, not alive and breathing anyway, and of course for her to show up, smiling with a plate of food would arouse suspicion in Frank and anyone else privy to what had happened only hours before. Emma and I couldn't be expected to do it either, not with our own anger boiling nor with knowing the type of man Frank was, we couldn't be put in danger and to ask Paul to do it would be begging for chaos. Then as if a gift from God, Elena heard Charles' voice as he crossed the driveway from the garage to the house. There was her answer. Quickly she suggested to Emma that Charles be the one to take down Frank's tray. Emma agreed and as she went to ask him, Elena took her chance. Peaking at Myrna to make sure she wasn't paying attention, Elena took the handkerchief from her pocket and poured into the soup its deadly contents, then taking the spoon from the tray she gave the soup a few quick stirs, watching with satisfaction as the chunks blended in nicely, looking like nothing more than bits of vegetable mixed among others. When she heard Charles' request for food a momentary panic set in that he might be offered this last supper that sat before her and she would have no choice but to pretend to drop the tray spilling its contents. Listening intently she was relieved that he had been made and accepted another offer and satisfied she took one last look at the soup with its seemingly benign ingredients and left the kitchen for the laundry room, praying to God that Charles would not sneak a spoonful on the way and seal his fate. Despite this one, albeit big, fear, as she began to fold linens a sense of satisfaction filled her. This would be it, a wrong vindicated, if not righted, and she smiled knowing that soon it would be Frank's turn to writhe in pain on the hard guardhouse floor.

Elena betrayed no emotion as she spoke. I asked her if she felt guilty over it, then or ever. She said she hadn't. She knew what needed to be done and she had done it. She never had any regret, except perhaps that she had not been able to witness Frank's pain, but she had been able to live with that unfortunate necessity.

I cannot say that I blamed Elena. I cannot even say that I thought what she had done was wrong, because I didn't, and I don't know that I ever will. As far as I was concerned I felt the same way about it then and now, as I did the day Frank died, the devil is dead, that's all that matters.

The day for my departure for Whitefish came quickly, as things of that nature often do. I woke up early as usual; with nothing much to do until the time came to set out. I had packed my belongs days before to give me something to do with the nervous energy that anticipation often brings and since then had been obliged to live out of my suitcase. It was turning out to be a beautiful day. The sky was clear and though the middle of June, it was not the normal color of a summer sky, that pale blue that comes from the unique tilt of the Earth during that time of year; it was a Fall sky, or a spring sky, that perfect rich blue that fills you with happiness when you look up at it. Spring is when new life begins and Fall is when things turn towards their end, I was doing both. Shutting the door on one part of my life and beginning another. It was as if the sky to which I had had spoken my vow, was once again speaking back.

    I felt a strange mixture of emotions; excitement, apprehension, doubt, pride, all swimming around in my chest fighting for dominance, but none succeeding. Instead they all mixed into an emotional stew that left me with a nice, easy peaceful feeling. Since none could exert enough power to cause a physical reaction nor could they settle enough to lay claim on my thoughts for any recognizable amount of time, I was simply left in a state of being, just being.

I stayed in my room for the most part, waiting for the time to leave to come. I didn't want to be in the way of those who needed to go about their work as usual, though those whom I was closest to made their way to my room at different points during the morning to say their farewells. I was touched that some of them had even brought me gifts. Peter gave me a brown cloth hardcover detailing the birds of

North America and Helen a well-worn volume by Alice Henkel on medicinal plants called *American Medicinal Leaves and Herbs*. They were heartfelt gifts, and it was touching that they had seen fit to part with them to aide me in my endeavor, and Paul thoughtfully packed me a large box full of goodies to munch on during my train ride and probably well beyond.

Joan came by, as did Darla, and even Henri. Emma continually peeked in on me throughout the morning as was to be expected, but Elena did not. I had not, in fact, seen her at all. Finally the time came and I picked up my suitcase and goodie box and headed to the kitchen. Smiles and more farewells came, and I quickly made my way to the front of the house. Myrna had offered to drop me off at the station early that morning on her and Stanley's way to get the next new girl, and while it was a kind offer, I thankfully did not have to take her up on it. Tom was home from university for the summer and he had offered to take me to the station himself.

Emma walked with me to the door. Tom was already there waiting. Standing with one foot propped up on the rear bumper of the car, he was deeply engrossed in conversation with Charles and hadn't yet noticed that I had walked out of the house. Without warning, Stephen came up from behind me and took the suitcase out of my hand, smiling at his having caught me off guard. Reaching under my arm he took the box Paul had prepared from me as well and placed them in the back of the waiting car. I searched for signs of Elena, but I still couldn't see her and wondered if I should go inside to look for her. I didn't want to leave without saying good bye, but I was also afraid to delay my departure.

Tom, finally finished with his conversation, looked over, and noticed I was there. He stood up straight, smiled and walked over to me.
"Ready?" he said. I almost laughed; he seemed to be more excited than I was.
I looked around once more. "I guess so." I said.

I hugged Emma, who had begun to cry and shower me with admonitions to be careful in every way she could think of offhand. I kissed her cheek and told her I loved her and thanked her once again for all that she had done and for bringing me to the estate. Stephen came over and shook my hand as did Charles as they offered their own wishes for a safe trip.

Tom walked around to the driver's side of the car as Stephen opened the passenger's side door for me. I began to lower myself into the car when I heard my name being called. I turned to see Elena running down the entrance stairs of the house, clutching something in her hands.
"Connie!" she gasped, out of breath from running. She stopped at the car and I straightened myself up, embracing her before she could catch her breath to continue.
"I was so scared I wouldn't get to say good bye." I said.
"Me too." She replied. "I was worried I had already missed you. I am sorry I was not able to come by your room earlier. I was working all morning and I wanted to make you something. Here." She handed me the box she had been holding tightly to her chest. "You do not need to open it now. I know you need to go."
"Thank you." I said.
We embraced once more and I climbed into the passenger's seat. Elena shut the door and waved as she backed away.

The ride to the station seemed shorter to me than it should have been. At first Tom had tried to speak, but he quickly gave up. I was too lost in my own thoughts to be much of a conversationalist. We pulled up to the station, rows of trains lined the tracks, some shiny, some dirty, but all like giant iron Sleipnirs ready to carry their riders to some other world. Tom waited as I went to the ticket booth. I held up the thin paper as I walked towards him and he gave a little cheer. Taking my arm in his, we walked to within feet of where I would board.

"Constance," Tom said." You have been a good friend to me and I hope that I have been to you as well. I want you to know that I think you are the bravest person I have ever known."

I laughed at the sentiment.

"It's true!" he replied to my disbelief. "You are! I've heard people talk all my life, but I have never seen anyone just risk it all to strike out on their own like you're doing now. I find it inspiring, and I respect it. For as long as I live, I will remember it. I will remember you standing here, shining like the sun. This, right here, right now, is everything that is good, everything that keeps mankind moving forward, small steps, big steps, just as long as there is someone like you who is brave enough to take them."

For the first time that day, my eyes filled with tears, my heart swelling with love for this man before me. I knew that I would probably never see him again once I stepped onto the train, but I knew that he had been dear to my heart and would always be one of my most treasured friends.

Tom took me in his arms and hugged me tightly, then taking my hand, he helped me onto the train. At the top of the stairs I turned and waved good bye one last time. Tom smiled, tipped his hat and winked, and then turning on his heel, he walked away.

I had been able to save enough money for a sleeping car, not a fancy one, but I still considered it quite the luxury and felt a great sense of pride entering the little room. The porter closed the door behind me and I sat down on the seat, taking from my purse the package Elena had given me. It was small, no bigger than a cigarette box and was wrapped in newspaper. I untied the twine and pulled off the wrapping. I could hear something sliding around inside. Opening the box a folded piece of paper popped up. I laid it aside. Underneath the paper was a pewter chain with a small gold daisy hanging from it as a pendant. Shocked, I picked it up and looked closely at it. I had never owned, nor had any of my family -not that I knew of anyway- a single piece of gold anything, in our lives. The daisy had a small orange topaz stone in the center and the top petal had been bent around the chain to hold it to the necklace. There was no clasp to the chain, it was fully linked together all the way around, but I could tell by looking at it that it would be long enough to fit over my head. I picked up the note that had accompanied it.

Dear Connie,
This daisy was part of a pair of earrings that had belonged to my sister Anoushka. I have the other half of the set. I wanted to give you something that was close to my heart, because you have been so dear to me. I had a sister and cruelty took her from me, and then I found you and it was as if God had given me a new sister, one that now hope takes from me. Know that as long as I live, whatever you do, wherever you go, my love goes with you.
Forever,
Elena

I refolded the paper and placed it back in the box and returning its lid, placed it on the seat beside me. I gently slipped the necklace over my head and leaned back in the seat, tears silently rolling down my cheeks, tears of sadness and tears of joy. I sat looking out of the window to the mountains in the distance. The train whistle sounded and with a jerk, one journey ended, and another began.

Made in the USA
Charleston, SC
11 July 2013